Will You Stay?

Vedant Saxena & Annie Pruthi

Invincible Publishers

First published in India in 2018

ISBN: 978-93-88333-22-1

Invincible Publishers

G-120, Sushant Lok III, Sector 57, Gurgaon-122002

Registered Address: Opposite Kasturba Ashram, Radaur, Haryana–135133

Printed at Excel Printers Pvt. Ltd.

In loving memory of my niece Chiya
For she was the bird that flew back home.

Acknowledgement

A writer is seldom at a loss for words. This is where I don't have any words in my arsenal to appreciate you all. My mere words won't do justice here.

Still..

I would like to thank my parents for having my back and ignoring the pressures of the society while their son was busy writing this book. There were tears in my father's eyes and joy in my mother's when I told them that I'll be putting my poetry "कभी तो मिलोगे" in this book.

This book is dedicated to your fight with depression.

My sisters Geetika and Prashi for believing that their brother is meant for something big, and for trusting and supporting my art.

This book is dedicated to you for believing in me.

My brothers-in-law, Nitin and Dheeraj,

I dedicate this book to you for showing me the strength and courage I never knew I had and for pampering me along the way.

To all my cousins who bragged about their brother being writer,

I dedicate this book to you in honour of the gratitude you made me feel by fuelling up my confidence.

To my friend Arush for his pep talks and diverting my mind from writer's block and frustration.

I dedicate this book to our friendship.

To all my friends (there are so many of them that I will have to write a separate book to mention them all), thank you for supporting and encouraging me to stick to my dreams.

I dedicate this is book to you all for encouraging me even when I was ready to give up.

To Meritt, for beta-reading and editing this book. You taught me that friends can be soulmates too.

I dedicate this book to you in appreciation of all that you've taught me.

To the entire team of Invincible publishers, Ajay sir, Ruchika, Aditi, for your support and encouragement,

I dedicate this book to you all for your unyielding faith in me.

ANNIE PRUTHI,

Thank you for always being there and believing in me when I couldn't believe in myself. You justified my choice of having you as my co-author. For all those 3 AM talks about plot improvement, character development, addition in plots and pitching in with the write-ups. You polished both my story and my writing.

This book is dedicated to our sleepless nights and hope for all those who feel as though they have none.

On behalf of Annie, I would like to thank her parents for believing in her, as well as Riddhi for guiding her little sister, Ayush and Paras for always encouraging her to follow her passion.

I dedicate this book to you in gratitude of your trust.

Last, but not the least, *I thank you*. Yes, you who are reading this, holding my precious in your hands. I couldn't have been anything without your faith and support.

All my readers and admirers,

This book is dedicated to OUR STRUGGLE through MENTAL ILLNESS, and to swimming back to the shores of normal being. We've SURVIVED AND CONQUERED. Continue to fight your fight and don't ever give in or give up. The fight isn't over, my friend. The fight isn't over.

"If all else perished, and he remained,
I should still continue to be;
and if all else remained,
and he were annihilated,
the universe would turn to a mighty stranger."

— Emily Jane Brontë , Wuthering Heights

Prologue

The chime of my bangles, sweet smile adorned faces, petrichor penetrating our nostrils; it all threatens me now. Is this the debt that I'm bound by fate to repay?

Eyes consumed by a dream, and future aflame in inevitable agony. Horrors of the dreadful past bring about unbridled memories, dragging me to my grave, to insanity.

Darkness haunts me and I cannot find him anywhere. I move my hands around, I collapse, I trip, I shout, I scream, I yell, but he isn't here. And suddenly with a jerk, I find myself surrounded by people who might never have experienced love at all. It's a grotesque gathering to experience the longing of love birds, diminishing away in dark twilight.

I call for him, I ask everyone where he is.

They laugh, they mock, they irritate me, for they haven't felt the ache of separation, the memories that haunt, the cravings that eat you whole, or the desires that wither you slowly; these gory elements never consumed them. It's eating me now, everything is consuming me. I am lost and falling into a vortex.

Then suddenly, everything comes to a halt, as if immobile, frozen to the earth's core. All the red runs clear, transparent and new. I can see him now, tearing the crowd apart, rushing towards me in a shroud of tears. In moments, we denude ourselves of every possession. I feel my bare body lying on a cold floor, his weight above me, running his fingers through my hair, his cheeks caressing mine. I feel captive in the chains of cravings.

My soul rises from my body, savouring his; our existence mingles into one, ending this drought of love.

Clouds blanket the sky and suddenly, it's dark again. I can't find him now, not on me, or in me, nor anywhere around. Moonlight filters through the curtains and illuminates the room. Now I see only pieces of broken glass on the floor and blood all over my naked body. I gasp for breath as I lie bathed in his blood illuminated in the naked moonlight.

My soul rises once again, observing every pair of bulging eyes that look right through me. My soul pleads, begs, and bellows like a banshee, "I want to hear from him just once, please help me," but the world is deaf to my pleas, and only the breeze howls in my ears.

"This pain is yours to bear alone. Let your soul ache and long for death, let him find you in heaven or hell," they laugh at me.

My defeated soul follows them, his blood dripping from my frail extremities and my exposed skin, a walking waterfall of vermillion. They look at me with ravenous eyes, like hungry wolves ready to pounce. Nothing is left, nothing keeps me sane now, everything has melted in me, and only a puddle of red remains, a mixture of blood, regret, pain, and tears.

I am nothing but this empty shell of a body with no heart or feelings. A hollow body without a soul, and then the memory's breeze howled again.

"Oh, poor Manya–it's love after all."

Chapter 1

Dawn cracked in with a soft soothing whisper amidst the dissonance of my chaotic life. Roads were clear, leaves hung loose on the branches with buds which would soon blossom. Following the soul-stirring camahanaich, dark clouds grew miffed at the azure beauty of a clear sky, and stretched down to the horizon. The morning ambience was now shrouded in grey.

I quickened my steps to evade the impending downpour. I didn't want to show up at college drenched; after all, it was my first day. However, the air thickened into fierce dusty winds in no time, slapping across my face as if it hated my guts for my stubborn strides against it. On any normal day, it would have been a lot easier since the P.G. house room which I had chosen to inhabit for the next three years of my college life was at a walkable distance, but these few steps were giving me a real tough time this day. Maybe it was a sign for the upcoming travails, or perhaps it was meant to encourage me to make an effort for notable achievements.

There was no trace of any mortal presence on my way. I reached the college vicinity, only to see a few guys hurrying through the large rusty college gates. There stood the magnificent monument of IHE–Institute of Hotel Education–my dream college. The infrastructure was huge and splendid. As I entered, a huge banner loomed above my head, sporting "Welcome Freshers."

Freshers, the word that unnerves every student on the first day of their college, and I was no exception. The word sent a chill down my spine, for something in my head said that the seniors were waiting ready with their arms and ammunitions, ready to greet their juniors.

I smiled at the old security guards seated at the gate. As if measuring my excitement and uneasiness at the moment, they smiled back generously and exchanged a few words amongst themselves. I closed my eyes and offered a little psalm to my guardian angels, for today, I needed a blessing to set a good impression.

I took a quick glance around the premises, as far as my eyes could reach. Sensing that it was getting late, I abandoned the idea of exploring the beautiful architectural marvel that was my college campus, and joined the crowd that had gathered at the reception. I decided to wander around later. While all the nervous faces were busy scrambling for their respective brochures, my tall frame allowed me to procure mine with ease. By means of courtesy, I handed a few extra ones to the petite girls behind me. The brochure was like an introductory pamphlet familiarising the new students with the Principal, the rules to be followed, the faculty members, the college nooks and corners, and the course time table. The orientation was to begin soon in the upstairs auditorium. The spacious interior was designed to contain more than 500 students at a time. As we had already been informed through mail, every student in the auditorium could be seen wearing dark grey trousers and crisp white shirts adorned with ties. No matter how old we grow, the utter distaste towards uniforms never subsides. To add further to the agony, boys were instructed to get their hair trimmed and faces clean shaven, while the girls had to assemble their hair up in a neat bun. It looked no less than an army boot camp.

Some seniors stood by the stage, chattering incessantly amongst themselves. They had on different uniforms. Except some hostlers, all the freshers sat there mummified.

As the Principal entered, we shuffled in our seats and the seniors rushed to occupy theirs. The Principal was dressed sharply, reflecting his personality a man of distinction. Looking dead serious, he began the most formal and perhaps the most arid lecture that novices were welcomed with every year. "Hello freshers, welcome to IHE, Dehradun, the most prestigious Hotel Management college in India. You've been meticulously selected from every corner of the country and brought here to be moulded into charismatic hoteliers. In the coming three years, we'll train you according to the industry's requirements, so that you can easily transition into the hotel industry work force." Everyone greeted this with loud claps. "We expect that you all will follow the rules and maintain the decorum while representing the college. I should remind you that failing will result in grave consequences." With this, the chaotic crowd went silent. He then left it for others to continue. Ms. Reshma, the girls' hostel warden, briefed the hostel rules and regulations that girls had to follow. This was followed by Mr. Thakur, the discipline in-charge, who told us further about the student guidelines, and was met with no applause. More speakers arrived on stage one after another, during which many seniors managed to slip away, but the freshers were left at the mercy of these old monks.

After hours of boredom, the tedious curriculum of the brochure led us to the 'college tour' where we were segregated into four different groups and were asked to enter into an empty room. It felt like kindergarten all over again. We waited there for someone to attend to our group when, to my surprise, we were greeted by a charming stranger. He had the most remarkable face with a chiselled jawline framed by a crown of wavy hair. After perching himself on the desk, he rolled up his sleeves and finally spoke, "According to the rules, it's my duty to show you around the college premises. I am in 3rd year, so you are all expected to call me Rohan SIR. Don't look so tensed, I don't bite," he laughed. This evoked a few chuckles from the attention seekers in the front. Girls drooled over him, while the poor boys had to fake it so they didn't end up on his bad side.

I smiled, mesmerized and astonished by his charisma. Unlike the other group leaders, he called out our names from the attendance sheet personally and asked the students to stand apart from the crowd. After attendance, Rohan Sir began guiding our group through the college. The campus was a thing of admiration. Situated on the outskirts of the town, it had a sprawling area within its boundaries. Every part of the college was designed to create a professional atmosphere with adequate space for all kinds of facilities.

The college had its own restaurant, bar and guest rooms, just like a hotel. There were kitchens and a bakery for the respective years, as well as a huge library and an equally large garden. Not only did Rohan tell us about the lecture halls and departments, he also added a few classroom stories about the faculty to keep the visit lively and exciting. Despite the popularity he commanded amongst the girls in the crowd, he remained calm, not bothered about the attention either. He was different from the image of a typical senior I had in my mind.

The visit ended in the vast food court which was facilitated and stocked with all kinds of beverages and soft drinks. Our seniors prepared and served food in the kitchen.

"Here you go, guys. Your induction program is over. It will take only a little time to grow aquatinted with the college. Do well, and just in case something comes up, feel free to ask me. Please proceed to your lecture rooms post lunch." Having said this, Rohan left us. Our nerves were now steadied by his generosity. The queue for lunch seemed endless amidst our seniors and super seniors. It was difficult to cut one's way out. To our relief, the mess in-charge told us to come around and fill our plates at the other end, as there was no separate line for girls.

Filling the plates came easy, but finding a place to sit did not. Most of the tables were occupied by seniors and their coveted bags holding up the sign 'not available'. I motioned ahead with a hope of finding a vacant seat. Instead, my gaze fell upon a familiar looking girl waving her hand at me, standing by the window. When I reached there, I recognized her from my P.G. "Clearly, we are not getting a table here anytime soon. Hop up here," she said, signalling at the vacant space next to her on the window sill. "After our brief meeting yesterday, I hope you remember my name," she said, looking up. "I am really bad at remembering names, I am sorry," I shrugged. "Never mind, my name is Riya. And you are Manya Sharma. See, I remember your full name," she chuckled. "Well Riya, this is not at all a bad place," I said, hopping up on the window sill. Dehradun's weather welcomed us with soothing rain and wind that tantalized our hair. ''Bewitching, isn't it?" Riya said, managing her hair. I nodded and kept looking outside. I had dreamt of a good start and it came like a blessing. Everything went on like a fairytale: a bonnie college, cool and composed faculty, and a not so nerveless Principal. I even came to appreciate the strict rules and regulations; they were like a talismanic protection for my scared soul. My batchmates were to my taste, but the biggest plus point remained Rohan.

"Hey l think we should hurry–it's already 2 PM, lecture time," Riya snapped at me, breaking the chain of my thoughts. We left the mess in haste with our bags. The lecture room was on the third floor. We rushed up the stairs, but found the doors already closed. I peeped through the glass and found that it was already full. Riya pushed the door open and we entered. Some guys were standing near the podium, and a few girls were sitting on the desk facing the class. We made our way to some empty seats. "So, everyone's here. Let's begin the introduction ceremony," the guy standing at the podium clapped, leaning onto it. The others standing near him burst into laughter. My worst nightmare was about to be realized, I figured. Introductions were never my thing due to my introverted nature. Then I found Rohan standing with them, which lifted my wits a bit. The seniors started choosing people randomly. Panicked boys and girls started blabbering their names, schools and hobbies which were ridiculed by the seniors who derived great pleasure from their nervous ordeal. 'How insensitive of them,' I thought while hiding behind my bag. I wanted to turn invisible.

When they were about to leave, Rohan's eyes met mine. For a moment, my scared eyes pleaded with him not to call my name, but he did, leaving me abashed. Everyone stopped there, waiting for me to take the centre stage. Riya tried to say something, but I stopped her. I was preparing myself for the commencement of my nervous unveiling when I stumbled midway and everything went numb. Embarrassing laughter echoed in my ears as I reached the podium. "Hey Barbie doll, what's your name?" a girl with curly hair raised her eyebrows. "I...I... am Manya."

"So, *I..I.. am Manya,* we want you to sing an old classical song for us, and then we'll leave," she chuckled and the rest of the seniors flashed their teeth. My mind started going over names of songs, trying to select one I could babble out with the least bit of embarrassment.

"This isn't a fucking audition. Hurry up, Barbie." Everyone started booing, which compelled me to start singing. As soon as I finished, I realised how awful it had been. Everyone in class was laughing at me, *including Rohan*. "Wow, what a voice. The crow voice'd nightingale of our college," blurted out the girl with the curls, clapping and laughing. Everyone joined her in her mockery of me. Filled with deep embarrassment, my eyes turned a fierce red and tears rolled down. With jittery steps, I took my bag and ran out of the class, pushing my way through the seniors. Riya called after me, but I couldn't be stopped. My world had come crashing down around me in just a couple of minutes. The corridor was empty, so I stood outside the lecture room aghast, still sobbing. It gets difficult to subdue your emotions and stand strong, especially in a foreign place. When I gathered the courage to leave, I saw a guy sitting on the stairs staring at me. He was quiet and looked serious, but with a sedate and earnest look. His hazel eyes struck me and for a couple of seconds, I was frozen. I felt a certain fondness towards him. It was hard to look away from those intense eyes. I gathered myself to leave, his eyes still following mine, until he was out of sight.

25th July

I remember not getting out of bed because I was too tired to do anything, staring at the ceiling, thinking about the void, suffering, withering, because of the deed I had committed, of loving someone, being so tired and so drained. Struggling to sleep, crying until my tears went dry. I remember feeling everything and nothing at all. I remember all of it.

I wanted someone to hear me, caress me and to accept me the way I was. To stand by me. But no one heard me, no one cared. They ignored my cries for help. They thought my smile was real. They thought my blank hazel eyes were alluring and my breath a signs of life they'd yet to unearth. The fact is, I was dead, a dead withered soul in a living body. That's when I stopped caring. I decided to accept things as they were.

Six months. Six long miserable months, I escaped from them. The reason was my own stupidity. While searching online, the tips to fight depression and anxiety disorders, I read somewhere that sharing helps. It didn't suggest who to trust, or whom to share with. So, I chose someone of my own liking. Since Deepika was so close to me and confessed all her insecurities to me, I felt inclined to share mine with her too. I thought she would understand me, so I bared all my insecurities to her. For a moment when she cried, "Oh Shreyansh" and hugged me after listening, I thought she would console me, prevent me from failing or falling. She did console me for a day or two, but when I told her that I never had feelings for her and that I was loyal to Vaani (the girl I loved until she betrayed me), something got into her.

I don't know what triggered her, but she disappeared, no calls, no texts–nothing. The next thing I know, she told everyone in college about me–my condition, whatever sins I had committed, how I tried cutting myself and thoughts of ending myself, even the medication I'm taking.

I had to go into isolation for the four months of my training and then two months of my vacation, in which I worked day and night in bars and cafes just to avoid questions and people in general.

When it's necessary to be among them, I am scared. How would I hold myself back from messing up again? For months, I've been trying to collect myself, gathering pieces fallen from me. Now when I've finally joined my bits and pieces, I have to let myself stand on the verge of vulnerability again. This time, with questions. But why should I answer them? I am not liable to answer anyone; even if I do, I know I'll be mocked.

This is what life has done to me. Or better, what I have allowed Vaani to do to me. No, no Shreyansh! No.

You promised that day to yourself, you wouldn't play the blame game, like she did. But why do I have to suffer like this? This loneliness won't fade away. I see her smile when I close my eyes. This is funny, isn't it? Having a soft spot for a person who has offered you nothing but pain, made you question your worth and left you with disappointment.

That smile feels like mockery now. Tomorrow, when I step back in college, I'll mind my own business and keep away from the crowd. Let them call me arrogant, I won't succumb to anything now. People exploit your vulnerability the way it's favourable to them. I didn't know humans could be this selfish.

But, I hope it goes well tomorrow.

I hope it gets better.

Chapter 2

I latched the door shut and locked myself in the room. My state of embarrassment and anxiety had been building up ever since I came back from college. I threw the bag on the couch and crashed on the bed face-down.

The hype inside me had died a cold death today. The humiliation I faced in front of the whole college had crushed my spirit to the ground. Why do people try to push you down? How can one show one's superiority in such a cruel way? What had been my mistake? Why did they choose me of all the people out there…why me? My stomach cramped and I felt very small and insignificant, as if all my feelings were nothing more than a speck of dust in the entire celestial space.

My thoughts turned to Rohan. He had been like sugar at first, magnetizing me with his generosity, but then he targeted me himself. He changed his colours like a chameleon. My head throbbed with all these thoughts. I squeezed the pillow with my hands and pressed my face into it. I missed home, I missed my people, and I missed everything that felt like home. This was a foreign place and I was losing myself. I felt extrinsic to this place, and this cognizance identified my very breath as non-native. I cursed myself for having ended up here. Had I fought my way out for this mockery? Were all those fights with dad, all those aggressive displays for this woeful day? It didn't seem like something worth fighting for anymore. I was afflicted with anxious uneasiness. I regretted fighting with dad. He had said that HOTEL MANAGEMENT was not for me, that I couldn't survive here. At that time, I had thought that he was being overprotective–a solicitous "dad" who considered me a kid, but now I realized what he had actually meant. Somehow, he knew I wouldn't be able to survive the people here. He knew I couldn't resist unrestrained expression or handle any kind of deception because I had never faced a backlash like this at school. Even when something happened, I could run to my dad and he would embrace me in his huge arms. Those were the comforts of my home.

Here, I felt homeless.

I decided not to call him, otherwise he'd find out how defeated his daughter was feeling. Somebody rapped the door and I dragged myself up to open it. Riya was standing there with her head tilted sideways.

"You haven't changed your uniform yet," she said, shutting the door behind her and crashing on the couch.

I remained silent. Understanding my refusal to speak, she got up and hugged me tight.

"I'm sorry, Manya, for whatever happened today. I wasn't expecting it. I wanted to object, but everything happened so quickly." Her tone was serious.

"It's okay, Riya. It wasn't your fault. I should curse my awful luck," I said, as tears rolled down my cheeks. "I didn't think I would face such humiliation and attack on my self esteem so early on."

"I can understand, Manya, but these things are common. Everyone new to a school or college faces this."

"Not everyone. We were helpful and sweet to new people."

"Strange. I was bullied first and then I bullied others. I was expecting this. Weren't you?"

"But this harsh?"

"It's okay, we will make amends. Don't worry. You and I together will kick some serious seniors' ass. Everything will be fine, I promise," she said, holding my hands. I smiled and nodded. I was happy to have a friend like Riya around.

"Now don't get too emotional, and change your clothes. We're ditching this boring food tonight. I know a good place, let's go there. You'll feel better too," she said, throwing her hands in the air.

"I am not in the mood to go anywhere," I said.

"Aww, I'm not gonna spare you. You've got to come. Get your lazy ass up and change your clothes," she said.

I gave up and changed into beige colour shorts and a black tee. Riya started whistling like a wolf. "Girl, you are going to kill masses on the road!" She winked at me and continued, "Bitch, I'm jealous!"

I slapped her back and pushed her out of the room, locking it behind us.

The road leading away from the PG was dark and shaded by a dense cover of clouds overhead. As Riya walked beside me, I noticed that it was I who should be jealous of her well sculpted figure, complimented by the pink shirt and denim shorts she wore. After that difficult day, I finally found solace in the cool breeze blowing my untameable hair all over my face.

"Were you pampered a lot at home?"

she asked, initiating another conversation.

"Kind of."

"Well, pamper yourself here."

"What are you here for?"

"To pamper myself."

Our laughter echoed through the cloudy night. A ten minute walk lead us to our destination. It was a small *dhaba* called 'Sardar Ji Da Dhaba' on the side of the road with colourful cots laid under a string of artificial lights. We sat on one of them and looked at the vehicles passing by; everything about that place was tempting. A young kid came to take our order and smiled at us.

"I've got to start working out again. I'm afraid you'll induce me into taking in a lot of calories over the coming years," she declared after hearing my order. "YOU brought me here to a *dhaba,* and expect me to order a salad?"

She laughed, "I have to be fit."

"You're already in great shape."

"My boyfriend Rehan is a gym freak, he pushes me to go beyond my limits." "See, you're pampered too," I smirked. "Yeah, he gives me the solace that my parents couldn't."

"Why?"

I asked regretfully. "The hunger for money keeps them busy." She smiled with longing in her eyes. "Not everyone is lucky like you, Manya." I smiled. "Working parents?"

"Family business and a practice of faking keeps them occupied," she sighed. "Yours?" "My father works for the government and mother is a housewife."

"I don't remember the last time my mother cooked for me. I wonder if she even knows how to cook," she scoffed. "You must feel lonely," I said. "No, my younger brother and Rehan keep me occupied."

"You're the lucky one now. I don't have any siblings, nor have I ever had a boyfriend. My childhood was lonely and my adulthood is lonelier."

"You've got me now, and I'll find you a boyfriend too," Riya said, patting my hand.

After stuffing myself on the delicious butter naan, daal makhni, and paneer masala, my stomach protested. I wanted to eat more, but couldn't do anything beyond licking my fingers clean. The sky began roaring wildly and we decided to rush back to the dorm. The cloud cover finally cracked open with sharp lightening and it started pouring and pelting. We rushed inside to take shelter from amidst the scuttling people on the road. Nature was at its ferocious best, mirroring the storm inside my head. The train of my thoughts came to a halt when I saw him.

He was standing there in the rain, his arms wide open and head tilted upwards. I wanted time to stop then and there, to run to him and hold him in an amorous embrace. He was a sight of art. People were running away, seeking shelter, but there he was – carefree and living in the moment, submitting himself to nature. He seemed different and I found myself unable to resist his appeal.

After a while, he came back in, entirely drenched. His shirt stuck to his tall chiseled physique, and water dripped from the mop of black hair one his head. As he came into the light, I realised that he was the same guy the college whom I had seen before, the one with hazel eyes. I flushed under his gaze. A craving to feel each heave of his chest, preserve his emollient lips, and tape myself to his magnetic looks and charismatic soul enveloped me. I sensed a kind of desperation running through me. It felt awkward because I had never melted so quick before anyone, for anyone. I smiled at him and he looked away, moving his hand through his wet hair.

Riya frowned at me. I expected him to turn back towards me, hoping that he would fall for me all of a sudden too, just like in the movies. However, he didn't.

"You're hiding things from me already," Riya snapped.

"I don't know what you're talking about," I gasped, breaking the trance I was in

"The way you were looking and smiling at him, someone would assume you know him intimately. You can't hide from my powers of observation," she chuckled.

"You have a dirty mind. And I don't know him." I went on to tell her about our brief eye contact in college earlier that day to satisfy her stubborn curiosity.

"That's intense, he seems quite enigmatic," she murmured, catching up to my pace. I nodded and marvelled at her ability to read my mind. God, he was alluring.

During our walk back to the PG, my mind was consumed by the thoughts of him. Not a single moment passed when I wasn't thinking about him. What was happening to me? I had never been like this before. Had something changed?

26th July

As I stepped into the college vicinity today, it was arduous to avoid eyes searing into my skin, needles burning in hell fire. I slid my sleeves down, the cuts on my arms...had anyone seen them?

Phoenix gathered more attention than me, I suppose. I am glad. At least there is something to take the attention of people away from me. For two continuous months, I worked vigorously in long shifts from outlet to outlet just to save up enough money for my dream bike, my Phoenix. It enabled me to avoid both my father's wrath and unwanted questions from nosy acquaintances. Home didn't feel like home anymore. I felt trapped there. A cage from which I wished to fly away. After Meet left to start her new journey post marriage, I avoided home as much as I could. To be honest, my absence doesn't really seem to matter to my parents. Maa packed some snacks before I left and asked when I'd return, but dad didn't care. In fact, even Maa's concern feels like a formality now. She is tired. Dad is tired. I am tired. Everyone is tired of me. I'm tired of this version of myself too.

A lot of them were still home. I wonder how it feels to be home. I'm actually glad that I'm here now at this time, to see nervous faces about to start their own journeys. Their parents are with them to wish them luck before they embark upon their new paths. I remember my own time, how alone and scared I was. Dad was busy and Ma never liked to travel, but who am I to complain? Those days were long gone.

I see them again, these sadist people never tiring of their ritual raging. I wish I could stop them. This doesn't feel right. Scaring the already scared kids. They'd rather spread animosity and anxiety instead of fostering unity and building community. Maybe that's how the world goes around.

"Pain Must Be Shared And Spread""

Something caught my attention though, rather SOMEONE. She looked scared and lonely, tears welling up in her eyes. Another victim of Rohan's nasty pranks. She looked at me and I saw helplessness in her eyes, as if pleading for me to save her. How could I possibly? I am the one who is in dire need of rescuing.

It rained today and brought with it a plethora of memories of how much Vaani loved the rains. Thoughts of her enveloped me, her quivering lips on mine and how she was no longer with me. My consciousness was shadowed by the memory of those lips. When I got hold of myself, I found myself out in the rain, drenched and shivering. Another blackout!

These things keep happening.

The rain distracted me for a moment, or I would've remained lost in darkness. I felt good. I felt alive. After a long time, the rain had calmed the chaos of my mind. Kuku paaji hugged me and said that he missed me, Raju embraced me too. They weren't lying; there was love in their eyes.

I had been missing everything.

I saw her again; twice in a day. Coincidence? She looked different, not like an exotic flower in an expensive flower shop, but like a daffodil dancing in the rain.

She smiled at me, and I didn't know how to respond. I had left my smiling face at home. I just looked away.

I hope she doesn't think that I'm arrogant or rude or an errant who only knows how to ignore people.

I am not myself anymore. I don't even know how it feels to be in my own skin anymore, that's how it is. That's how it has been for quite some time now.

When you lose someone special who has been the reason for your existence, you also lose a piece of yourself somewhere along with them.

Chapter 3

The next day was no different.

It was hard to ignore the leering eyes, knowing that they were waiting to slaughter me with further humiliation. Riya had fetched my syllabus the previous day after I had left the campus. I went to the girls' locker room and slipped into my chef attire for the first class of the day. This was the reason I had joined this college in the first place: BAKERY CLASSES, and my never ending craving for cakes. Guilty 'sweet tooth.' The bakery lab was empty when I reached it. I chose a table in the last row and occupied it with my bag and kit. Soon, more students started filling in, taking their desired spots.

The bakery chef was a slim man in his forties. He was dressed in formals, perhaps his best clothes, for the first class. I had expected him to be in his chef coat.

"Okay, silence everyone," he clapped to get our attention. "Welcome. I won't lecture you about the mundane rules and regulations. You've been chosen to be a part of one of the best colleges in India. Let that sink in. Learn as much as you can and enjoy your college life–love, friendship, team work–everything, because this time won't come again. And yeah, I am Rahul Sharma," he said, settling his spectacles.

"He sure seems cool, doesn't he?" said a guy with short trimmed hair, standing beside me. I shrugged casually.

"Our bakery assistant isn't here, so your senior Shreyansh will help you settle, while I do the paperwork." I was dumbfounded. It was the guy with hazel eyes again, and his name was Shreyansh. He looked quite different than yesterday, fresh as a winter morning. Even in the college uniform, he was beaming, His spiked hair were waxed and that intense look in his eyes was still there.

Shreyansh started grouping us in alphabetical order. I was paired with Manav, the guy with trimmed hair. Shreyansh looked at me for a while, and my breath got stuck in my throat. "Don't give her a hard time," Shreyansh said as he patted Manav's back, and walked away without looking back at me.

"Do you know that guy?" Manav turned to me and asked. "He seems so cool."

"No, I don't. He was just being nice."

"Maybe he was hitting on you," he said, shuffling with his backpack. "Are you serious? That can't be," I said firmly.

"You never know. Hotel management guys are really desperate when it comes to hooking up."

"I don't think he is desperate. Now keep quiet and listen carefully." I don't know why I was defending him.

Whenever my eyes met his, something sparked and my senses froze. His eyes were so intense and lonely that I found myself surrendering to them. The cool dark aura surrounding him calmed my nervous wits, and my fear of getting bullied once again evaporated. The whole practical went by smoothly. He guided us out of our doubts and confusions and gave us confidence. I knew this class would be thrilling to all the others too because it was the first one and we were bursting with curiosity. It was thrilling to me particularly because of him, the way he initiated us into everything. The clouds of my thoughts dissipated when Mr. Rahul called my name for attendance. I rushed to his desk and signed the register. When I turned back, I found the classroom empty and Manav waiting for me at the door. Shreyansh had vanished into thin air. With reluctant steps, I gathered my things and left the lab with Manav.

Everyone rushed for the mess, the very place I was trying to avoid. A huge crowd clogged the hallway leading to the mess. I tuned to slip the other way.

"Where are you going? Mess is this side," Manav interrupted.

"I am not hungry, you can have your lunch. I'll meet you back in class."

"You're hungry, I could hear your stomach rumbling and growling. You're just afraid because of what happened yesterday. Don't worry, no one will bother you anymore," he said in a matter-of-fact tone. So, everybody knew! I realized that Manav was sweeter than the rest. "I know, but I am scared. I don't want to face all of them in one place again and turn myself into a laughing stock."

"Uhhh, okay. I won't force you, but where will you go then?" He gave me a concerned look. "I'll meet you in class, Manav. You go and stuff yourself." I nudged him toward the mess and made my way over to a lecture room. As far as my eyes could see, the stairs were empty, the corridor deserted, and the classrooms locked. I decided to make myself comfortable in the soothing silence at the stairs facing my lecture room, the same stairs where my eyes had met Shreyansh's yesterday. A lot had happened in these past two days, and I wanted a moment by myself to let it all sink in. However, the alluring enigma of Shreyansh still whispered to me, *I'll bring you the rain of peace*. I was thinking too much. "Escaping the crowd already?" I turned around, surprised. Where had that come from? "Here." He tapped the railing

"Oh hello, sir. I mean, afternoon." My thoughts came alive at the sight of him.

"Oh, don't be so formal, Manya. It is Manya, right?" He looked at me. "May I?" He gestured to the vacant space beside me. "Yes…yes, why not?" I stuttered and made space for him. He sat beside me, a distant dream that I was living too soon. "So Manya, how are you today? And you may call me Shrey. I feel decades old when someone calls me *sir*."

"I am better today, thanks to you and the spell you cast in class, Shrey SIR." I smiled.

He smiled back. Oh boy, that smile!

"I am glad. You looked like you had seen a ghost yesterday. Did they give you hard time?

"Oh, I am afraid to say anything. I have now decided to absorb everything that comes my way.

He laughed. "They aren't my acquaintances and I don't participate in their shenanigans to harass kids who are already scared. You may share and bitch with me."

I smiled nervously. "Okay then, why do they do it?"

"A rather sadist trend of sorts, a long lasting one," he sighed.

"And for what good reason did you not join them?" I felt like I was talking too much. Hadn't he already explained it?

"First, I am not sadist. Second, I was blessed with good seniors, so I decided to be one myself," he smiled. Was this guy even real?

"Thank you, sir. When I had lost all hope of having a peaceful life here, you came to prove me wrong," I blushed

He laughed a little. "Don't mention it, you will be okay. Where do you stay, by the way?"

"Mrs. Shila's PG."

"Oh, yeah," he laughed, "She's hot, isn't she?"

I mirrored his laughter that echoed down the deserted staircase. Mrs. Sheila was in her mid 50's and dressed twenty years younger, sporting attires that oddly enveloped her plump body.

"Where do you stay, sir?" *Manya, behave like a good girl,* I told myself. "Two streets away in a studio apartment." He smiled like a child bragging about his belongings. "Where did you put up before? Your stream? How about your family?" I blabbered, failing to hide my nervousness.

"Hush..so many questions? I am from Delhi, with a non medical background. You tell me?"

I gladly took the opportunity to speak. I told him about the place I lived in Bangalore, my schooling, and how humanities provided no good advantage for Hotel Management. I told him about my father, his job, my mother and her exploits as a housewife. I confessed to him how lonely I had felt as a kid, with no siblings to play with. I held nothing back.

Like a good listener, he nodded. Most people crave for someone who would just listen to them. Maybe I had found that someone, or maybe he was just an oasis in a desert, soon to disappear.

The peace of the air that surrounded us vanished soon as a flurry of chaos came our way in the form of students with a satiated appetite. Mess time was over and I realized that we had been talking a long time. Two hours had passed as mere moments with him, like he was casting a spell on me and playing with time to keep my fears at bay.

"Afternoon, sir. Afternoon, sir." Everyone greeted him, and like a gentleman, he nodded and acknowledged everyone with a smile.

Since he was sitting with me, a junior, other batchmates of mine surrounded us. A barrage of questions and answers followed, but he graciously indulged in it throughout. When he left, they sang his praises, but only his eyes–his beautiful eyes–dwelled in my thoughts.

I stood up, inhaled the remnants of his aroma and moved into the lecture room. He'd left me hypnotized. That evening, Riya was waiting for me when I got back. "What took you so long?" she asked. "Nothing. I was just enjoying the walk back. The evenings are beautiful here."

"Really? Yesterday, it was morbid for you. You didn't like this place even a bit.» «This place is slowly growing on me now," I grinned. "Oh, come on. Tell me now. What's the matter? I know you're itching to blabber it out," she asked.

"I talked to that guy," I blushed. "Well, well, well. You're blushing as if he has asked you for marriage," she laughed. "Idiot," I exclaimed. "Alright, I'm sorry. Tell me more! What's his name? And which year?"

"His name is Shreyansh, he's from 3rd year. Same as that dog, Rohan. But he's nothing like him. He's sweet and generous, and all the juniors were heaping praise upon him.» "Don't jump to conclusions too soon. You don't know these seniors. And this place is weird." She didn't seem impressed. "Yeah, you're right. I shouldn't let my expectations drown me all over again. But, weird? How?"

"Well, I'll tell you everything I noticed, but later. Let me tell you something good first," she said. My eyes lit up.

"I am moving into your room!" she smiled and hugged me. I found out that my would be roommate had opted for the hostel, so Riya persuaded Mrs. Sheila to let her shift into my room. She even bribed her with a lip gloss she'd brought from Delhi. Clever girl!

When Riya showed me her things, I was bewildered. She had enough belongings for the entire PG. It took us 30 mins to move her four giant bags loaded with clothes, accessories, cosmetics, footwear and what not from her room to mine. The best thing she had was her giant teddy bear. She told me that her boyfriend had gifted it to her before she left home. It was fluffy and padded, covered all over in white fur, with a black ribbon around its neck that made it look like an advocate. It was big enough to cuddle with in bed. I wanted to ask her more about her boyfriend, mostly since I had never had one in my life, but I decided against it. I didn't want to come across as too nosey to my new roommate. My back ached after lifting all those heavy bags, so I turned down her request to help unpack them. She unfurled some melodious slangs popular in the North, and I simply laughed along, unsure of how to respond.

"So, you were telling me something?"

"Yes. Girls are so clingy here," she said while stuffing the cupboard with her clothes.

"What kind of weird?" I asked.

She laughed aloud. "Well, I was having my lunch in peace when a herd of girls attacked me, a mix of juniors and seniors. They were all from the hostel and tried to recruit me to their herd."

"What did you say?"

"I said, *I am not for sale, bitches*."

I laughed, "Seriously?"

"No. I didn't, stupid. They would've thrashed my face on the food plate." We burst into laughter. She asked me to keep talking to her so she wouldn't fall asleep on the pile of clothes she was folding. It took so long that I had to sneak some food into the room. We ate and tucked ourselves in.

"I want to meet that man," she whispered.

"Who?" I asked.

"I thought you had slept."

"Yeah, I'm sleep talking. I want to meet the guy who's making you sleepless."

"How do you know?" I asked. "Your bed creaks when you twist and turn, if you know what I mean," she winked at me.

"You are so dirty, Riya."

She laughed, "Goodnight, sinner."

27 July

I was never this way, or was I? I can't recall the last time I felt giddy. I am sure that I am more human now, but how can I be with a withering soul and a dead heart? I am a walking carcass with desires and cravings shedding from me until time unknown. And yet...

Today, the juniors looked at me as if I were a deity to be worshipped. I entered the bakery practical class to help Mr. Rahul, and they greeted me like they were my devotees. Poor kids, helpless with so many fears. I tried to be helpful, I decided to be.

Then, out of nowhere, she caught my eye again. I scrolled through the attendance sheet to find out her name and called them out individually. She responded to Manya, aah...what a beautiful name. She cheeped a faint 'yes'. I was hiding behind a mask of strength, yet she stood there with all her fears, agony and vulnerabilities bare.

There and then, I decided to dress her with my strength, or what little I had of it at least.

After the class, I looked for her everywhere. I found her alone, sitting at the lecture room stairs. When I spoke to her, I knew that she would be my deliverance. Words emerged from her mouth like a symphony, her eyes danced like rays of light as her lips formed two perfect petals. Her hair ran wild and lured me to her visage. I was the sailor transfixed by her siren song.

My memories were lost in that moment, and something, something flickered inside of me.

I absconded the questions surrounding me.

The next thing I know, it's 3 AM. I am restless, twisting and turning in my bed, but sleep eludes me. I wonder if I'll ever be sane again.

Thoughts of her are keeping me sane for now. I am willingly falling victim to them like a hypnotized prey.

I wish to find peace someday. I wish to not write in the middle of the night and confess my weaknesses in this way. I wish to feel normal. I wish good things for me.

Chapter 4

When I stepped into college the next morning, I wasn't walking–I was flying. I had the support of a super senior and two Delhites beside me. Oh yes, Mayank too. Delhi people ruled the arena, and the two bonded over their shared geography.

I surrounded myself with crazies and weirdoes. Normal people are boring. It's the crazies and the weirdos who make this world interesting. I felt much better than before. The seniors serving food in the mess stared at the three of us and muttered something to Mayank. He just smiled and I knew they had said something nasty. We were the only ones giggling and talking, while the rest of our batchmates stood in line like prisoners waiting to fill their hungry souls.

"Shouldn't we keep a low profile?" I asked.

"Shrey sir has our backs. We'll be okay," Riya winked.

"Speaking of him, where is he?" Mayank asked. I looked around, still holding my plate.

"There he is, come on."

"Damn, the one reading the book?" Riya asked.

"Yes, the cool one," Mayank exclaimed.

"Look, a threesome already." Some seniors sitting in a group laughed. Before Riya could say something, I elbowed her.

"Can we sit here, sir?"

"It's a free country, kid." Shrey looked up, "Oh, Manya. Come join." We sat around him. "I know you. You came into my room the very first day, right? With all the other guys?" he asked Mayank.

"Yes, sir. I'm Mayank. I live on the floor below yours," Mayank nodded, more like a bow out of respect. "He knows me, this is cool," he whispered to me, loud enough for everyone else to hear.

"And you are..." Shrey asked Riya.

"She's my frien..."

"Allow me, Manya," she cut me off. "I am Riya, her roommate, sir."

"Where are you guys from?" He put his book aside.

"Delhi," Riya and Mayank said in unison. "That makes the three of us," Shrey added.

"Cool!!" Mayank said and Riya imitated him. We burst into laughter.

"I am the only odd one out here." I made a puppy face.

"You're the only odd one in," Shrey winked at me. I blushed internally, he was acknowledging me as a part of this tiny group. "Did you guys like this place?" he asked.

"Yeah. But seniors here are crazy and rude," Riya said. I gave her a piercing stare. "I mean some, not you, sir. You're lovely. Manya was singing praises about you.»

Shrey laughed. The seniors on the other table looked at us. On no other table where juniors sitting with seniors, and we were hot property, or maybe a target. "Yes, you'll find exceptions everywhere. They're good people though. Well, some are," he said.

"Why do they have to bully us? We're already scared having come here, leaving our home and stuff," I said meekly.

"They've been victims of bullying themselves, so they bully others to derive satisfaction. Their seniors bullied them, and they bully you. But it's only a matter of time before they get friendly. They just want to give you a head start for things that will come in your way in future," he said.

"Such a bad and cruel head start," Mayank murmured.

"Cool, boy, nothing comes easy in life. It's the struggle and will to survive that makes life interesting and worthwhile," Shrey patted his hand.

"Then why didn't you participate? You weren't there at the introduction session, and I don't see you lurking around teasing juniors," Riya said.

"There's a story behind it. When I was in my first year, the second year seniors came to my room and tried to take my snacks. I was in a hostel back then, and snacks were no less than gold. I asked them to leave a few since my mom had packed them for me. Instead, he started making fun of me and my mother. I would've let him take them, but he dragged my mother into it. So, I grabbed him and punched him in the face." He shadow punched Mayank and we laughed. "Later that day, a group of second year seniors showed up to beat me up, and my roommate pissed his pants. I stood there shaking with fear, scared out of my wits, but I stood my ground. Some 3rd year boys were also present and they told me that since I had shown courage and stood up for right thing, they liked me and didn't let the second year bullies touch me. Soon, I was a part of their group. No one bullied me anymore. That's why I don't bully others. I want to be like that good senior I had."

"You're so cool and badass," Mayank exclaimed and we nodded grinning, mesmerized by him. He laughed, "Not really, I was fortunate. If the 3rd years hadn't been there, I would've wandered the college halls with broken plastered bones, bruises and black eyes."

"But what about the rules? I heard that colleges take undertakings from all the seniors before every session to prevent ragging."

"Yes, they do, but this just started after our 1st year. The college wasn't that high on rules before. We were free. Because of some clingy lovers, smokers, and bullies, the college authorities became strict. The culprit was our batch as they were running riots here. Stupid people," he sighed.

We talked as long as our break time allowed. His wit and charm ruled over our minds. His words created magic. We found ourselves fortunate to have met him. He was a lullaby to our ears. All these different people of varied shades, it was hard to figure out who was who. What were they? What did they want? It was a rude awakening here. I found myself caged in an unknown unparalleled realm–an alien planet.

I longed for a peaceful and calm environment. I wanted to be left alone to live in my shell. I had always been a shy girl, who minded her own business. I had refrained myself from connections and desires before, and here I was. There was something happening-something strange; something I had not yet discovered about myself.

28th July

I like to observe people when they are vulnerable or scared. Walking up and down, trying to escape everyone who encounters them, and avoiding further exploitation. The best part is when they manage to find hope in spite of their pain. It's a beautiful thing to watch them in hope of being understood and accepted. It's even more beautiful to watch them welcome those things into their lives.

"Hope. Hope is a dangerous thing to seek. Hope is the only thing powerful enough to sustain breath."

This is the hope I see in her frightened eyes, those agitated beautiful eyes. They say, "You can see someone's soul through their eyes." I see her soul right there, trembling within, asking to be honoured. I can feel her desperation to be honoured, her longing for acceptance. Who are we to deny her that? When did we 'humans' become so shallow?

Manya

I searched for the meaning of her name. 'Worthy of honour,' it said. Even her name demands and asks for the same. I shall give it to her. I will protect her; whatever comes to destroy her will destroy me first. It's too absurd to think about her, it's even stranger to write about her, but her smile is too captivating, and I wish to protect her.

But I feel too worn out now to struggle. I am stuck here in the abyss where every light is evanescent. I'm stuck to the bottom of this blackness where I lay deconstructed and defeated. From where will I gather the courage to stand for her? My mind, these thoughts are taking over. I'm not in control of me anymore. I often wander in this labyrinth and sometimes I don't come back. I wonder sometimes if I will meet Medusa's eyes and turn to stone. Maybe I already have. It's crazy to live so much in your mind that you've lost all hope of being a functional human being. I thought I'd lost all hope of living, really living, in any kind of reality.

But something strange is happening to me. I am coming back now. I am being redeemed. She has found me. She leads my way and lights my path. From the dark labyrinth, I come out, hand in hand with her. She kisses my cold stone heart awake. Medusa fears her beauty and I am free to wander with her.

This is unbelievable. I know nothing about her. She knows nothing about me. Yet, there is something which compels me to look for her. And I will. I'll help her because I'm selfish. Leaving her before she gets a hold on herself would not only be wrong, but also destructive to both our spirits. My soul demands her, demands to help this person longing to be saved.

Chapter 5

I lay there like a sloth. It was Sunday morning. My existence ached. The hectic first week of college had taken a toll on my body and I needed rest. One day wasn't enough to get rid of all this lethargy. Due to the introductory session on Monday, our Saturday off was utilised to compensate our weekly schedule. "No rest for the wicked," Shrey had said. "Manya? Manya?" Riya's sleepy voice echoed in my ears. "Uhhun…what, Riya?" "Do you want to grab something to eat?"

"What time is it?"

"11:30."

"Let's sleep some more."

"Okay, goodnight."

It was already lunch time when we got up. "Hey, just brush, take a dump, and run. Mealtime will be over soon," Riya shrieked from the bathroom. We reached there just in time, but received the cold stare of Mrs. Shila as if we were stealing her food. We sat in front of her like arrogant little thieves, looked into her eyes, and giggled. Like the bitch she was, she ignored us. Ironically for a PG owner, she really hated kids.

"Fat old bitch," Riya whispered. I nodded. This was the thing with me–whenever I was hungry, everything else faded away. Riya's lips moved at the pace of light. I simply nodded and nodded, not registering a single of her words, till my ravenous hunger was quenched.

"Manya, you listening to me?"

"Mmhmm…"

"Alright, so I was saying…" Blank again. "Can I join you girls?" asked a girl standing by out table. I hadn't seen her before in our PG. I looked at Riya, she shrugged. I shrugged too and she sat with us. She had a head full of curly hair falling over her pale face. We had the company of a stranger for the first time in our private space.

"And you are?" Riya asked.

"I am Soumya. Pardon me for intruding. We're in the same college." There were a dozen girls from our college in the PG, but nobody talked to us since all of them were seniors. I figured that Soumya must be a fresher. "Aren't you a week late?" I asked.

"Yeah, I had some issue."

"Well, you missed a lot, girl," Riya said.

"Oh, yeah? Tell me about it."

"Well, the college sucks. Boring classes, practicals are bitches that bite, food in the mess is like that in a prison. So, yeah — shit. You missed shit. And don't even get me started on the seniors. This woman right here was almost molested," Riya sighed.

"Calm down, girl." I patted her back. "Were you?" Soumya asked. "No, hell no. I mean, yes. They ragged me, insulted me, ridiculed me and stuff," I said.

"That's bad, will they do the same to me?" Soumya asked.

"You can't trust those suckers. They're an illiterate mob of piece-of-shit sadists. But don't you fear, we've got your back. We know a good senior now, but I am not sure if he's truly good or just pretending. Manya has fallen all over him," Riya said. I slapped her hand.

"Everyone's the same," I sighed. I could have protested, but what would that have achieved? I wasn't going to fall for sweet talk again. The world is mud and people only treat you well when they want something in return. When they want to move out of the mud and up the ladder, and after they've climbed it, they will throw the ladder back in the mud.

Mondays are like those ex lovers who's promises as hollow as they are. The college looked more crowded that day. One of the hostlers, Maryam, told us that a lot of seniors had come back from their homes just the previous evening. Suddenly, the college looked busier than ever with more seniors, and the threat increased manifold. My mind whirled when I saw Shrey talking to Soumya. She looked as though she had known Shrey for a long time — laughing, high-fiving, and hugging him. I frowned and wondered who she was. Had I made an enemy? Then, I grabbed their attention. The lamb walked by the bushes towards the water, but was seen by the predators and summoned. Their jungle, their rules. The prey must obey to survive. So I walked to them, accepting my fate.

"Hello, Manya. Meet my only bff, fellow comrade, acquaintance and part-time mother," Shrey grinned. Soumya slapped his arm and smiled at me. I stood there like a corpse.

"I know her," Soumya said. *Yes, you do, Soumya. And now you're going to fuck everything up. Holy mother of awful luck.* "Right, you both live under same roof of Mrs. Shila," Shrey chuckled. They laughed. I felt as if they were laughing at my fate.

"By the way, Manya told me a lot about her recent endeavours in college." There, they started preparing me for slaughter.

"Anything good? What about me?" Shrey asked.

"Yes, only praises." Soumya smiled at me and I sighed in relief. That was a close escape. I bid them both adieu and decided to run away before she could change her mind and allow the axe of slaughter to fall on me. My cynic conscience told me that Soumya was taming me to enjoy the fruits of my shame later. Or maybe not. Maybe she was actually sweet. Maybe.

College was a game of *maybes* now. I finished my practical first, then went straight to the mess. Rahul sir praised my hand in bakery that day, I was quick at it. I had always wanted to make cakes, from the time I first started eating. The science behind it excited me, the gastronomy and the texture. I used to call it 'fluffy heaven' when I was a kid. My sweet tooth which had no chill had led me to this college at last. If you gotta eat it, you should know how to bake it. "Move along fast, girl." The seniors didn't even look into your eyes while serving, like we were some underprivileged kids, begging for food. I took my plate and moved. Finding a vacant seat during mess time was like finding a needle in a hay-stack.

"Watch your step, kid." My shoulder brushed against someone. I looked up and frowned. My stars must have been aligned the worst possible way that day. "Isn't that the same girl from first day, Rohan?" the girl with curls grinned.

"Oh, yes she is," Rohan said, grabbing the bowl of salad from my plate.

"Sir, can I…"

"No, you can't till we dismiss you." The girl stared at me. She looked scary. I nodded like a lamb. "Let it be, babe. I am hungry. We'll play with the kids later." Rohan grabbed her arm and they walked away giggling, shouting at the other juniors. Play? We were no more than mere toys for them.

The lectures after lunch were pure torture. When your belly is stuffed, all you can think of is sleep. I tried hard to concentrate but the class was simply dragging on. I could see other students check their watches, waiting for the lecture to get over soon.

Most of these lectures were tiring. Some were about different cuisines, while my favourite was accounts — the only lecture where I managed to concentrate the best. Nutrition went over my head for the most part; I couldn't understand the composition of carbohydrates, protein, and vitamins.

Then there was Housekeeping where Reshma ma'am kept on giving us written work to do. Same was with Front Office. It was difficult to keep pace with the teachers and make notes at the same time. So, we simply swung to and fro to their beats. Like a pied piper, they charmed us to sleep and continued on with their teaching. I appreciated their enthusiasm. Despite knowing that they were making us drowsy, they went on and on. I wanted such dedication in my life. Once, I was giving in to drowsiness during a Nutritions lecture. Though Yogesh sir would say something funny now and then to keep us engaged, everything was in vain today. I felt for him, he was one of my favourite lecturers. My gaze wandered over to the corridor, and to my surprise, I spotted Shreyansh hovering around our lecture hall door. He was speaking to a junior who came in the room and said something to Mr. Yogesh.

"Manya, Ms. Reshma wants to see you. Please go to the staff room," Mr. Yogesh said. I nodded and left the class with my bag. Shreyansh was standing near the stairs, waiting for me. "Don't you have a class?" I asked. "Vacant lecture," he replied. "Lucky you."

"You are lucky too."

«How?»

"I called you out."

"So, Reshma ma'am doesn't want to see me?"

"No, but Shreyansh sir does," he smirked. "We might get in trouble."

"No, we won't." He held my hand and took me out of the college. "I want to show you something."

He led me to the lawns near the staff quarters. There was an abandoned cottage built under a huge tree. It was expansive. The corroded plaster of the walls and the cracks filled with algae gave it an old-timey aesthetic. It captivated the fancy of my wandering soul.

"It used to be a canteen," he told me. The place was barren inside, taken over by florets and wild bushes. There were benches laid around, blanketed by dirt. He dusted one with a leaf and we sat.

"A young guy used to come here with samosas, bread pakodas and tea. We used to sit here and enjoy it together, talking. He was a nice lad," he said.

"What happened to him now?"

"What usually happens, life. He lived with his mother and she was old and ill. Maybe they didn't have enough money for treatment, so she died. He never came back to our college after that. College decided to run its own tuck shop here, but failed to replicate the taste, the aroma of the tea and the feel. I can still feel it lingering around here. What once used to be life is completely barren now," he sighed. "Lots of love stories flourished here too, and behind those bushes. The first taste of love, weed and even alcohol," he winked. "Rohan first talked to Tanya here, after I pestered him for days."

"You were his friend?" I asked, shocked.

"Once," he said looking around, as if lost somewhere. There was something off about him that day. He had lied to call me out. Even though there were other girls far better looking than me who had been fawning over him since the first day, he had chosen me. Why? I couldn't fathom. I was not used to receiving such attention, and it had made me cynical about such gestures. Was he hitting on me? I couldn't gulp down being treated in such a special way.

I recollected my thoughts and looked around. I could hear birds chirping in the distance. My hand brushed against his fingers and I felt a sudden rush of something in me that I had never felt before. The feeling was alien to me. He put his hand on mine and smiled. His hand was cold and rough. My breath got struck in my throat and my heart thumped at the speed of light.

"Did you like this place?" he whispered. Like a song in my ear, it echoed through my consciousness. I wanted to grab his face right there and taste the venom from his lips. But I didn't have the courage. I never did. I only smiled and nodded.

2nd August

I look around and everything astonishes me. How easily these people get by their day, like it is nothing. They blink and their 24 hours are over. They giggle and run around happily. How can they be so happy? It's ridiculous. Why can't I be happy? Why can't I be at peace?

Here I am, struggling to pass each hour. I feel as if I am cursed to remain here for an eternity, stuck to a misery I never asked for or deserved. Someday, it will be okay. It has to be. Someday, I will be okay.

For now, I am not okay. It's disgusting to feel this way. I'm always complaining about my condition to myself. It is tiring. Everything hurts, but I don't feel like sharing anything with anyone at all. I don't want to come across as vulnerable and broken. This mask of strength and angry-man is working alright for me. I don't know anyone willing to hear me out. Who really wants to know about me? About me lying down on the floor aghast, or blacked out for hours in the shower or even these rants? None of them will ever care to listen. They don't know how I'm falling apart when it comes to reality. They can't know.

This is my only way to hold onto myself. It's the only way to struggle within, to fight within and grow stronger with the passing time. I get it now, life isn't about all this. This is all about getting through days, hoping for a better tomorrow. Maybe, maybe someday it will be. I'll work to make it happen. I'll work for it because I wish to.

Things are getting better. Soumya came back from home and brought me a lot of homemade snacks. She told me that she and her elder sister talk about me. Her sister talks to me often, she's sweet enough. Apart from Manya, I have Soumya too. College works fine and nothing hits during the lectures. I feel better and more content.

Everything was fine before I took her to the hut, where everything rushed back to me with the breeze; all the memories and emotions.

I was lost there; even with Manya, I felt lost. Why do people have to leave? Why don't people understand? Rohan should've understood me, after whatever we were and whatever we shared. He was that one person I used to look at and feel how blessed I am to have him as a friend. I used to imagine watching our kids grow up and play together. I was so stupid back then. I suppose, it just wasn't meant to be.

I get it, it's moronic to expect people to understand.

I'm deciding to let it go.

I let go of everything I possess, sooner or later.

Chapter 6

I sat wondering the entire night if they were acquaintances. He did say that he had asked Rohan to approach the curly haired girl, Tanya, which meant they were or could still be on talking terms. Who knew? The dilemma was – who should I ask? The only senior I knew was Soumya, but not well enough. I didn't feel comfortable asking her in any case. I had been trying to avoid her since that day. There was so much going on in my head that I felt crippled. The Basic Training Restaurant was filled with seniors.

It was on Tuesday during our food and beverages practical, and I wondered why they were hovering there. They had their own place in the Advance Training Restaurant. I put my bag in a corner and stood with my batchmates, hiding behind some tall guys when I saw Rohan and Tanya. Mayank then told me that we had to share the Food and Beverages class with our 3rd year seniors. They were to guide us through the practical. I sighed. One more place to feel too conscious, despite the attendant being there throughout to ensure that none of them bothered the juniors.

Somehow, the devil always finds a way to get to you. They threw all their work on us, and bossed us around. The attendant unfortunately turned out to have sworn allegiance to them, so he turned a blind eye to their atrocities. Curse them, hate them, but you couldn't escape them. No lecturer was present there that day. We worked there while the seniors escaped one by one from the attendant's eyes. Truth be told, he let them leave. Those were still early days for us, so no one really thought of bunking a class. "Are you coming to the mess?" Mayank asked after the practical was over.

I shook my head. "I am not hungry. I'll meet you in class." He nodded and left. I had some work pending, so I left for the lecture room which was vacant. I sat at my favourite spot near the window, since the only thing that could save me from the boredom of the lectures was the sight outside–the setting sun over farms, birds chirping, and trees dancing to the symphony of the breeze.

Above in the sky, Shrey's lost and lonely eyes danced in the clouds while thoughts of him rained over me. I finished my work and wandered in the corridor for a while as people started filling in at a snail's pace. I sat on the stairs and waited for Mayank and Riya. I hadn't shared anything with her about the events of the previous day. There should be some things which you keep hidden from the world, and that part for me was Shrey. Those parts now occupied me whole, consuming my every thought.

The heavy sound of footsteps broke my devotion and carried my attention to its source. I turned around to find Rohan and that curly haired girl Tanya, approaching with their group. Facing those monsters again was the last thing I had expected to do today. I got up in haste to leave before they had the chance to slaughter me again. I didn't want to bleed embarrassment. With quickened steps, I walked in the opposite direction.

The corridor was still empty and I could hear giggles and the sound of footsteps approaching me. I quickened my pace, exiting from the stairs at the opposite corner. While climbing down, I stumbled and tripped on something. Reel life seldom comes to fruition in real life, but this time, a movie moment found its way into my reality! It was fascinating how my heart conjures thoughts whenever I was around him–my knight with shining armour. He seemed to have come into my life to save my soul and equip me with confidence and security. Everything happened so quickly that I found myself dumbstruck in Shreyansh's arms, not even trying to gather myself back. I felt transfixed by his vehement eyes, making me restless again.

"Want to stay in my arms forever?" he smirked, staring into my eyes. Deep down, my heart whispered, *yes, yes, why not? You don't know how badly I want it.* Then I saw Soumya behind him, giggling at my stupidity. I gathered myself. There was a universe in his eyes and I couldn't break contact. I did not want this moment to ever end, but as fate had it, it did sooner than expected.

"Wohoo! Look at these love birds. Isn't it romantic? Loner got a girlfriend, and guess who she is?! Our very own nightingale," Rohan chuckled. His condescending look, with that objectionable comment further heated my already boiling blood. I cursed him within for spoiling such a good moment.

By then, Shreyansh had stepped forward and hid me behind him. Soumya held my hand. I felt protected. A crowd started gathering, as a tussle between two 3rd year students was no doubt appealing. The freshers looked rather excited amidst the chaos. Shreyansh looked calm and unfazed. I had never meet anyone so coolheaded as him.

"Look at cry baby. he's got the guts to speak up to his father. Looks like your he-man girlfriend is giving you enough courage. Right, Tanya?" Shreyansh laughed, and the crowd laughed with him. Fluttered with embarrassment, Rohan stopped Tanya from saying anything. It felt as if he wanted to win this fight on his own. My heart rejoiced as I watched them getting humiliated–an oasis in the desert of my previous shame. Rohan's gaze flickered to me and I knew he would target me next.

"Why are you laughing? Keeping crow-voice happy, huh? Elated to have your sugar daddy protecting you?" He knew his words against Shreyansh wouldn't affect him so he had shifted to me. I wasn't surprised. Hundreds of eyes stared at me, ready to tear me to shreds. I stood silent like a dumb bimbo, too frozen to react. "Rohan, how dare you say something to her? Don't drag her into our flight. Otherwise, I'll forget that you were ever my friend."

I looked at Soumya, and she nodded. "Yes, they were best buddies," she whispered. I wondered what had caused them to separate.

"We're not friends anymore, are we? I won't think twice before shredding you apart."

"You'll shred me, kiddo? Remember, I saved you from our seniors when you pissed your pants in terror." Another nuclear attack by Shreyansh.

"Yes Manya, he is the roommate I told you about," he smirked. Everyone laughed, even the people behind Rohan.

The whole mob endorsed Shreyansh, supporting him like a saviour. Flames subsided in the eyes of Rohan and Tanya as though the world had come crashing around them with no chance of rescue. Soumya patted Shreyansh's back and clutched his hand tight, smiling at him. I was glad that someone had taken a stand for me. A sudden realisation dawned upon me, however. Maybe I had underestimated Rohan. His silence bothered me. One couldn't expect a person like him to be silent for long, his tail between his legs.

The very next moment, he blurted out, "So what? I was scared, just like your whore Manya. At least I didn't attempt suicide like a loser. My girlfriend didn't cheat on me with her best friend. Poor Shreyansh, I pity you. Are you still depressed? What about your medications? I hope you are still taking them."

The crowd behind Shreyansh went silent. Rohan had stepped on a sensitive nerve. People in Rohan's group smiled, high fives were exchanged, and Tanya held Rohan's hand and grinned. I looked at Shreyansh for answers. Was it all true? I looked at Soumya and she looked away. He just stood there smiling. His eyes were sad and lonely. It was painful to look at him like that. He tried to hide it and was successful perhaps at suppressing it from others, but it caught my attention. My soul died a thousand terrible deaths within. He wasn't anything to me yet, but the look bothered me. It made me cringe inside with helplessness. He was hiding something traumatic, it was visible now. That visage of deep sorrow disappeared within a blink of an eye, and morphed into fury and furore. For the first time since I had met him, I felt scared of him. I could see Rohan getting tensed too. Everyone could sense something coming from Shreyansh and braced themselves for a violent reply. He stood 2-3 inches taller than Rohan and was more muscular. Everyone remained static as Shreyansh stepped forward towards Rohan.

"Cheap shot," he smiled at Rohan, patted his shoulder and walked away, leaving everyone stunned.

Rohan laughed and howled like a mad dog and everyone in his group followed suit, including his girlfriend Tanya. Rohan knew that he had made a narrow escape. Everyone knew. Soumya vanished after Shreyansh, and I was left stranded on the staircase.

The crowd dispersed to their respective classrooms and I rushed to my lecture room as well. I peeked into Shreyansh's class on my way, but he wasn't there. Soumya was. I couldn't find Riya or Mayank in my classroom. It was getting late, so I decided to sit alone by the window. I was in desperate need of fresh air. I couldn't stop thinking if Rohan had been right, if Shreyansh's past was that dark, and how I had ended up here.

All these questions kept bothering me during the lecture. I saw his melancholy eyes wherever I looked. I was desperate to know all that had happened to him. I looked outside the window – birds were chirping a song of loneliness. The atmosphere was growing soothing and dark. A gentle breeze cruised in, rafting through my hair and bringing with it the smell of longing and craving that I saw in his eyes. The enigma building around him seemed like a dark hazy evening. And here I was, craving to be submerged in it.

6th August

Do you ever feel tired? The kind of exhaustion that grows within as days pass? Its roots settle in the nerves and turn dense. Yes, that tiredness. The one that destroys you from within.

I am tired now. I feel tired of everything around me, but no one understands that. No one will. I wish they could know the things I struggle with, maybe they wouldn't mock me then. I wish I could scream at the top of my lungs and tell them about this sadness that eats me from the inside How it feels to be ten feet under water with your body tied to an anchor that's pulling you down, down, down. You know you need to find your way back to the surface, but you can't seem to untie yourself. Your will-power has been reduced to nothing and you have become a victim of your own circumstance; a victim of your own apathy and inability to fight.

Of course, nobody bothers to ask. They find it easier to pretend that there is nothing wrong with me. When my parents look at me, they think of me as an innocent boy from childhood. I think they want me to remain that way, frozen in time. They need me to remain unchanged–it's more comfortable for them, probably because they can't imagine or think that the happy child they nurtured has turned into such a sad soul. Maybe they just don't want to face the reality of their own flawed parenting. Perhaps they see their failure in my face. If only I could make everyone understand. If only my parents understood how tired I am! I'm tired of everything happening around me and I don't know when it'll end. Sometimes, night haunts me. No one saves me, no one tries. Those who try, can't help either. They can't understand the mess that is inside of me and my brain. They cannot fathom the idea of a human being in so much pain, pretending everything is fine.

The worst part about being consumed by love for someone is that you lose yourself to the point of no return The other person monitors you and maintains a surveillance on how you move, what you think, who you speak to, and everything you have to say. It becomes a routine that never breaks. It just sticks with you, even when they are gone. The worst part isn't when they leave, it is when you lay awake in bed, basking in twilight, and all the memories that are buried inside of your wounds begin to burst and expose themselves You wait for someone to stitch them back, but no one comes. So you leave them open to fester. The hardest part is having to come to terms with their absence and finding yourself unable to accept it.

Worse yet is preparing the other side of the bed and waking up in the morning to see that it has remained intact. What's more horrific than giving your whole being to someone in its entirety, unconditionally, and suddenly being left with nothing when they abandon you? There you are stripped bare, skin and bones.

Goodbye cuts deep and the pain is released slowly in waves, the blood of regret. I need someone to help me. I need to help myself.

Chapter 7

My first few days of college life were a roller-coaster ride. I managed to get through two weeks of the first semester despite all the confusion. I had still not gotten rid of the uncertainty regarding whether hotel management as a career was the best option for me or not. Every passing minute left me more muddled with my thoughts. I had no control over them; I had no peace.

My career wasn't the first priority; the main focus now was dealing with the chaos that would surround me for three straight years ahead. I could build my career after that if I could just get through these years unscathed. Trying to survive under the influence of a strict conformist and binding environment was no easy task. Rules are for lambs, while wolves wander free.

The daily ache of practical classes was like surviving a Zombie apocalypse. There was no escape, but to tackle the situations ahead. An escape only invited the sharp bite of short attendance and a marksheet teeming with bright red. My schedule had Bakery, Food and Beverages Service, Front Office/Housekeeping on the same day and then Food Production last on all individual days. Food Production and Bakery practicals lasted 4 hours, sometimes more, without any rest. For four straight hours, one stood there whisking eggs, making dough, frying vegetables, peeling potatoes, cutting vegetables, and what not.

Housekeeping and Front Office were arid and weary. Food and Beverages got nasty when we were told to work with the seniors. It was simply unbearable. As far as college was concerned, it was way better than a hotel where you'd have to work for at least ten to twelve hours per day. After practicals, we had our lunch break, but that joy was never long lasting since we had to face the trauma of theory classes soon after. People outside the college wondered what and why we learnt cooking and serving. They believed that Hotel Management was a downward spiral where we were doomed to a life of chef/cook or waiter. I faced these remarks from neighbours and relatives.

One has to make the effort and swim through all the hardships that come in the way. Waves shall come to collide with your courage, shatter against your will and confidence, but you can conquer the ocean. It was all about tackling challenges and getting through.

Migratory birds always fascinated me. They left their nests as though they never had an attachment to it and searched for a new home far away. When seasons changed and resources decreased, they moved to another place for resources, food, a favourable climate and shelter. While moving away from home, humans desire the same, but we don't adapt so quickly.

I had been a baby bird myself when I left home. My destiny had led me to Riya and Mayank. The clouds of isolation and solitariness over me vanished when I got together with them. I had found myself a flock that didn't judge me and accepted me for who I was, rather than for what the world wanted me to be. In an ocean of callous people, they were like ripples of compassion. I was free with them. Yet, shelter was something I still craved for.

I was still homeless.

My potential home was lost.

It was lost in the storm of his homelessness. The puzzle of my life was inching towards completion, but the piece containing Shrey was still missing. We hadn't spoken after that incident with Rohan. I felt as though he was running from me, or perhaps from himself, the murk of his past. I dressed in questions and roamed for answers to denude me. It's not that I didn't try, but those hazel eyes kept me at bay through those nervous glances shared between us.

The sound of a ghazal filled the room as I lay there, succumbing to the symphony of the slow track, trying to find some peace. Riya was absorbed in her phone, grinning stupidly. People in love seem no less than fools to me. I had never thought I would ever be a victim, but we don't have a say in this. Love chooses its victim on its own. "Why are you smiling like an idiot?" I asked.

"Nothing, Rehan and his stupid jokes." She put her phone aside.

"Tell me something, what's up with you and Shreyansh? Didn't you guys talk after that tussle?"

How could I answer the same question I had been asking myself. "Can we skip this?" I sighed.

"No, we aren't. I know something is bothering you."

"Okay. We haven't spoken since the fight."

"Why? Did you try?"

I sighed, "Nothing more than just some nervous glances. Do you think it's because of his past?"

Riya nodded. A brief silence followed.

"The look in his eyes rejects me. I feel them yelling at me to not approach him. I don't know why he is behaving so strangely."

"Maybe he wants to escape and your face looks like a big question mark. Should I ask him out for you? Or how about proposing to him on your behalf?" she grinned.

"Hahaha, very funny, Riya. Should I laugh?" She threw a cushion at me.

"Yes, you can laugh, you confused melancholic creature. Talk to him or else you'll die in suspense, and I won't be able to drink and dance at your wedding." I chuckled. Perhaps she was right, perhaps Shreyansh wasn't comfortable enough yet to open up to me about his past. Maybe all he needed at the moment was a time out from his miseries.

"Do you think Soumya will be mad at us?" I asked.

"I don't think so. She would've come to us by now if that was the case," she replied. I nodded, yet still suspicious. While I tried calming my mind, someone knocked at the door. Riya, the lazy ass, asked me to open it, and I dragged myself up. Soumya stood on the other side in her PJs, smiling. I felt a wave of nerves course through me for a second, but her smile didn't seem like a storm's arrival. I could tell a lot about people by their smiles. Rohan smiled like the devil incarcerate, Tanya like a witch, looking to slaughter her prey, Riya like a trusted sister, Mayank like a mischievous kid, Soumya like a mother, and Shrey...I hadn't been able to deduce anything from his mysterious smile. It had been both charming and sensuous until that day it lied to me. That lonely, lost, and scared smile had been hiding millions of emotions behind it.

She came in and sat on the couch. Riya looked at me and frowned. "Ma'am, I didn't mean to insult seniors that day. There are exceptions, like you," I said meekly. "It's okay, girls. You didn't offend me," she smiled. "I am not like Rohan and his friends. I am here to make you guys comfortable so you can stop the hiding game."

"We were scared that we had got on your bad side," Riya said and I nodded. "Well, you did nothing to offend me," she said. "And our differences are with the hostlers, the rest of us should stick together."

"Differences with hostlers? Why?" I asked.

"Another long hold-up like ragging. They feel that they are superior, when in reality, they are clumsy informers and boot lickers," she groaned.

"Just because they got a hostel by a good rank, they think they rule the college. They are Mr. Thakur's spies." We laughed. Mr. Thakur was always serious about rules.

"Why did you lie earlier when we first meet?" Riya asked.

"I just wanted to know about your troubles and the things I missed on my extended vacation."

"Aren't you concerned about short attendance?" I asked.

"It's just a myth to scare the new kids. Attendance doesn't matter," she sighed. This college was a world of lies. I wanted to ask about Shrey too, but I refrained. I wanted my answers from him directly. I wanted to tell him that I wouldn't exploit his vulnerabilities. I was vulnerable myself, and two vulnerable people can't manoeuvre each other.

I didn't want to be his end. I wanted to be his beginning.

11th August

My mind isn't under my control these days. It travels in spirals of thoughts and questions, but without any answers. It feels like I have no control over my body now. I am a possessed corpse, a zombie.

I am surviving this life for now. I have promised myself a thousand times to not give up, but that's all I wish to do once and for all. But, I won't. I won't, because I shouldn't. I cannot. I have to survive until I can learn to live.

If I can learn to live, I will have to fight. I will have to convince myself that my sadness is a condition that lives under the layers of my skin, which I can't get rid of. The only remedy is to add a layer of armour over it. This will make me a 'survivor'.

I can't give up just yet. There's something in me that still wants to fight. Though the tunnel seems long and I've to travel far, there has to be a light at the end of it all and I have to find it, for the people who still care for me, but most of all, for myself.

Somedays, I promise myself that I won't give up. Other days, I struggle thinking of reasons to live. Sometimes, I wonder how long I can survive this way. How long can I breathe until it doesn't feel like a burden? I always end up choosing life.

"Trauma victims cannot recover until they become familiar with and befriend the sensations in their bodies Being frightened means that you live in a body that is always on guard. Angry people live in angry bodies. The bodies of child abuse victims are tense and defensive until they find a way to relax and feel safe. In order to change, people need to become aware of their sensations and the way that their bodies interact with the world around them. Physical self-awareness is the first step in releasing the tyranny of the past. " — Bessel A. van der Kolk I can't find a way to accept this body and all these cravings and desires it demands. I have to try and embrace this sensation somehow. I live in the body of a soldier who is at war with himself. In order to accept myself, I've got to embrace these *desires and cravings, and somehow win myself back from them. I know I will.*

Chapter 8

I couldn't sleep well the following nights. Over thinking was killing me, but I couldn't stop myself. If only there were a switch to flip and shut off my thoughts, I would have had peace. My heart, the untamed beast, wanted whatever it wanted. It wanted to wander wild and free into the arms of Shreyansh.

The entire college talked about the fight for a whole week. It wasn't new for the seniors, but it amused us juniors rather much.

"Shreyansh sir should have punched that dog Rohan," I heard someone whispering in a lecture.

"I wonder what he would've done to Rohan's pretty face. I go to the same gym Shreyansh goes to. That guy is a beast." *Yeah, a hollow beast. A hurt, scared thing wandering around with broken pieces of himself.* Nobody talked about what he was going through. Even the generation most prone to depression wasn't ready to talk about it. Maybe they weren't able to believe that a guy like him could be depressed. If only they knew, that happy face hid scars and unspoken pain.

One day, Riya and I had gotten late and rushed through the empty corridors of the college in terror.

"Should we bunk?" she grinned.

I pushed Riya into her class and walked towards mine, only to find it empty though. A hand reached my shoulder and I turned around to find Mayank standing there with a crooked smile.

"Princi called a meeting, Mr. Yogesh is there. No practical today," he said excitedly. "Isn't it cool?"

There it was — his pet word 'cool' he used with everything. Apparently, even while mourning over a death, he would say, 'WHAT A TRAGICALLY COOL DEATH!'

"Where should we go now, Mayank?"

"The library, or there is a cool lawn near the college gate where all the other students are."

"I am not so sure about sitting with the crowd."

He repeated my words back to me in a mocking fashion and said, "Fine, we won't sit. Come now, or I will drag you."

The said lawn was just before the main college gate. I had seen it when Shrey had taken me to that cottage. The lawn was mesmerizing. It was lavishly built, covered with florets on both sides, alluring enough to catch your senses off-guard. The ground was covered by a carpet of grass, the kind where your toes digs in and make you feel as though you're standing on clouds.

Some of my practical classmates were sitting there in a group and chatting, mostly hostlers. Mayank and I made our way over to them, but the look they gave us barked 'stay away', so we did.

"They hate me." I crashed down to the ground under the shade of a tree.

"They don't hate you, they hate us."

"You know about it?" I asked. He nodded. "But why?"

"Well, I'm sure there's a super cool story behind it," he said. "I'll find it out soon."

"Creepy people," I said, digging up dirt.

"Where else can we go? These hostlers are everywhere."

"Come, I'll show you a place," I said and stood up.

We crossed the lawn and walked over to the college building near the staff quarters. There were some couples snuggling beside the cottage that Shrey had taken me to. Mayank looked surprised. "Yeah right," I whispered. "Keep following me." I took him inside. There was no one there.

"Wow, Manya. How did you come across this place. It is so cool!" He was elated like a child who had found a secret hiding place away from the world.

"Because of me." Shreyansh was standing by the door, smoking.

"Cool place, sir," Mayank said, "Can I have a puff?"

Shrey and I gave him a surprised look. He grinned. "You take this, I'll light another." Mayank took the cigarette and walked out. I didn't find smoking cool at all, neither did I know that Shrey smoked. I wondered what else I didn't know about him.

The chaos outside sounded deafening because of the silence between us. He took another cigarette out and lit it.

"So, Shreyansh sir has got the time to talk to his juniors at last," I muttered, kicking dirt. I don't know how I got the courage to be blunt, but I did. Maybe his presence was enough to conjure up courage in me. He finished his cigarette in a few puffs, took some mint out of his pocket, slipped a few under his tongue and passed some to me.

"Not every other junior, only you," he smiled, those hazel eyes twinkling. My heart skipped a beat. Without doing anything, he moved me strangely. "I was walking by when I saw you both."

"The same junior you have been ignoring for a whole week?" I asked, looking away.

"I wasn't ignoring you, I just wasn't ready to talk," he answered.

"Is it ready now?"

"Maybe, because it doesn't want to escape anymore," he shrugged. I looked at him in disbelief, not satisfied with his answer.

He smiled, digging up the grass by his shoes. "Aren't you happy with my presence?"

"It's not like that, sir, I am just surprised by your sudden approach. You can't just come and go whenever you like."

"I am here to make amends," he said.

I nodded.

"Would you like to go out tomorrow?" he asked, looking down. *Was he asking me out? And blushing?*

"Are you asking me out for a date, sir?" I voiced my thoughts.

"Don't flatter yourself, lady," he grinned. "I am just offering to show you around."

"Can I refuse?" I said, playing with him.

"You can't refuse your senior," he smiled. "I'll pick you up tomorrow at 11 since you wake up late."

"And how do you know that?"

"Riya enlightened me. She also told me that you didn't have your breakfast today," he said, taking out something from his bag. "So, I fetched some sandwiches from the college kitchen."

I took it and smiled, wondering what else must Riya have blabbered to him.

"One last thing," he said, half-turning to leave. "You should call me Shrey, I am *sir* only for others."

I nodded and smiled.

Mayank came back in shortly after Shrey left. We settled ourselves on the grass that had grown all over the floor. Beams of sunlight peeped through the holes in the roof and danced around me. I undid the foil and took out a sandwich from it, offering one to Mayank. It was delicious. We then walked back together. The air felt good on my skin. Mayank mumbled 'so cool' with the first bite. I rolled my eyes at his favourite catchphrase.

The upcoming date excited me to no end. Though it wasn't an official date, I flattered myself all night thinking about it. I surrendered myself to the exquisite thoughts of Shreyansh and his hazel eyes, hypnotizing me as I dissolved into gentle slumber of the night.

I woke to the annoying chants of my alarm. "Can't you shut that thing off?!" Riya shrieked, "I am trying to get some sleep!"

I tip toed my way to the bathroom. The wet floor felt cold under the soles of my feet. I slipped out of my night clothes, and my skin tingled all over as thoughts of Shreyansh returned to my mind. I stepped into the shower, while his keen eyes still dominated my thoughts.

Wrapping myself in a towel, I tip toed back into the room and reached the cupboard. After an eternity of looking though my clothes for the best thing to wear, I found a grey long-sleeved top and paired it with black jeans and sneakers. I had finished brushing my hair and was ready to leave when Riya woke up.

"Where are you going, girl?" she asked, rubbing her eyes. "Did we have any plans for today?"

"Umm...I am going out," I replied, appreciating myself in the mirror.

"With whom?" she asked, getting up. "Are you ditching me today?"

"No, I am not. I am just going out with Shrey sir."

"Goodness gracious, look at your face. You are blushing, and you didn't even tell me about it."

I looked at her and smiled. She was about to say something, but a loud horn interrupted her. She rushed to the window and peeked out.

"Your saviour is here!" she exclaimed. "I want every detail of your romance when you come back," she continued, patting my rear.

I rushed to the door in a hurry. Shrey was sitting astride his bike. It was a classic vintage bike that made a lot of noise. Mayank was mad about it. He wore a black shirt over blue denims, like a knight on a black horse.

"You're on time," I said, looking at my watch. He shrugged and gestured for me to sit behind him.

"You look gorgeous," he whispered. I thanked him and the engine roared to life.

The silence between us was palpable but I refused to take any initiative this time to flicker up a conversation. I kept myself occupied looking around.

The city was new to me, yet the people around looked familiar. I'd never been to the north in all my life. Yet, it felt like I had some transcendental connection with it, like I belonged here. The city intoxicated me. As the sun rose up in its path, its light filled me with great ecstasy. The city was gradually coming alive around me too. The wild breeze played with my hair hung loose. I didn't know where he was taking me, but the urban was slowly giving way to nature on the highway. The wild bushes and trees surrounded us now, lush green and wild. Each slap of the wind filled my nostrils with aroma. Only a handful of people recognise what a joy it is to see sunflowers dancing with the arrival of sunlight, daffodils smile, and tulips welcoming you. Give heed to the rustling of leaves, and you'll hear the song of salvation echoing through your consciousness.

"These are the hills of Mussoorie," he pointed ahead, breaking the silence. Sunlight breaking through the punctures in the clouds coloured the hilly terrain ahead. Everything was so serene. Suddenly, I felt a chill in the air that made me feel renewed. He stopped his bike in front of a small eating joint by the side of the road.

"Are we here already?" I asked.

"No, I am just fetching something to eat."

"Taau, aloo-pyaz pakoda kardi aadha kilo." Aaaah, pakodas! We took the parcel, paid and left.

A raw muddy path lead us to an old rusted gate covered in fresh moss. The board over it read 'Godwin Park', perhaps from colonial times.

"Is this where you wanted to bring me?" I asked, peeking inside.

He took off his shades and said, "This is my shelter when I am down and low."

A guard sitting by the entrance smiled at us and waved at Shrey. He waved back with a smile.

Taking long strides, we passed over uneven ground covered in shrubs and wild flowers. Huge trees as old as time stood sentinel on either side. It was the perfect picnic destination and I spotted some families out with kids, celebrating their Sunday together.

"This is the best place to relive one's childhood memories," I smiled.

"Yeah, this is nostalgic, but this isn't the place I want to show you.»

I looked at him puzzled. He muttered 'follow me', and I did. Like a hypnotized prey, I followed him to the far end of the park, which was completely deserted. Under one fenced corner, a narrow stairway led down. They were carved in asymmetrical marble, and taken over by moss and algae. The orange ball suspended in the clouds created scenic view worthy of surrender.

I almost slipped twice, but he held me by my waist. Blood rushed through me at his touch and my skin rose in goosebumps. The stairs led to a narrow isle, then opened up into a wider space outlined by a railing. I looked up and the orange ball suspended amidst the clouds created a scenic view worthy of surrender. Benches on other side had been engulfed completely by the trees above them, hiding them from the world. I stood at the exit and marvelled at the beauty.

"Come over here," he said, pulling me over to the railing. I stood beside him, and the railing felt cold to my touch. The lush green hills lay in front of me, so close that I felt as though I was standing on clouds. I looked over the railing and noticed a narrow stream of water running through the green fields below.

I closed my eyes, ensuring that I had captured it in my mind forever to cherish. A gentle breeze danced across my face, the fresh aroma of soil right after a rainstorm.

For a moment, I wasn't there. I was somewhere in the clouds, floating. When I opened my eyes, the trees were alive and the birds chirped a song of salvation. I wasn't alone, yet the solitude of being in this natural paradise was overwhelming.

I heard a gentle noise behind me and turned to see Shrey shuffling his feet. He had his hands folded across his chest and his lips curved up in a smile. He was a treat to watch. I settled my wild strands behind my ear and asked, "What are you looking at?"

"You," he smiled. "You're blazing with joy. It's satisfying."

I sat with him and held his hand, sliding my fingers through his. They were cold and rough.

"Why are you doing this?" My gaze was fixed on him.

He smiled, "Should I lie and be sweet? Or be honest and bitter?"

"Spoil me with truth," I mumbled. He turned to me and looked directly into my eyes. I was getting all the attention that I had been craving for. "When I saw you the very first day, you were a terrified, scared, helpless soul. The next day, when I met you in class, you were all alone too. You didn't feel safe and I didn't know what to do about it." He took a deep breath, and I felt its warmth on my shoulder. "I saw the reflection of my old self in your eyes. I had no one to save me from the things that were destroying me. So, I decided to save you from it."

His eyes were lonely and his hands turned sweaty. He pulled them back.

"What happened to you, Shrey? Why aren't you telling me?" My voice was unsettled.

"I want to skip this conversation. I'll tell you someday. "

"No, don't be silent. Say something-anything."

"The only thing you should know for now is that I am doing well. With you, Soumya and others, I feel content."

"Rohan said a lot of things that day. Were they true?" I regretted the words as soon as they escaped my lips.

"If I say they were true, will you abandon me?"

"Why would I?"

"People love only the good parts of you, Manya. But when you bare your dark places to them, they run. They just want to love the good parts of you." He looked away.

"I won't. I am not someone who only enjoys the light and runs from the dark." I grabbed his hand, "Show me your dark places."

He turned and smiled with his lonely eyes. "The moment won't allow me to spoil it."

I smiled and nodded, wondering how long he would try to escape me. A day would eventually come when he would have to utter his story, and I would listen. For now, with expectations in my eyes, I just smiled.

"Can we eat now, my belly is churning. Do you hear it?" he grinned. We ate, as the chirping birds filled the silence.

14th August

She saw me smoking today, and I am glad that she didn't ask me anything about it. Maybe she understood that she will have to be patient with me. It's funny how everyone thinks I am tough, rough, and that nothing affects me. They think I possess an iron shield, which is quite funny to think of. It amuses me.

The truth is, I am fragile and more broken than anyone knows. Sometimes, it takes hours, sometimes days, weeks, months or even years to collect all the scattered pieces of me and put them together in a complete frame. I could see that she wanted to collect me, pick up each scattered piece of me and make a whole NEW out of those shards.

There's a reason behind my decision to stay alone. I frequently say that it's good to remain aloof because it's a way to protect yourself. Instead of laying yourself bare and stripping down to your vulnerability, you can save yourself. What if it didn't work out again? Frightening! The prospect of another failed relationship scares me out of my wits.

What if I express it and she takes it lightly? What if she takes it for granted; me, for granted? What if I have to live all those nightmares again, plus new ones? Nightmares have already kept me from sleep all this while. In my nightmares, I'm peacefully sleeping in someone's arms, but when I wake up in the morning, I am all alone, forgotten, withering and diminishing. I am nobody worth remembering. Am I strong enough? Brave enough? Is there any way I can allow myself to expose my vulnerability all over again?

I know she has questions about my existence, and questions it is built on. Manya will forever be someone whom I will try to keep hidden from the world. I need to keep her safe. If people ask me about her, I wouldn't tell them anything, since I don't want US to be an open book. I want US to be a diary I can lock in my heart forever. Whenever I look at her, I feel how I felt for the first time. It's something, something that's talked about in the books.

People will talk about us; I want us to be that book. But they will never be able to decipher us. Never.

Chapter 9

We met the following day in college and continuously after. We talked a lot, but this time it was all about him, as he had promised to bare himself and the murk that surrounded him to me. Still, I felt that he was keeping some details about his personal life a secret. It occurred to me that it would take a lot more from my side to unravel it all. He was an enigmatic masquerader.

In my dreams sometimes, we met and talked, but he would vanish at the first light of dawn. My hand would reach out for him, but he would resist the embrace. I did not know why he restrained himself so, but I was determined to help him.

While Riya and I were sat on our terrace, following the date night, she asked, "So, what did you guys do out there?"

"Nothing that can satisfy your wild imagination," I answered.

She frowned, "Won't you share anything with me?"

"We just talked."

"About?"

"Life."

"Are you serious, Manya?"

I nodded.

"Are you from the 90s?"

"Why?"

"Who talks about life on a date?"

"We did. And it wasn't a date."

"I know right, he is a saint," she chuckled.

"You know shit. And yes, he is a saint," I said, stopping her with my hand.

My life at college was finally coming under the rein of my will, except for the occasional perturbations caused by Rohan or otherwise.

Soumya introduced us to some of her friends too. There weren't many girls in our college to begin with. Of the fifty total, twenty lived in the hostel, and the rest were scattered outside. Mrs. Shila's PG housed only fourteen of them, including us. The PG had started to feel like home now, we were a family with Soumya as our mother hen.

"Did you like the city?" she asked one evening while we were having dinner together. I nodded. It occurred to me that since she was best friends with Shreyansh, he must have shared it with her.

"We went to Godwin Park," I replied.

"Shrey took her out?" Mansi asked and the other seniors turned to look at me.

"Yes, he did. Leave her alone, jealous people," Soumya laughed and they laughed with her. They treated me and Riya well.

Amidst the chaos of college life, clouds of the first internal tests arrived and left us stranded. Since college began, no one had given much heed to studies until now. One of the major hurdles was Nutrition. The lectures weren't much help, neither did any of us had enough confidence in the subject to help each other swim through. Riya was from the humanities background and Mayank had non-med. I was a commerce geek.

So, we decided to meet two hours before exam time and study together to share whatever our little brains could remember from the classes.

"We are going to fail," Mayank said, plucking his already short-trimmed hair. "Why the hell do they expect us to learn carbohydrate formation or structure?"

"Or what protein is doing with its life?" Riya chuckled.

"Maybe sugar broke up with protein," Mayank grinned.

"Their love story is casting depression upon our lives," I tried to rap. Half an hour passed in our nonsense, and we didn't cover anything besides a threesome story of protein, carbohydrates and sugar.

"Look at you guys, and I thought you were worried about the exam." Shreyansh came down from the stairs and approached us, looking fresh as a winter morning.

"How come you're here so early?" Riya asked bluntly. I pinched her and smiled at Shrey.

"I had no intention to be. Mayank summoned me," Shrey replied.

"Why?" Riya asked again.

"To save you from banishment, my child," Shrey replied and we all burst into laughter, except for Riya.

"He scored the highest marks in nutrition," Mayank said, "That's why I asked him to save us. Isn't that cool?"

Riya frowned. I didn't understand how someone could hate a winter morning sun, the first bud of spring, or the first rain of monsoon. He was all that and more.

He lured our focus back to the subject and taught us enough to get through. Putting her hatred aside, Riya dived into the subject along with us.

We came out of the examination hall the next day unscathed, satisfied and overwhelmed by his magic. The fear of flunking had turned into the joy of relief.

Mayank mumbled 'such a cool exam', while Riya was quietly satisfied with her performance. I mouthed a 'thank you' when I saw Shrey outside his class, and he replied only with his eyes.

The results of the first internal exams came out within three days and I fared pretty well. And by pretty well, I mean outstanding–I had managed to be in the top three. The best scores of two out of three such internal exams were going to hold weightage in the final semester score, so I was happy to have got a good head-start into the academic year. I was getting everything I desired for the first time in my life.

Riya started behaving strangely immediately after the results.

"Can you put your smelly lingerie away in your cupboard?" she said one day at our room.

"Are you even in your senses?" I replied. "You're being flip and rude."

"Yeah, like your wet towel on my bed, your undone laundry on the couch, and..."

I cut her off, "Shut up. What's your problem, Riya?"

"You are," she snapped and left.

She ignored me all day at college that day. I could see the frustration on her face. Something was eating her up. She had scored averagely, but I knew Riya never gave priority to academics anyway. Mayank was cool with everything. He barely passed, yet he was happy for me. After being ignored for a week, I decided to finally confront her.

"Sit here, Riya. I want to talk," I told her one evening.

"I am busy, Manya."

"NO, you're not. Just sit here," I ordered.

Like an obedient kid, she followed my instructions.

"What's wrong with you, Riya?"

"Are you asking me this again?" she yelled. "You're my problem."

"WTF? Why?"

"You're so involved in yourself that you didn't see the things I'm struggling with. Rehan fought with me, I nearly flunked my tests, but you couldn't see it. Instead, you're revelling. Do you even know how ridiculous it feels?" She had this sadness in her eyes that I hadn't been able to understand before. "It's just that your life is smooth as butter right now, while mine is like sandpaper…" she trailed off. "And you couldn't care any less."

I got up and hugged her. Tears flooded her eyes and streaked her cheeks. I caressed her hair, but she pushed me away and left.

I felt bad and convinced myself that I was indeed guilty. Happiness can spoil sometimes and turn us arrogant. We forget the people who held us when our chips were down. At the same time, we envy others, unappreciative of what we have already, feeding ourselves with the illusion that 'happiness is just a myth', a delusional path of self-pity that leads to destruction.

Riya ignored all of my twenty calls, ten long texts and an SOS through Soumya ma'am. Instead of getting mad at her, I understood and waited for her, skipping my dinner, penning journals, calling and texting all the while.

She came back to the room at twilight, her mascara smudged all over her face, eyes red and hair a tangled mess. She looked devastated. She entered the room and crashed on her bed, upside down, hugging her pillow. I went to sit by her and started caressing her hair.

"I am sorry, Riya. I got so busy with my life that I forgot about you," I whispered. She hugged me by my waist and started sobbing. I gently supported her head in my lap. "I am an egotist Manya…I end up pushing everyone away," she said.

"No, you are not, Riya. Rehan will agree to this."

"No, he won't. I fought with him because I wanted to meet him, but he refused because his exams are approaching. Like a pampered baby I threw a tantrum and accused him for derailing the long distance relationship," she said, still sobbing.

She had told me earlier that they used to meet daily, and never in their four year long relationship had they parted for so long. It was too hard for her to bear. "I hope he will understand and meet you after his exams," I consoled her.

Long distance relationships can be tough, testing and very delicate, requiring tremendous love, trust, time and will. But it is also the most beautiful because once you overcome the distance, it becomes a testimony for the two people of having passed the tough test of love to be together. It is the kind of love we all seek.

"You know what? Let's go out tomorrow, it will freshen you up."

She smiled, wiping her tears. "Are you trying my way of cheering back on me?"

"Yes," I smiled.

"Thank you, Manya. I don't know what I would've done without you."

"You would've turned into Devdas," I chuckled, "And Rehan Paro!"

She threw a pillow at me and we burst into laughter.

25th August

Sometimes, she would tell me her insecurities.

Sometimes, she'd show me her fears and let me take them away. Sometimes, she'd express her desires, but be sceptical if I addressed them. Sometimes, she'd cry in her longing, but wouldn't let me wipe her tears away. Sometimes, when her wounds became unbearable, she'd let me cure them. Sometimes, when everything around her caused her to question her self worth, she'd run into my arms. I would share the aches with her as she'd take refuge in me. Sometimes, she'd approach me with questions I wanted to avoid and I wouldn't budge as I'd denied. Sometimes, she'd tell me about her conservative past and how she wanted to change everything. Sometimes, she'd want to run away with me to the palaces of her dreams. Sometimes, she'd tell me everything, while sometimes, it got a little difficult for her.

Sometimes, she'd hold enough strength to move mountains, while sometimes, she'd be as frail as a flower. Sometimes, she wished to fly high and solo. Sometimes, she'd hide all her emotions. Sometimes, she accepts that she's falling for me; when I am trying, she doesn't.

Chapter 10

The next morning, I got up early with the agenda of cheering Riya up, and ran to Soumya's room. Rubbing and shielding my eyes from the early morning sun, I bumped into a chair near her room and yelped. The corridor was empty and deep silence prevailed.

After knocking furiously for what felt like an eternity, she finally opened the door with weary eyes and disheveled hair. She was still in her tiny shorts and spaghetti top that she must have slept in. "Ma'am, we're going shopping. Since we don't know anything about the city, you've got to accompany us," I demanded.

She rubbed her eyes and looked at the wall clock. «It's six in the morning. Don't you think it's a little too early, Manya?"

"Don't get irritated, I just wanted to confirm."

"Okay, I'll come. Now let me catch some more sleep. Shush…shush…shush…" She slammed the door in my face. I walked back to my room grinning, then dozed off for a little longer.

After fussing over clothes for a good while, all of us were finally ready by 10 AM. The reason girls want to be appreciated is because we put a lot of effort into getting ready. One compliment can make our day, and one remark can spoil our week.

Soumya told us about a place that served the yummiest paranthas in town, so we decided to get breakfast outside.

Mrs. Shila scolded us for wasting food and not informing her beforehand that we wouldn't be taking breakfast at the PG. Soumya's scooty was spacious enough for a tripling, though the daunting task was to avoid the traffic police. Riya did a great job by hiding the number plate with her handbag. The policeman could only roll his eyes and make faces as we zoomed past him in good speed and giggles. It was business as usual for Riya, as she bragged about such stints during her school time. While Soumya talked about her driving skills, I stayed silent, for all of this was new to me.

We let Soumya choose the market for shopping, and she took us to a hub in the centre of the city. Paltan Bazaar was old and vivid, filled with a variety of people exploring a variety of shops with an array of accessories, clothes, footwear and bags on display. Soumya told us that the place was best known for bargaining and window shopping, and if your tummy just happened to start growling, many lip-smacking street food options were also available to grab a delicious snack.

The excursion was a happy and welcome distraction for Riya. After touching base with every corner of the market for about an hour or three, we were left exhausted and decided to halt our expedition for some fresh Nimbu Paani.

We sat under a neem tree and sipped on our refreshing drinks. The cool air was soothing on our tired sweat-drenched bodies.

«I feel hungry after exploiting my father's earnings. Thank you for this, Manya." Riya's eyes twinkled like a kid. I nodded. She went ahead towards the parking lot, while Soumya and I followed. "She seems quite excited. Why did she thank you?" Soumya enquired. «She's being generous," I smiled.

The eatery Soumya had selected was quite far and in the vicinity of Mussoorie hills. We decided to stop by our PG to deposit our shopping exploits before moving on. The sun was beaming down over us, but the cool breeze relieved us from the scorching heat. Riya sat sandwiched between Soumya and me this time. I let my hair loose, allowing it to succumb to the breeze.

As we entered the outer area of the city, the magnificent hills of Musoorie appeared before us. The hills wore a blanket of green shimmering in the sunlight. While it was a usual sight for Soumya, Riya and I cherished the natural artistry and marvelled at it.

The eatery lay on the road side, with tables laid under the shade of trees against the backdrop of the beautiful hills and a valley. The gentle breeze tantalised our hair and pampered our lethargy.

The owner greeted Soumya and a young boy cleared a table for us. I wondered how many innocent children served labour and were consumed by poverty. We ordered Paneer paranthas with tea. Riya pointed to the butter dripping off of the food and said, "I'll have to skip meals for a week to burn the calories I gain today today, but I'll fucking eat it!" We burst into laughter, catching the stink eye of other guests around us, but one mean expression from Riya was enough to make them look away. Those paranthas were delicious and the tea was heavenly. The view of valleys and vehicles passing down the zig-zagging road, made it surreal and I made a mental note to visit again with Shreyansh.

Just then, Riya's shriek broke the chain of my thoughts, "Is that Shreyansh?" I looked behind me and saw his black vintage bike, and himself sitting on it. It was like he had stepped out of my thoughts. I was about to call out to him, but stopped as I saw him smoking with another guy sitting by him. Upon a keener look, I recognized Mayank. "He is smoking a joint," I heard Soumya say with irritation. "I told you he isn't a good guy. There had to be something fishy behind that charming facade," Riya added, igniting me further. My ears burned as I heard her chastise him, and my eyes burned as I saw him smoking weed. "This same thing led to the fight between Rohan and Shreyansh, and eventually the rivalry between day-scholars and hostlers.

But he won't quit it. Stubborn bastard," Soumya sighed. I looked back at Soumya puzzled, Riya was astonished too, but Soumya looked down and held her hand up, as if to stop us from asking anything further. My mind fuzzed over. I stole a last glance at Shreyansh, but he had his back turned towards us. We decided to ignore them and not ruin our outing, but the damage was already done; the day was already ruined in my head.

The following day at college, I was unable to concentrate on anything. Of course, the boring practical classes weren't any help either. My mind was constantly flipping back the image of Shrey smoking weed, and Soumya's words stuck to my brain cells like threadworms sucking blood from my capillaries. *Could a drug really wield that much influence?* I wondered.

I wanted answers that only Shreyansh could provide. I looked around, everyone was busy with their work, even Mayank. I looked out the window and caught sight of Shreyansh passing by the corridor. I immediately went to the attendant and asked him for a water break. He gave me a weird look and conceded. I rushed out of the class without looking back and called out, "Shreyansh."

He turned around, his eyes twinkled as his lips curved up in a smile. "Morning, Manya. You seem to be in hurry." I looked away, catching my breath. "I wanted to talk to you." "You left your class for that?" He raised an eyebrow. "Yes." I was on break as far as the attendant was concerned, but I decided to bunk it altogether. "Where're you headed?»

"Library. Come along."

I pulled out my phone and texted Mayank to bring my bag and try for proxy. I followed Shreyansh into an almost empty library since most students were in their classes. We chose a vacant table beside the book shelves, hiding our presence from other people. "What do you want to talk about?" he asked me as we took our seats. "I saw you yesterday." "Me? Where?" «At that famous dhaba on the highway to Mussoorie.» The look on his face changed. "Yeah, I was there with Mayank for breakfast."

"Yeah? What else?" I fired back.

"What else? I don't get what you're saying, Manya."

"AND, I saw you smoking." I looked into his eyes He turned his gaze away from me. "It wasn't me."

"I left my class just to talk to you about this, and you're ignoring me?" I asked standing up.

"Okay, sit," he said, pulling me down. "I was smoking. I haven't told you this, but I'm addicted. It's the perfect getaway from everything bad in my life." "Why? What's eating you up? What are you running from? You know you can share anything with me, Shrey," I said in distress.

"I'll answer everything in time. It's just my veiled past, casting an evil shadow on my present,» he replied.

"You always deviate from the topic. I found out something about your addiction from Soumya."

"Oh, Soumya and her blabbing mouth. Shoot."

"You and Rohan had a fight over the same reason. The college is now divided into outsiders and hostlers because of the fight between you guys. Is this true?"

I asked with hesitation. "I told you, I'll answer everything in time," he said dejectedly.

"Shrey, tell me now. I want to know why they hate me," I ordered. "Okay, fine." The look in his eyes changed into rage. "That bitch Tanya is the reason for everything."

I looked at him puzzled. "Yes, I'll dig from the start," he said. "Rohan and I were best mates: in college, hostel, everywhere. He met me on the day of registration. He was the guy I was looking for as a friend. We fought with the warden to have him shifted to my room till he gave in to our request. Our bond grew stronger after that. We were no less than brothers," he chuckled. I smiled with him as he continued, "Our batchmates relied on us a lot, as he was the brains and I the brawn. Even the seniors respected our bond and stayed away from us and our circle." He smiled, recalling everything. "Rohan and Tanya got along and started falling for each other. Slowly, the addiction of weed began to catch up on us in college. Even Tanya started smoking weed in between classes and breaks." I looked at him in surprise.

He nodded and continued. "One day, Tanya asked me for a joint. She wanted to take it into her hostel for her roommates. So, I asked my friend who lived outside to get me a joint since he used to fetch weed for us. I got it and gave it to Tanya."

"AND?" I asked with curiosity. "I don't know what happened. Her warden caught her smoking weed. She shifted all the blame on me and my friend," he replied. I looked at him in astonishment. "What happened after that?" "The hostel faculty and both the wardens turned to me, and I had to defend my friend. How could I have betrayed him? I defended myself too, because I knew my father would throw me out of his life if I got expelled. As fate would have it, I got expelled from the hostel for bringing weed in." "This was the reason behind your fight?" I asked. "No. There's more to the story," he replied. "I was expelled from the hostel, so I had to settle outside. It took me two days to find a flat and settle in, but thankfully I had the help of my friend. When I came back, I found out that Tanya had started fanning the rumour that I had informed the warden on her and that was why they had been caught. To make matters worse, I was blamed for defending outsiders over hostlers, bringing dishonour to the hostel. As a result, the hostel restrictions were made even more strict." He clinched his fists and slammed the table with them. "Are you okay?" I confirmed.

He nodded and continued, "Rohan turned against me, and all the hostel clan followed. I was thrown out like a fly in a tea cup. Everyone despised me, even my best friend. My only fault was that I defended the truth." I put my hand over his arm. "Don't worry, Shrey. Everyone loves you now. Why are you still bothered about them?" "It still hurts, Manya." There was pain in his eyes. I tried to placate him by caressing his shoulder. "Rohan will understand someday that everything he believed in was nothing but a lie, and his relationship with Tanya was build upon a foundation of lies. He'll turn to you and he'll regret everything he did," I exclaimed. He smiled and nodded, whispering, "Thank you." The librarian asked us to leave as he was going out for the break. We left the library and turned to the water cooler, where we found a group of students gathered around the notice board. "What is this about?" Shrey asked in his husky voice.

Some juniors turned around in excitement. "Sir, it's about the Freshers' party. It's due next week," they said in unison.

I looked at Shreyansh in panic, but he grinned at me. The Freshers' party was finally here after a month and a half of waiting and torture. An island of hope in a sea of distress.

4th September

My conscience is as black as my lungs.

I love to smoke. I love to slip it between my lips, puff it, and then exhale everything out- anxiety, depression, over-thinking, my so called 'mental illnesses'. Smoking enables me to forget about everything. I call cigarettes 'metal illness killer,' because they do wonders like a boss. Light it up, smoke it up, SHUT THE FUCK UP. It helps me be in control and stay sane. It helps me stay alive, at least until I die.

She caught me smoking again. It was weed this time. I couldn't abscond from the questions anymore, so I gave in, I let her take a peek. I decided to show her inside, guide her into my conscience. That way, at least she wouldn't drown in my murk. She asks me things I can't remember anymore. I try at times, but can't recall any of them. There are times when everything becomes too heavy to bear. I don't know when I last remembered these things. Maybe it was when people started walking away or when it didn't matter to me who stayed or went anymore. Why don't people take their miserable memories with them? Why do they leave that hole in our hearts along with a void in us to suffer with? It pains me to think that I couldn't do anything about it. It gets nearly impossible to bear this pain sometimes. The anguish runs shivers through me and I wonder if I can change something, or everything. If only I could find a tiny shred of who I used to be. But I can't. There is nothing but darkness, but I'm not going to stop searching for light. I'll live yet.

Chapter II

My steps were timid and my mind occupied as the sun descended into oblivion and the breeze got heavy in my hair. The path to my PG from college was filled with enough greenery to re-energize my tired soul.

Riya waved at me from the balcony, talking on the phone. I took my time to freshen up, prepared coffee and when I came back, she was still busy chatting. I gave her a stern look and she demanded five more minutes. After taking twenty instead, she decided to hang up.

"You're early," I said, and noticed her panicking about something. "What's wrong?"

"You read about the Freshers'?" she asked. "I can't decide what to wear."

"You're panicked because of that?"

She nodded.

I could not help but burst into laughter. She threw a puppy face at me, "Alright, I'll help you select something." While she was worried about what to wear, I was wondering about the events of the party.

The next day, the college was abuzz with chaotic and nervous freshers. All of us had clamoured into the auditorium, awaiting a briefing by the head of the Cultural Committee. Some seniors from the Cultural Committee were lurking around the stage.

Mr. Thakur's blabbering lasted for half an hour at the beginning. He went on and on about our prestigious college, its old traditions and the importance of its reputation, putting special stress on how it shouldn't be maligned or degraded. It was indoctrination at its finest. Whatever we did, we had to keep in mind that one naive action of ours could land us straight in trouble. Everyone sighed.

Soumya had told us that if we enrolled for events, we could bunk our classes and still get attendance, so we did. I got myself onto the decoration team. I wasn't good at it, but figured it would require the least amount of talent.

I found out from some seniors that Mr. Thakur formed a cultural committee every year to organize college events. Rohan had been heading the group for the past two years. Shrey had told me that they were Mr. Thakur's eyes and ears.

People quickly began working the following day. The committee, along with Mr. Thakur, prepared an action plan for the performances, limited of course within the commandments of our holy college. The plays were about the hotel industry. Hip-hop & contemporary dancers were forced to move to slow classical beats. It seemed like a warped circus in slow motion.

The participants, even though rebellious, had to stay mum. No one wanted to stir a riot against Mr. Thakur's supremacy, but I sensed something brewing amidst the junior participants. Who likes to be bossed around and ridiculed anyway, especially at an event which is solely meant for them?

I could see the more laid-back participants being ridiculed. They weren't allowed to rest for even a bit. A revolt was boiling and it soon erupted. Vikram, one of my batchmates, was finding it difficult to groove on classical music. Not to mention, he was being pushed to the edge by the seniors.

"Move your ass, dude!" Sarthak, one of the seniors, shrieked.

"If only he had an ass."

"But he does have a figure like a ballerina." People laughed and mocked Vikram's tall and lithe frame.

"Fuck it. I am not doing it." Vikram walked away and the rest of the bunch followed him.

"Get on that stage right now!" I heard Rohan shouting. Everyone in the audience turned towards them.

"We aren't dancing anymore," Vikram reverted back in frustration. «You can't treat us like shit."

"This is my place, and you'll do whatever you're told." Rohan stepped ahead, staring at him. With a stern look in his eyes, Vikram shook his head. Rohan was about to charge towards him when Shreyansh, who had been sitting in the front row, intervened.

"Okay guys, cool it now," Shrey said. "Rohan, they are not classical dancers, don't push them to dance on classical beats."

"Shrey, don't poke your nose into this matter. I am the cultural representative and I must maintain decorum," Rohan replied.

"Decorum? You of all people shouldn't talk about decorum after the things you've done in your time," Shreyansh smirked.

"You were involved too, and we both paid the price for it."

"Both? Yeah, right. You're ruining their fun for extra credit, extra marks. Don't be a boot licker, have a life and let them breath some fresh air. Don't be a pawn," Shrey said. By then, everyone in the crowd had surrounded them, sensing another tussle between the two arch-enemies.

"Are you their saviour? You're challenging authority? You're challenging Mr. Thakur's preferences? Let's go ask him, so he can decide everything now." Rohan turned to the exit with his team.

"Yeah right, run to your daddy now," Shrey followed him.

We all accompanied them, but Mr. Thakur called in only Shreyansh and Rohan to his cabin. Both the groups outside waited in anticipation. There the college stood, divided.

We began losing our patience when they didn't come out for the next fifteen minutes. I don't know what took them so long, but when they came out, there were more happy faces than disappointed. Rohan came out with his asshole smile plastered on his face. He high-five'd people from his group and said something I couldn't hear. They all broke into laughter that burned my ears. Shrey came out a few moments later, his brows furrowed. Without saying anything, he walked away and vanished before I could tear through the crowd and reach him.

The juniors danced to the tunes of Rohan and his group for the rest of the day. I wondered if this mess of a circus would ever improve. The next few days weren't great either. Riya enrolled herself for Ramp Walking. I saw her and some other chicks getting acquainted with Rohan and his group. Some junior boys were lurking around them too. I wondered how quickly could things escalate. First, they were mocking them, and now they were getting comfortable with them as though nothing had ever happened.

The absence of the guy who had stood up for them wasn't missed in this chaos, at least not by me. I felt for him, while he was wandering off somewhere all alone, all because of one sole reason. He took a firm stand for what he thought was right, for the things that were actually right, but he always seemed to pay the price.

Shrey never visited the auditorium again in Rohan's presence, not that anyone stopped him. I once saw him talking to Reshma ma'am who was looking after all the practices. Professors adored him. At least, some did.

After a week of practice and tantrums from the seniors and the Cultural team, everything was settled and prepared for the freshers. The Cultural head, Reshma Ma'am, and others sat there examining the performances in chronological order.

Shrey sat in a corner, away from people. I went to sit with him. There was so much to talk about, but words didn't escape my mouth.

He laughed as a boring dance performance came to end.

"What?" I asked.

"They call this a performance? A show? This is going to be a horrible and boring event."

I smiled and clutched his hand. "I'm sorry about that day."

"No, it's okay. I had to try," he said. "I just wanted them to have fun, like we did."

"By the way, what did you and Rohan do?" I asked.

"Well, in our first year, we mixed whiskey with coke and got everyone drunk. Then in the second year, I recited a poem mocking girls, while Rohan arranged a classical dance on a seductive song. Since he was Mr. Thakur's spy, he got away, but I got in trouble because I refused to be his ladle."

"You weren't wrong, Shrey." I clutched his hand tighter, and he smiled at me. The practice show was about to end when the comparer asked him to come on stage. Some people from the second year cheered along with some juniors who admired him, while his haters, Rohan and his group, rolled their eyes. I noticed Reshma Ma'am smiling.

He stood and smiled at me, then walked over to the stage. The comparer gave him the mic and smiled at him. Instead of standing at the podium, he took centre-stage. I didn't know what he was up to or why they had called him.

"Here we are again, welcoming these new fresh faces. These people will welcome others next year and they will welcome others the following year and so on. But you won't get a better show-stopper than him, I promise you that," the comparer said.

"Yeah, yeah, but you aren't going to get anything out of me today. I like my poetry to be a surprise, hence I will recite it on the final day itself," he smirked as Rohan stood from his seat in anger and Tanya pulled him down.

This guy, there was nothing he couldn't do.

Days passed in the blink of an eye. It took Riya six hours, eight different shops, piles of dresses, and countless tantrums showered on shopkeepers to select her dress for the freshers' party. As for me, it only took me one glance at the mannequin to know what I was going to wear.

All this while, I had suppressed my urge to talk to Riya about Shrey. I also wanted to discuss her regular talks with Rohan and his acquaintances, but for the umpteenth time, she wasn't able to focus on anything other than herself. As usual, I decided to let my problems get marginalized and listen to hers. I wished to change myself, for my own sake, but I knew this was not going to happen anytime soon.

Chapter 12

The morning panic on the day of Freshers' foreshadowed how the day would turn out. Riya's bed was empty. She was up early for the first time in long. My intuition led me to the bathroom, only to find her doing something to her face. "You're going to scratch you

r face off, Riya!" I exclaimed.

"You should try it too!" she shrieked. "Maybe for Shrey!"

I decided to stay calm.

She took her time to get ready, but when she slipped into her dress, she was a sight to behold. She was the kind of beauty that sinks in and settles into your thoughts, then hits deep in your conscience and leaves traces of stardust. The maroon gown she had selected after turning the market upside down looked ravishing on her. The colour was meant for her, along with the emerald of the necklace that embraced her neck. Riya's beauty was fatal, her attire her weapon of choice.

"How do I look?" she asked, still looking in the mirror.

I wrapped my arms around her waist and whispered, "You're going to be death." She giggled and hugged me back, and I realized I had yet to bathe and change.

I rushed into the shower and was quick to get ready and slip on the black saree I had chosen.

"If I am death, you're hell," Riya winked at me.

Soumya had booked a cab for us which was waiting outside. She had told us that she didn't want any roadside romeos to feast their hungry eyes upon our beauty, true to her role of the mother-hen we desperately needed. We even called her 'mom' sometimes.

The decoration around the college's gate made it look like an old man dressed in a tuxedo. The old gatekeeper's wrinkled cheeks curved into a smile and he mumbled blessings at us. His words always made my day better.

Today, we walked with authority, as it was our day. Frills and flowers adorned the reception, and the floor was embellished with a rangoli, bordered in rose petals. All the first years had collected around it, guys in formals and girls in either gowns or sarees, looking like they'd spent an entire week preparing for the occasion.

After taking some selfies with and pictures of the rangoli, we moved on to the auditorium. The hall looked alive with frills, balloons and lights contributing to the overall ambience. I rejoiced within for having done a splendid job. A red carpet stretched from the gate all the way up to the stage for us. The chairs laid facing the stage wore black covers with red ribbons. Some sofas in white were placed at the front with glass tables ahead of them.

I found Mayank sitting in the front row and approached him.

"Ma'am, I am saving this seat for my friend, can you please...holy shit! Manya? YOU?" he exclaimed upon seeing me.

"Last time I checked in the mirror, I was in Manya's body," I replied.

"You look dashing, dude." He straightened his violet three piece and smirked at me. "What have you done to yourself? You look…umm…"

"Gorgeous?"

"Yeah, don't read my mind. I can't believe I'm actually telling you that you have the ability to look beautiful," he chuckled.

I slapped his arm playfully and grinned. People rushed in and occupied all the seats. Very few came to sit in the first few rows. Those who had enrolled themselves in the disciplinary committee stood around us, but there was no discipline monitoring necessary today. All the lecturers were sitting in the row ahead of us, while the sofas were reserved for the Principal and his chief guest.

Someone vacated the seat on my right and Shrey came to sit beside me. "You should've saved a seat for me. You knew I wouldn't sit anywhere but beside you," he whispered. "And damn, you look ravishing," he coughed. I blushed under my breath.

"Here you're blushing, while the guys around you are already planning their future with you," he grinned.

I laughed and hit his shoulder. "You too?" I asked.

"You keep flattering yourself, junior."

He wore grey trousers with a black shirt. The stubble on his chin invited me to feel it under my fingertips. For the first time, his hair weren't waxed and spiked, but fell over his forehead.

The auditorium bustled with excited chirping. Everyone was smiling and enjoying their time at the college for the first time in a month. Rohan, Tanya and the rest of their group were busy licking the boots of our professors and ordering the juniors around to start the program. It was all the same for them; bullying, bothering, commenting and making fun of others was part of their daily routine.

The hustle bustle stopped abruptly and everyone rose from their seat as the Principal entered the auditorium. He wore a dark brown suit, and had paired it with a striped tie. Some head lecturers walked behind him. The peaceful clapping turned into whistling and hooting as the chief guest entered the auditorium. The curve on Shrey's lips widened too as he saw Nalini Sharma entering. He turned to Reshma Ma'am and bowed down to her. She smiled back at him. Shrey had always talked about her, how her books and life's story had motivated him, how desperately he wanted to meet her, and how gorgeous she looked in pictures. She was wearing a pink saree and looked gorgeous indeed.

They reached the stage for the lamp lighting ceremony. The cultural group and Rohan rushed about in panic, and I heard someone say they didn't have a matchbox to light. The Principal glared at Mr. Thakur, who in turn glared at Rohan. Meanwhile, our charming Principal did his best to keep the chief guest occupied to hide the embarrassment.

Shrey laughed like a kid at a circus. "Why are you laughing?" I asked him.

"Because of their stupidity," he replied.

"It's a matter of our college's honour and you are laughing?"

"What am I supposed to do then?" he said, still grinning.

"Stop grinning. If you can't help, at least don't make fun of them."

"You are no fun, Manya." He stood up from his chair and walked over to Rohan. "Hey, chief," he yelled, "Take it." He threw his lighter at him and winked. To my surprise, Rohan smiled back.

"See, I can be of help," Shrey said, sitting down, when he returned.

"Yes, you are a saviour," I smiled at him.

This was only one hurdle amidst the many to come. I feared the college would embarrass itself in front of a renowned outsider, but didn't we bring this upon ourselves?

As everyone settled down, lights were diminished. Slow music wafted through the air. The spot light shifted from centre-stage to the comparer whose spectacles gleamed in the light.

"Hello, people!" his voice echoed through the hall. "Are you ready for some fun…?"

The gathering yelled back in affirmative. I mumbled too.

The curtains rose and what transpired next was nothing less than a disaster. The performances that followed were coerced and messy. More than hard work, their struggle reflected forth. The skit was the only saving grace and commanded everyone's attention. It was about the prejudices associated with people in the Hotel Management industry which made them be classified as waiters, cooks, and bellhops. Media persons were also called in to see the skit in hope of attracting more youth to the industry.

After the performances, it was time to choose a king and a queen. Eight guys and eight girls from our batch had been selected for it, and everyone wanted the title and the spotlight. They had to walk the ramp first, and Riya stood there like the North Star, glowing brighter than anyone else. The boys and girls were paired with each other and walked down the ramp to the beat of loud music.

After the walk, it was time for questions. 'Beauty with brains,' they called it, but how they could measure that with questions asking the rupees in a dollar, the measurement of an average tea cup, and the alcohol volume in beer, I couldn't fathom.

After the gimmicky round, the comparer took the mic again. "While we wait for the results, I present to you, the BEST. I have been hiding him all this time. Some might have vanished, or grown drowsy or annoyed, but get ready to wake up now because this guy is worth your while." The crowd shrieked in unison, "Shreyansh!"

The hibernating auditorium erupted into a chaos. The discipline committee stood there baffled. Mr. Thakur shrieked at the top of his voice, but it faded away in the excitement of the crowd.

Shrey smiled at me and walked up to the podium, took the mic and sat down on the stage.

"It's spring, and I see love blooming everywhere. In movies, in reality, in dreams too. Hah! Not mine. I have to sleep to dream," he started and some chuckled with him.

"The thing is, I don't believe in 'love'. Do you, guys? Those who shook their head are listening and those who didn't aren't. You too still have to pretend to listen. I'm going to dilute your thoughts. I don't believe in love anymore. All I know is that love is not always beautiful. Does love make everything gracious? Is it about happy endings or about fascinating relationship goals? For me, it's not about such things. My definition is beyond people's imagination. The truth is, everyone wants love and rushes for it. Yes, at some point in time I would want it too. Maybe. But I won't rush for it, I won't be desperate.

"But, tell me, does love include courage to leave the dark tunnel behind and walk into bright light and bathe in it? Is love all about getting close with another? The way you giggle at my ugliest jokes, is that love? And if we love each other, would you stay there forever? Isn't forever an illusion, like an urban legend? Will someone prove it wrong or will someone show us that legends do come true?

"Oh, I am naive. As you must have come to conclude by now. Perhaps it's immature to have a deep understanding of love. But whatever I've studied about it, I can tell you this: love is nothing but a Pandora's box of stones of commotion, beads of distaste, and pearls of confusion. However you end up adorned, a veil of emotions with holes of longing condemned to misery will hang on your very soul, ultimately pulling you down into the oblivion of regret.

"You don't want to explore or indulge yourself with people or the moment then; you just want to get that person and love anyway, anyhow. You want to win them as though they're a trophy in a competition of sorts. People are in such a rush to get into relationships and love someone that they often fall prey to false *promises, feelings and emotions. And when they get hurt, they blame love and even start hating it.*

"Instead of blaming love, blame yourself for flying fast, so blind that you pushed yourself into a bond of false reality and cherished momentary happiness. Nothing is forever, everything fades away with time, and even the most sparkling thing does. I was always told that love is forever, it remains forever in our veins. If you are bleeding in love and still surviving, then my friend, you're on the right track, you've found that love. Hold it and cherish it forever."

His eyes lit up and he smiled, the same smile I wanted him to wear *forever*. It's astounding to see someone's eyes light up when they talk about their passion. Words were his instruments and he played them like Beethoven and Mozart.

The auditorium echoed with the sound of clapping, and everyone was awestruck. He held his hand up and there was silence again.

"I know I am not supposed to lecture you. You get that enough here," he smirked. "We talked about love, and now we shall talk about its arch enemy–'longing'. That's something I'm good at."

He started reciting:

"अपनी आहें बचा कर रखना,
मेरे शब्द घाओं बहुत दे जाएँगे"

"कभी तो मिलोगे यही सोचकर
ज़हर जिंदगी का पिए जा रहा हूँ
सदियों से लंबी ये खामोश रातें
हर पल मुझे घेरते ये अंधेरे
उस पर जुल्म ढाती तेरी यादें
हर रात जलते हैं ख्वाब मेरे

रो ना पड़े वह कहीं देख कर
रो ना पड़े वह कहीं देख कर
मैं जख्मों को अपने सिये जा रहा हूँ

कभी तो मिलोगे यही सोचकर
ज़हर जिंदगी का पिए जा रहा हूँ

ढलती उम्र है
लंबा सफर है
कितना अभी और चलना पड़ेगा
कितने भी बरसे सावन ए दिल
कितने भी बरसे सावन ए दिल
तुझे तो यूँ ही जलना पड़ेगा

डालेंगे मिट्टी खुदी वो आकर
डालेंगे मिट्टी खुदी वो आकर
खुली कबर में जिए जा रहा हूँ

कभी तो मिलोगे यही सोचकर
ज़हर जिंदगी का पिए जा रहा हूँ ..."

They shrieked and shouted his name like madness unleashed. Nothing stopped them. Shreyansh stopped at the exit and bowed, acknowledging the praise.

The comparer then invited Nalini Sharma on the stage. She shared some motivational words with us and praised Shrey's thoughts and his poetry. She waited there while the comparer took his time to announce the winners. Riya stood there tensed. I had a feeling that they would choose the winners from the hostel group. Mr. & Ms. Freshers were announced and were, as I assumed, from the hostel. The other outsiders and I flashed a fake smile as they were presented with the crown.

Riya stood there quietly, her toes tapped the floor rapidly. 'Mr. Personality' was selected from the hostel group again. Riya's eyes were now shut, her jaw clenched. I felt for her.

"And Ms. Personality is…RIYA SHARMA!" he announced. Riya's face beamed wide in a grin as the auditorium was filled with the sound of hooting and whistling from all the outsiders. I yelled her name as loud as my vocal cords allowed.

Mr. Thakur called everyone who had contributed to the event onto the stage, including the cultural committee, Mayank and I, and some others to meet the chief guest. Shrey wasn't called. He had no worries as he stood there surrounded by juniors who were busy clicking selfies with him. The chief guest got pictures clicked with us, and when we left, she called out to Shrey. She took a selfie with him, while Mr. Thakur and Rohan looked at them, pissed.

After all the professors left, someone changed the music. Loud music blared through the speakers and everyone started hooting. There was chaos, but a certain peace in it too. The moment was surreal. Shrey dragged me in to dance. The beats were fast and sharp, and everyone threw themselves in like they had no care in the world. I tried matching Shrey's pace, but he was so absorbed in the moment, his eyes closed and his hands floating in the air.

Riya danced with Rohan and his people. It didn't bother me. We were free. We were happy. I wished for time to just freeze then and there. I saw Shrey signalling to someone, and the music changed to a slow beat. The light dimmed with it too. His feet shuffled towards me, he leaned forward and whispered in my ear, "May I?"

I felt his warm breath on my neck, and a thousand emotions rushed inside my heart. I did not utter a word, but only gasped. After wandering on my back, his strong hand settled at my waist. I raised my brows and he smiled. My hands crawled over his shoulders as he pulled me closer to himself, yet maintaining enough distance for decorum. He was such a gentleman.

We moved with the music. There was something defiant about him, some part of him that wasn't ready for anyone to understand. Yet, I read his silence. Was I falling for him?

The warmth between us crept into my soul. I tried to match his rhythm and lost myself with him. I convinced myself that I wouldn't care even if my breath was taken away by the end of this dance.

After an hour of feverish whirling, we crashed on some chairs lying around. Shrey pulled a flask out of his pocket.

"What's that?" I asked.

"Vodka," he grinned, gulping it down. I raised my brows. "Don't tell me you're not thirsty," he shrugged.

I took the bottle form him and smelled it. He laughed. I hesitated, then took a small sip. It tasted like apple juice, so I drank some more.

"It helps bring emotions out. Now you know the secret to my poetry," he grinned.

"I wonder, if I will ever get an evening like this again at this mundane college." I sighed.

"I will cherish this day forever, all thanks to you," he said.

"Why?"

"Because, my lady, you make me feel alive." He kissed me and my longing obliterated as the stars bid goodbye to the morning light.

17th September

I look at her and notice how flawless her smile is, how truthful her eyes are, how beautiful her soul is. I wonder if I'll ever find someone so beautiful and substantial in my life as her. You can't count on things that surround you. Light escalates over darkness, dawn arrives, dusk falls, seasons change, and years pass by. You grow from a kid to a teen, into an adult, become old and everything ends one day. Maybe the cycle restarts after it, or maybe there is nothing but your name carved over a tombstone in a graveyard or ash.

People come into your life through an open door and lock it behind them. Once they leave, you believe that you should not allow anyone else to come through it anymore. Nothing is in your hands and you possess power over nothing. Heck, you can't even stop yourself from withering away. You diminish with time.

No one rules me; no one has power over me. But when someone comes and questions my existence, about everything I hold dear, how can I focus? She questions everything. Sometimes, she keeps me awake at nights, but sometimes, the thought of her makes me sleep peacefully. Sometimes, I don't know who I am with her. I forget about the dead me and bloom in her spring, only to wither again at night, little by little...

But, damn, I want this girl. I need her.

I want to feel what it is to be alive with her, to dance with her in the rain and not get burned, to live without a shred of the past in sight. I enjoy the lively presence that this girl brings to my struggle.

Chapter 13

We'd completed three months of college as the semester folded to an end. Somehow I had survived, evolved, and managed to conquer the challenges of college life that I'd thought were insurmountable. The time after freshers passed by rather quickly, maybe because I didn't have to struggle so much to fit in anymore. Teachers knew me from the event as well as my grades. Two more unit tests came and went and I improved, each one better than the last, including Nutrition. The architect of my success, Shrey, refused to take any credit.

My exposure to the silverware, getting good grades and a good reputation, in college led to a reshuffling of my social position. The people who hated me, particularly some seniors, started settling in my presence. There were some exceptions, but I counted them amongst my permanent critics. Some people would hate me without any rhyme or reason, so I embraced my fate and no longer allowed their behaviour to bother me. I found solace in this new life, but craved to perfect it more.

Meanwhile, Riya and Mayank enjoyed the company of 'others' as well, specifically Rohan and his folks. Surprisingly, that didn't bother me anymore, as long as Riya and Mayank were both 'cool' with me. Their absence or presence did not bother me. I enjoyed the company of Shrey and Soumya, and some of Shrey's groupies a.k.a. 'fan folks'.

They were so mesmerized by his thoughts that they hovered around him all the time, just to get a chance to sit and listen to him talk about anything. He would often ask my suggestions and opinions too, maybe because he wanted to shift the attention to me, or maybe simply out of kindness. As I would speak, he'd listen to me intently, stroking his chin, drinking all my thoughts in, giving me all of his attention. He listened to every sane suggestion and each dramatic opinion and pondered over them. He was doing everything to make the phoenix in me rise from its ashes. I, being uncertain within myself, always agreed with whatever he said.

However, there was one thing about these discussions that frustrated me. He wouldn't ever allow me to counter his views. He wasn't arrogant, but he was a selective listener. You can't penetrate through the minds of selective listeners, nor can you break the walls around them.

Everything he had said in his speech at the Freshers' bothered me. It was an honest speech hidden in the folds of anecdotal advice. He had bared his soul, but concealed it under layers of denial. Maybe it was just a performance for the others, but I could see his heart crying with every word he uttered. The rage of pain and agony in his eyes was enough to trigger a chaos inside me. I struggled not to talk about anything related to that day. He had the tendency to evade every question. Whenever he got tired doing it, he'd come back to me with his answer.

Here I was like an open book that he was reading from. I didn't usually allow anyone to read the secrets of my inner sanctum, but his piercing gaze corroded my defences and I obliged him. Without a concern for any impending hurt or betrayal, I allowed him to wander inside my soul. Till now, he hadn't disappointed me. In just three months, he had transformed me into a better person.

Exams drew closer and brought the usual anxiety with it. Everyone started completing journals and practical files, even the ones who didn't normally show up for class the whole semester. Such was the fear of our practical exams. Nights passed in scribbling journals and completing practical files. The dark circles under our eyes emerged like fine art.

"I look like a nocturnal animal awake for centuries with these shadows around my eyes," Riya said one night, looking at the mirror.

"And I look like the daughter of Dracula," I chuckled.

"Anyway, did you ask Shrey to help with the notes and studies? We need it bad," Riya asked.

«Ahan? Last I remember, you were cursing Shrey and passing rude remarks at him. What changed?" I teased.

"Yeah, I know. I am selfish and he's not. Are you going to ask him or not?"

"Yeah, I'll ask him, but I'll only help you if you promise to treat me at a place I like," I grinned.

She flashed her middle finger at me and I reciprocated by flashing both my middle fingers and even my toes.

The next morning, I found Shrey having an animated discussion with someone. I looked keenly at the person, but I had never seen her in college before. She was waving her hands frantically, her bows furrowed, but Shrey looked composed and at ease. He patted her back and she left.

«Shrey sir!" I called out as he turned.

"Ufff. I have told you not to call me *sir*.»

"It's mandatory to call you sir here in college, or the others won't respect you."

"Fear doesn't bring respect. It comes from within. If this respect is from the fear of getting ragged, I don't want it."

I looked at him in awe, then regained myself and asked, "What was that about? Who was she?"

"Nothing. She's your senior, just came back from training, came to say hello," he shrugged.

«Okay, okay, but that was one heated *hello*," I grinned.

"You use your brain for all the wrong things, Manya."

"You are bad. By the way, you promised to help me study for the exams. When do we start?" I asked.

"We'll start tomorrow. Today, I have some matters to deal with."

"That girl? Ehh.."

"Again, don't use your brain cells so much, keep it for tomorrow." He pulled my cheeks and disappeared.

I wondered what the matter could be. Perhaps he was right; I was using my brain for unnecessary things, but then, he had left me with so many questions.

Time passes by slowly when you are in wait for something to happen. I couldn't help fantasize about me and Shrey studying together in some far corner of the library alone. I craved for him so badly that it gave me sleepless nights. Was this love?

I deduced it to be first signs of fatal attraction towards someone. Whenever I was with him, all I thought about was the time when we would meet again. I had him, but it was never enough and I craved more. I don't know what I was getting into, but it felt real; it made me feel alive.

At last, Monday arrived with much anticipation. The exams were near and my attendance was under control, so I bunked the revision classes to concentrate on studies alone.

To keep me out of my misery, Shrey skipped his classes too. We did this for a whole week, until I was brimming with enough knowledge to top the class. "You look like a tired nocturnal creature," I said after we were done with our studies for the day and were out in the garden. He looked exhausted. The weather was overcast and hazy. This was the last Friday before the exams so there were very less people in college.

"Yeah, I had to revise some parts to teach you. Plus, I had my own course to study," he sighed.

«Oh. I'm too much of a burden, aren't I?"

"No, don't bother over it. I enjoy it," he smiled.

"That means, you enjoy my company?" I asked, lowering my gaze.

He smiled and his eyes twinkled, "Yes, you can say that."

"Alright then, I'll give you a treat for spending so much of your time with me," I said excitedly. «Tomorrow?»

"Yes."

"Okay, I'll pick you up?"

"But where will we go?"

"I've some more places to show you around," he said. "Be ready by 10." I smiled and as usual, my mind started framing events of the next glorious morning.

25th October

Have you ever wondered if we ourselves are to blame for our so-called heartbreaks? We rationalise everything way too much and start expecting everything to be in alignment with our own liking. We make plans in our subconscious minds, and then expect it to play out the exact same way in reality.

How badly we want the 'frame' of our life to be perfect with them, whether they want us to be a part of theirs or not. We look forward to their daily pleasantries and feel disappointed when they don't consider us important enough to greet us anymore.

We wear our hearts on our sleeves and try to keep our heads high with pride. Yes, we are so rigidly good, right? We try to spread love and care, shower it around. Then why do we cry when it's not reciprocated?

I don't believe it is wrong to love someone wholeheartedly. I think it's okay to see a future with them, to have dreams of ending up together, but it's not right to assume that nothing will change. Situations, time, and feelings are momentary.

Guess what? We are our own worst enemies, ever ready to serve our hearts on a platter. People might squeeze it hard and leave it to bleed. Yet, we're ready to take the risk.

How ridiculous are we?

We either take too many chances or none at all, which is quite often the only option we think we have to pursue.

Chapter 14

This time, Riya didn't complain. She wanted to dedicate her time to studying and her tension was obvious. She didn't study before, and now when the exams were over our heads, she was panicking.

Shrey was on time again and waited for me while I got ready. It was like **déjà vu.** I took a decent amount of time getting ready and was not apologetic about it at all. He looked sharp as always in an olive sweatshirt and denim jeans. I was my usual self with a button-down denim jacket and black jeans, paired with leather boots. I had left my chestnut hair untied and unadorned.

"Where are we going today?" I asked him.

«You'll find out,» he replied as I sat astride his bike.

We crossed the city limits and entered the woods. It was the end of October and there was a chill in the air percolating through my clothes. The sun felt good on my skin and the aroma of greenery around me, mixed with his cologne, numbed my senses. After a while, the chill began to get to me. I began to feel terribly cold, so I clutched him and looked away as our gazes met in the rear view mirror.

"Are you kidnapping me?" I asked.

He laughed, "Why?"

"Because you still haven't told me where we are headed, and I'm jittery with anticipation.»

"Alright," he coughed, "I am taking you to a cave."

"A cave?"

"Not a nomad's cave, a tourist attraction," he replied.

I stayed silent, bewildered and excited. My mind flushed with the thoughts of our last escape, the quaint park and the view. I remembered how it had taken my breath away and how he had captured a place in my heart that day.

We turned away from the road onto an isolated path. He stopped and parked his bike next to a few other vehicles. For a moment, I thought we were lost, but we were found again by the wilderness.

"Are we here already?" I asked.

"Yeah. We'll walk from here, into the wild," he said.

Our feet sunk in the mire as we walked further, surrounded by mountains. The path we travelled led us further to a pavemented bridge, a cliff to one side and fencing on the other. A narrow stream gushed beside the iron railing and I could hear it roaring as we walked beside it.

At the end of the path, there were makeshift eating joints with temporary setups. Some people were relaxing and enjoying the scenery. Some of them had spread their tables and chairs in shallow pools of water made by the stream. People were enjoying their snacks, with their feet submerged in water. Some even sat on the large rocks scattered in between the stream. The vicinity brimmed with wild flora and fauna.

The aroma of snacks filled my nostrils and made my tummy churn.

"I am hungry, I want to eat."

"We'll eat there," he said, pointing ahead.

I stood there flabbergasted. I was living in a dream. I bit my tongue to come back to reality. The mountains that surrounded us met ahead in a scenic view. The stream fell through the rocks and had corroded the cliff face into a cave-like structure. It was both intimidating and serene.

"Whoa!" I exclaimed and clutched his hand firmly. "Let's go in there."

He looked at me and smiled. "Let's eat first. My stomach is rumbling too."

Taking careful steps downhill, I stopped for a moment and breathed in all the beauty around me. The aroma was refreshing–it smelled like wet soil.

We found a vacant table by the entrance of the cave and took it. The water under my feet was cold and fresh. I rolled my pants up and dipped my feet in. There wasn't a single soul around who wasn't mesmerized by the beauty and peace of this place.

"What do you want to have?" Shrey asked.

I thought for a moment, but had no clue.

"Maggi, maybe? Masala Maggi?"

"Yeah, of course. Anything would do with *adrak chai*."

"Sure, I'll return in a moment."

Shrey went to place the order.

"So, what was that tense conversation with that girl all about?" I asked when he returned.

"Don't ask. You will regret asking it as much as I'll regret telling you."

«Why?»

He shrugged. I pressed his hands and glared into his eyes. His resistance broke in seconds.

"It's an old matter, running fresh again,» he said.

"What do you mean?"

"Here's your order, sir." The vendor arrived with our savouries.

"Thank you." I paid him and turned back to Shrey.

"When Deepika first came to college, she was too scared of her seniors. Some of them took advantage of her fear and bullied her. One of her classmates came to me and asked for help, since I was anyway helping their batchmates regarding the Freshers." He paused. "So, I talked to her and consoled her. In the process, I helped her be strong and face the things that lay ahead for her.»

"Okay, where is the part which I was going to regret asking?" I asked, taking a little sip of the chai.

"She fell in love with me. I didn't give her any indication that I was into her. I was acting more like a mentor to her. I don't know what went wrong. I cursed myself for this, because I didn't want to hurt her, but I couldn't love her back." He looked away.

"It wasn't your fault, Shrey," I looked at him concerned.

"It was my fault, I shouldn't have initiated things. She pleaded me to be with her, even begged me to stay, but there wasn't anything I could do. I told her that I couldn't love again and that it was not in my power to love anyone now. I was tired. I wasn't able to love myself, how could I have loved someone else? I was helpless, but I didn't leave her. I remained with her, consoled her at times, and remained her emotional support throughout, but even that broke me. Yesterday, she came back from her training. I had parted ways with her after she blurted out my secret to the whole college. We hadn't spoken since then." He sighed and looked away.

"Your secret?" I asked, although I already knew the answer.

"I felt like a scared puppy back then. Since she shared everything with me, I felt like sharing things with her too. I told her about my breakup, how I was cheated on, my depression, my panic attacks, the suicide attempt..." he trailed off, but I grabbed his hand.

"Why are you blaming yourself? It's natural, love comes naturally and you can't force yourself to love anyone. It was your good intentions and pure heart that you remained with her as a support. People choose to leave without thinking about the consequences, without thinking about anyone else. It was selfless. It was her fault, you know. People ask you to pour out everything to them, and when you do, like every other hollow person, they don't know what to do with it. If love was easy, life would be smooth like a fairytale."

His lips curved into a weary smile, but his eyes still had that touch of sadness.

"Are you okay?" I asked.

He nodded. I clutched his hand and got up. "Let's go," I said, pulling him.

Sunlight made the water look like a blanket of crystal. Pieces of marbles in the stream glowed and shone like emeralds. The cave was dark and eerie. There weren't enough souls to admire the beauty, but many faces captured themselves while posing for selfies.

"Fold your pants up to the knees, the water level is high inside," he said and I followed.

We went inside the cave, all the way back to the source of the stream. It emerged mysteriously from between the rocks. I stood there and held his hands firmly.

"Shrey, you are the most beautiful soul I've ever come across." I said in a hushed tone, "Thank you for bringing me here. I needed this. I needed this getaway, this escape."

"You have to be beautiful yourself to be able to see the beauty in others. You're beautiful, Manya. I haven't seen such a beautiful soul in a long time. I hope you don't do anything that Deepika did," he said, looking down.

"I won't, never ever. I'll adore you forever," I said. "You're someone whom I will always treasure and keep safe. I cherish my luck for having met you so unexpectedly. I just can't stop looking at you. Those gleaming hazel eyes always drive me crazy. I lose myself in them. You make me feel things I thought I would never feel."

"What if I am not real? What if I am not what you see in me? What if I am not the person whom you want me to be?"

"What if you are everything I say you are, and you're hiding behind someone else, and you don't want to be seen? What if I bring you out of it? The mask? The skin?"

He was standing close to me, and the space between us decreased further. I inched closer to him, feeling his warm breath against me. His aroma was doing something to me. I stood on my toes to inch closer towards his lips. He closed his eyes, tilting his head down. My quivering lips craved to taste those venomous lips. I wanted to contain myself in that moment, but I spilled out.

I don't know what happened, but he broke off in a split second and resisted. «I'm sorry," he whispered.

My face flushed with embarrassment. I couldn't understand what had happened. Something in me told me to run and I bolted out of the cave. He yelled after me, "Manya, Manya..," but I ignored it.

The only thing that remained echoing in my mind was '*I'm sorry*' and his reluctant face. I left the place, alone and shattered.

2nd November

Her skin brushes against mine and something ripples through me like a thousand lightning bolts. I've felt emotions, desires and cravings before, but this is different. I might even call it strange, because I've never felt so occupied with someone and so overwhelmed by them simultaneously.

Her eyes peer through all the barriers and hit right at my fragile heart. I know this isn't supposed to happen after a heartbreak. I've tried to enter into relationships after that event broke me apart. I even degraded myself with flings and casual intercourses, but I never felt such peace as I do with her. Somehow, she frees me from the haunting.

I wonder how strange it is, despite those efforts to move on, I couldn't really come out of my past. But now, when I've stopped trying and surrendered myself to fate, I am being rescued by this equally fragile victim. How fascinating it is, two fragile people trying to rebuild one another.

Something happened today at the cave. She held my arms and it felt as if this is all I'd ever wanted in my life. Her shy yet mischievous eyes penetrated through my consciousness. I've never felt so lost. The world around me stopped, and there we were, the two of us and nothing else, no fear of betrayal. Her breath on my neck awakened my cold heart and blood began to rush into it. I finally heard it beating for the first time in very long. My hands quivered at the thought of holding her, but I didn't. I've never felt these emotions before. Her lips brushed against mine, and I knew I had tasted nectar. I have never felt this lost in a kiss. Yes, I've kissed before, but nothing felt like this. I tasted her and I realized I would be thirsty without drinking from her again. I've loved before, but this feeling is alien to me. I can't grasp that such a beautiful thing could possibly happen to me. I've been searching and wandering, and have since then resigned myself to defeat. I knew I wouldn't get salvation, home, or the feeling of it, but this girl is questioning everything and proving me wrong. I realize that I've been searching for this, wandering for this, waiting for this. I've been waiting for this girl since forever.

Now that I know this, I am afraid. I tremble with the thought of being left alone again; torn into shreds. If that happens this time, I know I won't be able to revive myself; I won't survive that kind of torture again. She's reincarnating me, investing in me. The intensity of it makes me more afraid, I don't know what I might do to her. How could a guy like me handle such a fragile beautiful thing? I might destroy her. So, I decided to run away today. I pushed her away to the point of no return. I don't want her to come after me, searching for her answers. She's better off without me. People like me don't deserve love; we are toxic to the purest souls.

Chapter 15

I ran out of that place, his words echoing in my mind. My legs gave up and I collapsed in the mud under my feet. I stayed there for a long time. Then it dawned on me, 'He is there, back there, and he won't come.' I stood up to leave, mud dripping from my jeans.

Somehow, I walked back to the road; it was deserted now. The sun was slowly descending into oblivion. A gush of wind blew through my hair; it felt eerie. Birds were flying back home and I wondered how I would get back. I wish I had wings too.

I must have walked for over thirty minutes in the dark before I reached the main city. People who saw me on the way stared at me, I wondered why.

I reached my P.G. and saw my reflection in the mirror at the gate mocking me. My pants were soaked and streaked with mud; my kohl was smudged all over my face, my hair were pretty messed up and my eyes, blood red.

I rushed to the common bathroom before anyone could see me. No one used it because it was in a dark corner of the building. It didn't scare me anymore, but my own reflection in the mirror did. Even my conscience appeared soiled in the mud of unrequited desire and untamed feelings. I didn't know that to feel and have desires was no less than a sin, else I would've kept it to myself. My reflection intimidated me that day.

I rubbed my face with water to get rid of the kohl. I could just as well have gotten rid of my skin too. I didn't want it anymore. After that, I walked straight to my room and crashed on my bed. Riya sat there ready with her questions.

"How was your date?" she chirped.

"We'll talk about it later," I replied.

«Tell me now?»

"I want to sleep, don't disturb me," I replied and hid my face in my blanket.

She didn't ask me anything after that. Maybe she knew. Anyone would've known by seeing the helpless situation I was in. I slept for almost a day. My mind was a mess, my life was a mess, my hair were a mess. I decided not to make our lives more complicated, so I didn't bother Riya about it. I pretended that it didn't matter anymore. Riya continued not asking anything. Even if she had asked, I wouldn't have told her anything.

I had this thought at the back of my mind that he would call, or maybe talk to me at college or something. But no texts or calls came. For a week, he didn't show up at college at all. Soumya had told me that it was normal, since people often vanished before the exams and went back home for a while, but he hated going home, *so where was he?*

I tried to push everything aside to concentrate on my studies. We had a leave of three days before our first semester exams. I wasn't tensed as Shrey had taught me how to overcome almost everything I lacked in, even my place in his life.

"You didn't tell me anything about your date," Riya said a night before our first exam.

"But I did tell you everything you need to pass. Sleep now."

"That means, you aren't going to say anything."

"What do you expect?"

"I expect to know everything, of course."

"Sleep and let me sleep, I have to wake up early." She threw a pillow at me, as I threw myself into yet another miserable long night's sleep.

The exams went pretty well, and the study time spent with Shreyansh helped me. I expected yet another semester of brilliant performance and outcomes. During the exams, we tried to ignore each other as though we never existed for the other. I wasn't ready to face my fears yet, but it hurt me to not talk to the person without whom I wouldn't have survived this semester.

The session was over, the year was over. Everyone was packing their bags to go back home, but instead of missing my home, I missed being in Dehradun already. I didn't want to go back.

Riya came flitting into the room as if she were a bird chirping a song, and smiled stupidly at me. "Why are you sitting there mummified?" she asked. "Are you down? Mood swings?"

"No, I don't want to go back…»

She cut me short, "Home, I know that, kid. That's why I have some wonderful news for you." I looked at her puzzled.

"We're going on a trip, Dhanaulti!" she grinned.

«We?»

"Yeah, my guy is coming. Then there is you, Soumya, Mayank, and…»

"And…?"

"I asked Shrey to come along too and he agreed," she winked.

I threw my clothes away and got up to hug her tight.

I called my parents and told them about the trip, not mentioning the presence of any testosterone with us of course. Mom allowed it, but dad was sceptical. After a few tantrums from me though, he allowed it too.

It was a dark night and there was a freezing chill in the air. I waited for the others to join us, while Riya and Rehan collected the tickets. I wrapped my arms up, hugging myself, though the chill seeped through my cardigan anyway. Soumya arrived with Mayank. Something had been brewing between them for sometime. Shrey came in at last and stood with Mayank and Soumya, a little away from me. He didn't even say hello to me. I felt cloaked.

Riya and Rehan came back holding hands, chirping and laughing.

"Guys this is Rehan, my..." Riya started, but Rehan cut her off.

"I am the luckiest guy to have her." He wrapped his arms around her shoulders. Both Soumya and I looked at them in awe. Mayank hugged them, shouting, "You're so cool together!"

Shrey stood at a distance like a zombie, lost in his own thoughts. It was almost as though this romance and affection repelled him.

"Hey, big guy! Shreyansh, right? I've heard a lot about you from these ladies." Rehan stretched his hand towards him and winked at me. I blushed. I had talked about Shrey and my fondness for him with Rehan over the phone quite a few times.

"Pardon me, if that bothered you," Shrey smirked and shook his hand.

"He's kind of an angry young man," Mayank whispered to Rehan.

"I heard that, kid," Shreyansh said. Mayank squeaked 'sorry, sorry' and grabbed Shrey's hand, much to our mirth.

"Guys...let's discuss things later, eh? The bus is about to leave," Riya yelped and ran towards the bus. We rushed after her, giggling and laughing.

We boarded bus at around 10 PM that night. Riya sat with Rehan and Soumya with Mayank.

"You're left to sit with me," I whispered to Shrey.

"I don't mind that," he smiled. «Do you?"

"I thought you would."

"You overthink."

We took our seats and the bus engine roared to life. It was already dark and there weren't a lot of people on the bus. A dense fog descended from the hilltops and obscured any view outside. The night was cold and I squeezed my hands into my thin cardigan for warmth. I cursed myself for not having carried warmer clothes.

"How were your exams?" Shrey asked.

"Went well."

"Did whatever I taught you help?" He smiled and patted his own back.

I shrugged and looked away, out at the darkness and a soothing silence.

"Still mad at me?" he whispered.

"Who am I to be mad at you? I am mad at myself and how my unrequited desires lit up."

"You are human, everyone has desires."

"Are you not? Don't you?" I asked.

He smiled, "I stopped having desires long ago. I stopped feeling too."

I looked into his eyes; he couldn't hide the hollow loneliness that night.

"But if you have, like I do, you can't force them on people. I forced myself on you."

"You expressed. It's brave to express. Not everyone can do that."

"But it was wrong, Shrey."

"To feel isn't a sin. Don't feel bad."

"Then why can't you feel it too?"

"I don't know, Manya. I built walls around myself after she left. And I'm afraid now to tear them down and let anyone else in."

"I am here, Shrey. I will always be. Don't be afraid, for I have only love to give, not hate." He remained silent and soon dozed off into a world of dreams.

I was very conscious of his presence next to me, his scent filled my nostrils and he climbed into my thoughts yet again. I wondered how someone could numb themselves and their thoughts without any effort.

We reached our destination in the very early hours of the morning.

It was dark and eerie, and the bus stop was lonely. We took our bags and alighted from the bus. Rehan embraced Riya and Soumya snuggled up against Mayank, while I craved for a presence. Shrey slipped his fingers into mine and ignited me again. I burned in that frigid winter night.

It was around 3 AM and the chill made me quiver as I shifted my weight from one leg to the other. Mist embraced us as we walked in silence to our hotel nearby. Never before had I walked like this in the dark, on a lonely and strange path. My parents had never allowed me to go outdoors after 10 PM. But I was free now, I didn't feel shackled, except only by my thoughts and feelings.

I looked to my side and saw this guy holding my hand, oblivious. I wanted to stop him, to whisper, or shriek, "I am falling for you, Shrey. I need you, I want you." But then, I couldn't afford to push him away again.

I wondered how long I could keep torturing myself and fear losing him, when I didn't even have him in the first place. I had a lot of expectations of this tour, and I didn't want it all to come crashing down on my head in the form of disappointment. I was desperate to hold on to everything. Hold Shreyansh, and *never let him go…*

5th November

I really don't know where to start today. One evening while I was trying to kill time during a lonely twilight, I read this in a book, 'People fall in and out of love.' It bewildered me. For the next five minutes, I thought hard, trying to figure out how such a thing could even be a possibility. It is weird to think of someone who was once completely and madly in love with you, being incapable of seeing stars in your eyes anymore. One day you're everything to them, and another day you're nothing. Suddenly, your voice is no longer melodious and talking to you doesn't produce the same glow on their face.

I'm no longer in love. Or am I? It sounds harsh, but maybe that's the only truth. I keep dropping hints and even confronted Manya with my sadness twice or thrice but no, she didn't believe me. She just couldn't understand, no one does. I know this is devilish of me to say, but my guardian angel commanded me to scream it. I sob and cry, and she cannot take the sight of my red eyes, and so I tell myself that she's still here and she won't leave, but for God's sake, my heart knows the secret.

Sorry, but not so sorry.

I don't blame people for leaving. I didn't blame Vaani for leaving. I don't blame anyone for leaving. I won't blame Manya for leaving. How could I when I am the one who pushes them away?

Sometimes, that's the best thing to do. Let someone loose, let them free, let them go. If they return, they were meant to be. They returned because they wanted to; because you meant something to them. If they don't, they were never meant to. They never wanted to stay. You were just caging them.

This case with me is alien. People never stay or come back in my life. You see, my life is kind of a public loo. People visit, shit and piss in it and leave without flushing, leaving the rotten emotions and memories behind them. My nights reek of it and since I can't quit, I stay there decimated by them.

I am not a quitter. But what path do you take when that's the easiest option?

Quitting?

I crave her arms. I want to lie in serene ecstasy, cradled to sleep.

No, I'll quit on this.

I must. I'll quit because I believe quitting is the easiest option. I'll quit to avoid worse scenarios.

Chapter 16

It's okay to wander around, in hope of getting found one day. All our life, we yearn to find pieces missing from our lives, to run away from the monotonous moments we dwell in. But then, we often find ourselves stuck in a web of lies, and it gets tough to redeem ourselves. So, we decay there until we find an escape.

Eighteen years of my miserable life, I lived in Bangalore and never stepped out of the border. Most of the time, I desired to escape, particularly because I was sick of all those skyscrapers, the mundane weather, and the rotten air. With the first sight of snow in Dhanaulti, I knew my salvation lay there. When my feet trudged over it, tremors rushed within me, feelings I'd never had before. I had dreamt of this, craved for it. This chill, this calm was possessing me, numbing me and making me feel alive all at the same time.

Dhanaulti, a small town near Mussoorie, boasted of lush green mountains cloaked in snow. The fleeting sun rays that escaped through the dark clouds made it appear like a blanket blazing in a golden light. A well preserved forest cover, the main tourist attraction of the city, with trees standing tall with pride, birds singing ballads of salvation, the frosty air caressing our skin–everything was tempting and exotic about this place. A snowy track led us up to the top of this heavenly place. When we reached it, a thick mist enveloped us. Tree-tops peeked through and it felt like we were floating in the clouds, walking over a white blanket. I felt blissfully lost.

"I want to build a cabin here in the woods and stay here till my end," I said and everyone laughed.

"Someday, we'll build it together," Shrey whispered in my ear and I blushed.

The locals predicted a storm that night, so we ditched the idea of seeing other places. We wanted to chat a bit and get to know each other better. The boys went out to fetch food before the storm struck, and us ladies sat on a mattress rolled on the floor, having wrapped ourselves up in a huge blanket.

"What must they be up to?" Riya asked.

"I don't know, maybe getting along," I replied.

"Maybe drinking," Soumya said.

"My Rehan won't."

"I can smell a junkie from a distance," Soumya replied.

"You must have sniffed Mayank a lot then," Riya said, and we laughed.

"There's a real person inside that junkie, a lonely, scared, fragile kid hiding from reality," she sighed. "I don't blame them."

"Are you psychic? I seriously think you don't need to read any Psychology books. If I were you, I'd focus more on production and housekeeping for the semester exams," Riya said and Soumya hit her playfully. I joined the fight too. It filled the void of siblings that I always wished to have.

The boys came back after a while, high and wasted. More bottles jingled in the poly-bags they were carrying. I had this thought at the back of my mind that I could have my first real experience with alcohol on this tour. Though Riya had warned me that alcohol brought out emotions from the very deep recess of your mind, it only left me wondering how something could pull down the walls I had hid my thoughts behind for ages.

"We stumbled upon this cool Chinese food joint, while we were dri.."

"Drying ourselves from the cold and frost, right Mayank?" Rehan rolled his eyes at Mayank and he nodded.

"I know what you were doing there, bub. You reek of alcohol," Riya said and looked away.

"Alright. I'll let you fight later. Let's eat the food first. I'm hungry."

Soumya grinned and snatched the parcel from Mayank. The food was great. I was amazed that these three drunkards had managed to fetch food this delicious.

We sat around in a circle, still wrapped in our giant blanket. It was getting colder as the night progressed. The storm was here already. Howling wind could be heard beyond the windows.

"Alright, it is getting boring out here. We should play a game," Rehan said. "This game is *tell the truth or drink*."

I had never heard of this game before, particularly because I had never drank before. Shrey grabbed the blanket and sat on the couch away from us. His eyes were glued to me, sending jitters down my body. I felt something strange. His blood shot eyes scared me, yet I could feel a temptation.

"Shrey you should join too," Rehan said.

"No, spare me this kiddish melodrama," he replied.

"It's good to be a kid sometimes," I said meekly. He obliged and stood up.

"Share your blanket at least," he whispered.

He wasn't weird, neither arrogant nor rude. He was just himself, walking away from these things like an old soul trapped in a new world. I think he sometimes found it difficult to settle, like he had experienced everything and seen everything, and now such things were just awkward for him.

"So, here we go." Rehan spun the bottle and it stopped at Mayank. He grinned like he had won a lottery.

"So the question is, are you and Soumya dating?" Riya chirped.

Soumya punched Riya in her arm and glared at Mayank. Like an obedient kid, he obliged by gulping a sip from the bottle next to him.

I found it rather cute how they wanted to keep it a secret. The world feeds on our emotions. The more we make ourselves vulnerable, the more we're prone to exploitation. The best way to survive is to keep personal thoughts, feelings, and emotions limited to yourself.

The bottle swung again and pointed to Shrey. "So, Shrey. Dude, what's up with this angry young man personality?" Rehan asked.

He smiled, "It goes around pretty well. No one bothers you much. No one asks you silly questions."

"Man, I like this guy." Rehan high-fived him and they laughed. I wondered if Rehan got the sarcasm or not. Poor guy.

The bottle rolled again and it was my turn this time. "So Manya, how many guys have you dated before?" Rehan asked.

"Why do you get to ask questions every time?» I asked. He shrugged. I looked at Riya who was grinning and fondling him. They were playing with me. I grabbed the bottle and gulped it down. Everyone booed. My throat burned, for it tasted like rotten cough syrup. I felt like puking, but controlled the urge somehow.

"That was impressive," Shrey whispered in my ear and I blushed.

We played the game for a while. Shrey drank half the bottle, skipping every personal question thrown at him. The bottle rolled again and it pointed to Soumya. "Why do you care for everyone so much? Why so selfless? Why so mother-like?" I asked.

Soumya smiled at Shrey. "I never got the privilege of knowing my mother, and she died when I was just three." I grabbed her arm and whispered, "Sorry, I didn't know..."

"It's okay," she smiled. "I was deprived of that love. I had no siblings, so my childhood was lonely. When I came here, Shrey taught me what it feels like to shower love without expectations. It's divine. I still remember your words, they'll remain carved on my heart forever. He told me, *I save them in order to save myself a little.*»

"Not so selfless after all," Shrey smirked at Soumya and she nodded, smiling.

The bottle was rolled again and it was my turn. I couldn't skip more questions after having drunk my first and last awful sip. This time, it was Shrey's turn to ask. I glared at him and he smiled. "So Manya, what's your worst fear?" he asked.

"My worst fear is being alone or left alone. People say solitude is bliss, but I don't believe that. It eats me alive; the thought of being alone on the long journey of life haunts me."

Shrey held my arm. "I'm okay," I whispered.

"Okay, so this is getting serious now. We should stop, I want to sleep. I don't know how long I would get to cuddle him," Riya said, looking at Rehan.

"Damn, you've changed. Where is my shy little baby?" Rehan chuckled.

That night, I woke up with a start, my mouth dry and throat itchy. Shrey wasn't around, so I checked all the rooms, the bathroom, everywhere, but couldn't find him. The balcony door was latched from the outside, so I cleared the frost off the glass and peeked outside. He was there, strolling around like a nocturnal being. He opened the door after a couple of knocks.

"What's up with you? Still up?" I asked, suddenly realizing that my head was spinning.

"You look possessed. Medusa-like," he laughed. "And yeah, I'm insomniac. I haven't slept properly for months," he whispered like it was normal.

"How can you stay awake? I mean, I can sleep for days, even weeks straight." I took a seat beside him.

He held the rum bottle high. "This keeps me awake and well."

It was dark; even the moon was shy that night. My bones clattered while my hair bristled on my back. I looked down at the snow cloaked road; it was a beautiful sight. Snow covered everything–trees, bushes–in a blanket; their white goddess. It seemed as if the land beneath had decided to wear a white wedding dress that night. Shrey pulled me into the blanket around his shoulders and wrapped his bulky arms around me. The air around him reeked of alcohol and smoke.

"You've been smoking too?" I asked.

"Alcohol and smoke are like bread and butter."

"Whatever," I said.

He took a long sip and looked at me, his hazel eyes twinkling like diamonds in the darkness.

"What are you looking at?"

"You, you're beautiful, like snow on a rose bud," he said smiling.

"That's why you run away from me every time, right?" I squinted at him.

"I run away from myself. I don't want you to get caught up in the storm inside me. I wouldn't be able to save you from myself."

"The storm inside you needs solace. You just have to accept people into your life instead of pushing everything and everyone away, and churn in murk on your own.»

"I am used to this loneliness. Everyone leaves one way or another, so it's difficult to digest when someone actually decides to stay." He gulped down a big sip from the bottle. I took the bottle from him and took a sip. I was starting to get the hang of this cough syrup, though I acted like I was going to throw up. He laughed at me and I hit him with my elbow.

"See, you laughed! Why can't you keep on doing that?" I asked.

"Because, Manya, you can't remain happy forever. It's just about moments, little moments that define who we are and validate our existence. These little moments don't last forever–we don't need to smile in order to live."

"But we can always try to be happy, Shrey."

"When you start trying–trying to be happy, trying to live–you actually die inside. Happiness isn't about trying, it's about feeling, embracing the little sparks of joy in your life and keeping your internal fire raging. It's about having the desire to be alive and live like nothing else matters. We're so busy trying that we stop living. It's like we're already dead inside but have to survive till the excess fuel inside us runs out."

I looked at him in distress. How could he be so honest? How could he say the things most people only think of or are afraid to admit? People easily accept that life is supposed to be good and pretend they're happy while they're struggling to survive and carry on with their lives. How easily they lie to themselves and to one another.

When you ask *How is everything?*, they reply with a fake smile and say *Awesome*. I think and tell myself daily that life is good, life is beautiful, I have everything, I have everyone. Yet when I lay in bed at night, I struggle to keep my mind blank as I attempt to sleep. Everything that's happy around us is a mirage and we're living a lie. He snapped me out of my thoughts and handed me the bottle. I gulped a mouthful now. It felt okay now, and I felt a sudden rush of heat inside. I liked rum. "So, when were you happy then? As I can see right now, you're not."

He laughed and lit his cigarette. "I don't know when. There was a time when my sister wasn't married and I was a kid. We used to go to this small restaurant back in Amroha where we lived. The food there was delicious. I always used to order 'Dal Makhni'. It was my favourite. We were a happy family back then. I still remember that time. Maybe the only good memory I've had with my family." I looked at his face that was shinning; it was good to see him opening up.

"What about the time when you were in love?"

The eyes that twinkled before turned gloomy, and I regretted asking the question suddenly.

"You won't leave that topic, will you?" He took a long drag. "I still remember the times when she used to call me at midnight and tell me that her mother thrashed her or her father scolded her, because they had caught her talking to me. Sometimes, her sister would rat her out, but she wouldn't let me speak trash against her family. I admired her love for me, for them, but I never felt sorry saying that her sister was a bitch.»

I laughed and took the cigarette from him. I hated the smell of it, but I still wanted to try. My lips touched it and I could taste the flavour of his mouth. I took a small drag from it and coughed. My eyes teared up. Shrey patted my back and passed me the bottle of rum. "It's okay, it always happens the first time. You have to inhale it and feel it in your throat, and then slowly blow it out." This time, I did okay. The smoke or whatever it was, hit my throat directly. The feeling was strange; like my throat was burning from the inside.

"Why did her sister hate you?" I asked.

"I don't know. Her sister, friends, parents–everyone hated me. Maybe they were astonished about how someone could love so much. I guess, her sister and friends were jealous," he smirked.

"What happened after that?"

"What usually happens, humans and their never ending desires. She wore a skin of desires and searched for someone to denude it. I wasn't the one, I couldn't be the one. She got tired of me, so she cast me out of her life. When she started changing, I kept waiting for the exact moment she would tear me apart. But that moment never came. I told myself that she must be distressed. Since I was in training, I couldn't fix it. I let my guard down because I felt sure that she wouldn't leave me. I mean, how could she? After four years of a relationship, how could she flip the switch and just move on? You can't do that if you are truly in love. But eventually, the moment that I had dreaded came rushing to me and the storm blew me away. I think I knew she would tear me apart all along, but at a certain point, I was so happy in my delusion and fooled myself into believing that she wouldn't ever leave me. I didn't want to let myself believe it. "

I held his hand. "I don't know how to respond to it. I have never dated anyone."

"Well, that's why I shared it with you. You would be neutral," he sighed.

"I don't have anything to say, but let me tell you this: it's their loss that you're not a part of their life anymore. I'm glad that you are here with me, and I want you to stay. I'm glad you finally shared everything today, though in bits and pieces, but at least you tried." I squeezed his hand gently. His eyes were dull and dark now.

«See, I'm not prone to it either. Alcohol does that to you, brings out everything you don't want to share. I know I am a complicated person and I don't deserve love, but I deserve to live, right?" He looked deep into my eyes.

I wanted to tell him that he deserved every kind of love possible. I wanted to give him that, shower it on him. I wanted to tell him that it would be fine. Life might be tough, but he was tougher, maybe the toughest person I had ever met. But all I did was to put his head on my shoulder. My lips ceased to utter anything.

I wrapped my hands around him. He tilted his head up and those gloomy eyes looked right into mine. His lips inched closer and I could feel his warm breath on my face. The hair on my nape bristled as his lips brushed against mine. I wanted to resist it, resist him, resist the kiss, but I gave in. Dawn was falling in and I was falling for him.

His hands wandered to my hair, while mine explored his back. His tongue found his way into my mouth, where our tongues collided and fought for domination. Neither of us was ready to give in. He slid his hands inside my pullover. His fingers traced my back like it was a treasure map, or perhaps he was creating his own. The touch felt warm and rough. It was him who gave in and left me gasping for breath, just to take it away again.

My earlobes found themselves in captivity of his lips now. He sucked and bit them. I was ecstatic, shivering helplessly in his arms, moaning under my breath.

I grabbed him tighter, pulled him by his hair and tangled myself in his arms. He held my head close to his chest, embracing me whole. I wanted to submerge into him tonight. Snow began falling and I drifted off in his arms.

24th November

It's been more than two years now, Vaani, and you're still stuck to me like my shadow. And shadow you become, dark and non-existent, when there's no light around me. Though it's been difficult, I've decided now that it's time to let you go. It's not something I ever wanted. It's not something I'll ever fully accept, but I have to. I must.

There was a time when the thought of leaving you would send tremors down my spine. Now I feel nothing. After you left, I stopped feeling everything all at once. Your absence left a void of numbness and sorrow, where I live now. Sometimes I wish I could stop thinking about you the way I do. I wish I could stop caring about you and your existence, especially when I am extinct in your world. I can't seem to help it. I cannot stop.

You came into my life and constructed this huge mansion for yourself inside me, and then you abandoned this home, leaving it empty and loveless. I can't seem to forget about you. I deleted all the photos and I deleted all of our messages, but I can't delete our memories and I can't delete the things you said to me. Did you ever mean any of it? Did I ever mean anything to you? Did you even care about me at all? God, I'd give anything to know what I did to make you hurt me so badly.

You know...

My soul is caged in limbo, belonging neither here nor there or anywhere. And there is nobody around to give me a heartfelt condolence, There is a heavy weight sitting at the back of my mind, In this silhouette, I breathe daily to ensure I stay alive in the chains of my confinement, I once heard this song on loop, It was about a young man who held his shit together and did not let life get the best of him, I gulped down bottles of vodka until it burned my throat, I tasted glasses of wine to see if bitterness or sweetness was anecdotal. All this while, my soul was screaming out loud, But I couldn't gather up the courage to imagine myself lying in a shroud, For days and nights I lay there without moving, Thinking of tragic ways in which to bring about my demise, I sought my angels, Called upon them,

But demons raged and barred them, denying approval, I struggle, I writhe, I cry, With a wish to mummify, Again, I answered the missed calls, And ensured I am all right, Crack stupid jokes on love birds, And laugh as loud as I can whenever they come up in my sight, Don't ask me- I don't know how to eradicate these demons, I don't know the art of summoning an angel to come to my rescue. So, I'm pushing myself out to reach greater heights, I'll try to learn how easy it can be to climb, Because for heaven's sake, you cannot ever whisper, that you don't feel fine. I don't feel fine...

Chapter 17

People flocked back to college in huge numbers, as opposed to my wishes of being amongst the few to arrive in college this soon. This never happened in school. Students used to come a week or two after the vacation ended. Here we were, all grown up, rushing back into the den, too scared to lose attendance.

To my surprise, Rahul sir and Reshma ma'am were still dwelling in their school times and had decided not to come. We sat there in the housekeeping lab alone.

"So, we drag our asses back here and no one is even around to record our attendance?" Maryam said.

"Where did you go for vacation, though?" Sagar asked.

"Are you kidding me?"

"I'm not. But you can still smile. It's good to be human sometimes, instead of being a bitch all the time," Sagar smirked.

"Excuse me. Did you just..."

"Yeah, he called you human too," Mayank joined.

"Guys, leave her alone," I sighed, scribbling in my textbook. The pending work just kept building up.

"Yes, we will, but what are you going to do with her alone?" Sagar grinned.

"Son of a… You really have a dirty mind." Nisha hit Sagar on his forehead, and he grinned like an arrogant brat.

"Are you girls raising your weapons against us?" Gaurav, who had been silent all this while, decided to pitch in. That guy was always looking for a fight.

"We speak 'grenades'. We don't need weapons," Maryam chuckled.

"Yeah, I have a bazooka in my throat," I said.

"I didn't know you were into deep throat," Mayank grinned. I punched him in the face.

"You are an asshole," I glared.

"Owww!" Mayank hid his face, "You're certainly a southpaw, Manya Tyson." Everyone burst into laughter.

"Did you go home?" Shruti asked me.

"No, we went on a tour. What about you?"

"I went home. Where did you go? And with whom? Parents?"

"Nope," I paused. "Mayank, Riya and her guy, Soumya ma'am and Shrey sir."

"Shrey sir?" Nisha asked. It was fascinating how his name always caught people's attention.

I nodded.

"Wow. You are so lucky," Nisha said while Shruti rolled her eyes at me from behind her funny spectacles.

"What? We're good friends. Don't let your dirty imagination run wild," I said and Nisha made faces. Shruti meanwhile, smiled. She understood me well.

"No, you can't be. A guy and a girl can't be JUST good friends," Maryam said. I didn't answer her but just rolled my eyes, I knew she had a crush on Shrey.

"Ignore her," Shruti whispered in my ear.

The rest of my fellow classmates arrived after a week, and it was then that the college decided to drop the bomb, declaring the results of the first semester. Everyone's eyes were glued to the notice board, so I decided to stay away and let the others discover their fate first. I knew I was at my destination.

"I think you should look at your result now," Riya said with a poker face.

"How did you do?"

"I barely passed, but I'm content. Go and check yours." She nudged me with her elbow.

Some were celebrating, some stood there with gloomy faces. Results change people and not in a good way. If they do well, they are under the pressure to perform better. If they don't, they are under the pressure to cover up. In either case, you fall like a house of cards.

My eyes seeked out my name, while my heartbeat gave the background music. When my eyes finally rested on my name, thunder clapped my world into two. I had barely passed, and slipped in accounts. I had managed to fail in the only subject I was good at. I had been hopeful that I'd scored well. Riya grabbed my arm, but I looked at her helplessly.

Intense emotions rushed through me as I pushed her away and ran towards the girls' locker room. I turned on the tap in haste, but couldn't feel the cold water flowing out of it. I splashed some on my face, but nothing. It was getting harder to breath. I had never flunk before.

"It's okay, Manya. You'll be fine." Riya patted my back. The locker room was deserted.

"Riya, leave me alone," I muttered.

"No, I won't. Honestly, I cannot keep myself from saying this, but you dug your own grave. Look what you've done to yourself."

"What?" I shouted.

"As if you don't know. The frequent meetings with Shrey in the midst of exams..."

"Shut up. Just, shut up. You think you're helping me by saying all this? And why do you always drag him into everything? Why do you hate him? What has he done to you? You were the one who wanted me to approach him for studies."

"You think it's all about me?"

"It's always about you, Riya!"

"Manya, you know what, you're in the mud. And people in mud often throw dirt on others. I tried to extend you a rope. Now, I take it back. I'm leaving you on your own," she said and turned to leave. "Sink or swim, I don't care."

I sat there alone, my head spinning. I had seen people collapse under the burden of expectations, now I knew how it felt to be in that situation. I was not ready to accept it, but the truth remained unchanged. Riya was right. I had dug my own grave, but it wasn't Shrey's fault.

My phone vibrated, bringing me back to reality. I looked at the screen; five missed calls. It was Shrey, no guesses. I told myself, 'I won't ever blame him.' No one should take the fall for my poor choices. It vibrated again and I picked up.

"Manya, where are you?"

"College."

"Tell me where you are. It's 5:30 and everyone has left." I looked at my phone; I had been alone in the locker room for three straight hours. Had I had a blackout?

"You there?" he asked.

"Yes," I replied meekly.

"I am waiting for you at the gate, come out," he said and disconnected. I grabbed my bag and left. The empty corridors of the college seemed creepy and haunted. When I came out, I found Shrey talking to *kaka;* they looked happy.

"Shall we?" he asked and I nodded. Kaka smiled at me and I felt a glimmer of warmth for the first time that day.

"Where's your bike?" I asked.

"I gave it to Mayank. I wanted to walk with you."

"Listen, you don't have to do this. I'm fine."

"Well, I just wanted to walk, the weather is good today." He looked around at me and continued, "Since you said it, you're not okay."

"I am fine, don't feel guilty about anything."

"Why shouldn't I? I always manage to pull people into the murk with me."

I knew Riya had said something to him, but he wouldn't mention it. "No, you didn't. I don't blame people for my bad choices. My conscience takes the blame for it. With you, I see no murk, only light. I wouldn't run away from it anyway. I'm not a coward, Shreyansh Thakur. "

"Well, I warned you before and I'm warning you now. If you want to be with me in this murk, we'd better find some light together." He wrapped his fingers around mine. It felt like the first time, the adrenaline rush…

"You're coming out with me tomorrow."

"College?"

"Let's bunk it," he whispered.

I knew this wasn't right. I was already in the mud, sinking deeper, and yet, I decided to swim.

The next morning, Riya shook me hard and I woke from the dead.

"Don't you want to go to college?"

"No, I'm not feeling well."

"Alright, bye." She left without asking what was wrong.

It didn't bother me. I had stopped giving people the leverage to upset me. No one could disturb my inner peace.

It was one of the many things Shrey had taught me. I rolled in my bed, pulling the blanket on me.

"NEVER GIVE ANYONE THE POWER TO DISTURB YOUR PEACE OF MIND. NO ONE IS THAT IMPORTANT."

30th November

Now that I've tasted from her, I know I will want to drink from her forever. She's a fine vintage wine and I cannot help but savour her. I remember that night because I relive it in each and every moment. I remember it in every breath, how her lips sent shockwaves down my body and caused my blood to pump at the speed of light, how her velvet skin brushed against the roughness of my body and soul how I treasured her inside my veins. Everything was so real, I drank her in and we became one.

She was a fragile showpiece, hollow among those filled jars. Little did they know, if love was poured into her, she could turn into a masterpiece, an artefact that must be cherished for its imperfections.

If I could make people aware of the pretentious nature of the so-called perfectionists, I'd break the world. People run after perfection only to come to the revelation that they were chasing a lost cause, an ephemeral entity of themselves. They chase an ideal they can never even hope to become.

'The only way to reach perfection is to understand what your imperfections are, and wear them like an armour.'– Tyrion, GOT series.

People are so scared, so dissolved in their own insecurities that they get lost. They are walking to no destination in particular, as those insecurities manifest within them.

It's ironic and funny since I too walk with my insecurities. I worry that I'll never be human again. I know I won't be able to feel again. I'm worried that I'll meet every next girl with arms and ammunition ready. I'll wear a tattoo on my forehead telling them to keep at bay. If they insist on pursuing me, I'll show them places they would hate, places where light doesn't fall and night never ends.

Oh, how inhumane I've become!

It's all because I was hurt by someone I loved the most.

But then, we all are a part of this vicious cycle, we all are a part of this karmic wheel. Somebody has to be the heartbreaker, someone has to be heartbroken. Someone is going to fall and be wounded while someone else is going to heal. Some will think of life as nothing too important to cherish, while others will take extensive care and still reach a dead end. That's how it is. That's how it has been.

Chapter 18

I walked to Shreyansh's flat. It was two alleys down the road from college. The usual busy streets were deserted, barring some people who sat around fire logs by the road. Winters in Dehradun could be bone chilling. Cold breeze seeped in through my jacket, freezing me. My hands wandered from my jeans' pocket to the jacket's for warmth. I should've worn gloves, I realised.

Through the mist, I saw his silhouette by the street near his flat. He had never invited me to his flat before. I wanted to see how he lived. You can tell a lot about a person just by the sight of their place where they live. It was hazy; I couldn't really see what he was doing. When I drew closer, I found him sitting on the footpath with a cigarette pressed between his lips.

"Is this your breakfast?" I asked, irritated.

"Hi. You're early. I thought I'd finish it before you arrived." He crushed the bud and stood up.

"Can't you quit?" I asked.

"How can I quit the only thing that keeps me sane? Though sometimes, I wonder if I'm smoking the cigarette or if it's smoking me, the price we pay to live," he sighed. "Mayank took my bike to college, so let's walk. The place isn't far."

We walked out of the street and onto a wide damp road. Naked winter trees surrounded us. Our breaths rose up in a visible vapour and dissolved in the frigid air. Brown leaves and broken twigs crunched under our feet. His cheeks were red like fresh strawberries. I held his hand, cold as usual, and rubbed them with mine to warm them up. He smiled at me.

We stopped in front of an old building. It looked deserted.

"Are we going in there?" I asked surprised.

"Yes, we have to trade drugs from here," he laughed and moved into the building. It was dimly lit, paint corroding from the walls. An old lady greeted me and hugged Shrey. We followed her to a staircase which had broken steps. It led us to a large hall upstairs. Some ragged sofas lay beside the wooden staircase. Some kids occupied the tables and plastic chairs lying around. Their tongues were curled over their lips and their eyes glued down over whatever they were scribbling or painting. Some of the younger ones sat on a tattered carpet that stretched across the floor, old toys surrounding them.

"An orphanage?" I whispered.

"A home for the lonely and underprivileged kids," he whispered back.

Some young ones rushed to him and held his hand, one even pulled him over to play with them. Like a weary traveller on a road from eternity, Shrey found his home that day. That time. That moment. I could see it in his eyes. I sat there looking at him; they were all over him, on his lap, on his shoulder, around him, embracing him like he was their own.

After a while, he came to sit beside me. I was busy drawing a duck for a small girl. I handed her a plastic crayon to carry it on. I turned to look at his glowing face and couldn't suppress my smile.

"Do you come here regularly?" I asked.

"No, it's today after a long time," he replied.

"Why?"

"Today's my niece's birthday," he said.

"Why didn't you tell me before? How old is she?" I asked.

"She would've been two years old today. Like that little girl there," he said smiling.

"What do you mean?" I asked, holding his hand. I hoped I'd misheard him.

"She died."

I looked at him in disbelief. I bit my tongue and it went numb. I had never taken death easily, never been able to digest the idea of it. The thought overwhelmed me and my emotions. A child who had never had a chance, hadn't even started talking or walking, was never able to make it through life. It hurt me. How could life be so cruel?

It reminded me of a quote I read:

'Only a moment you stayed, but what an imprint

your footprints have left in our hearts.'–Dorothy Ferguson.

"I'm sorry, Shrey."

"Its okay, Manya," he sighed, looking down.

"I didn't mean to..." I couldn't speak. I didn't know what to say to make him feel better, "I am really sorry..."

"Everyone is sorry. You, people around us, our relatives, our neighbours, they all were sorry. Even the doctor came out with a 'sorry'. The God we worshipped said 'sorry,' but were they? Were they sorry to the mother who carried that baby for nine months, only to see her dead face after three months of her birth? I remember my sister being so lazy when we lived together. Then, when she was blessed with the kid, she changed. She used to wake up during nights, just to check up on her and feed her. She transformed herself for the kid. Then after that 'sorry', it transformed her again–into a morbid, lost, mourning mother. I know how hard it was for her to walk out from the shadow of herself to start living again."

"Three months?!" I couldn't believe my ears.

"Yes. When I think about it, I wonder…what about the father, rejoicing in the blessing of his angel, and planning to build his world around her? Or those grandparents looking at their son who was overjoyed about being a new father? Or my parents? I won't talk about myself; I am a cold heartless bastard. But when I held her in my hands, I did feel something flicker in my chest. I know that I won't ever feel it again." He hid his face in his hands.

"Shrey, I might not know how it feels to be in your shoes and I won't bullshit you that everything happens for a reason. What possible reason could there be for this cruelty?" I sighed. "But instead of mourning over her, smile because she happened to you. She walked into your life and bloomed the barren land of your soul. If you destroy it now, you'll stop the love she brought into your life, and allow the void devour you. Hate her, hate everyone, but would that bring justice to her memory? You have a choice. Dwell in hatred and loss, or you can live, love, and move on."

For she was the bird that flew back home.

He smiled at me, that broken smile with gloomy eyes. We stayed there for some more time and then left. That generous old lady bid us goodbye. "I had a good time today," I said, walking out into the street.

"I wish I could say that too." He smiled, "But I am glad that you were with me today."

I snuggled up to him. "You don't have to thank me." We walked hand in hand. Silence filled our surroundings. Chaos pounded inside me, trapping itself in a ball of anxiety, but I looked at him and settled myself in the peace of his silence. I knew this chaos. It wasn't anything in comparison to the storm brewing inside of him.

"Do you want me to walk with you?" he asked when we reached his flat.

"No, don't be generous. We are good without it," I bid him adieu and walked back to my PG, lost in thought. My teeth chattered and hair bristled all over me in the cold wind.

Riya was waiting for me, still in her college attire, tucked in her quilt. It was cold inside. "So, finally tired now?" she snapped at me as I came in.

"What's up with you? So snippy?"

"Well, everyone who saw you bunking college and giggling on the street is snippy with you."

"Why do they care? This is my life." I threw my jacket to one side and crashed on the bed.

"It's not your life, especially when others are involved in it."

"What do you mean?"

"I am being dragged into it too. They're making jokes about you and Shrey. Rumour has it that you're dating him."

"If you don't wish to be dragged, then don't be, but don't put everything on me. Tell them that you've stopped talking to me. You already have, right? Whatever they say doesn't bother me."

"Someday, it will bother you, and you'll be sorry."

"I'm not sorry now and I won't be sorry in future."

I pulled the quilt over me. "Goodnight, I am tired."

I turned to see her again, and said,

"It would be better if you don't believe in those rumours."

5th December

December, a fascinating month of loneliness and love. A month where love blooms and lonely hearts wither. The frosty air sways the garden of lovers' hearts while blanketing the grave of the lonely undesirable heart.

When I held my niece in my arms, she was so fragile that I was afraid a monster like me would hurt her. Her birth invigorated me. I miss her sometimes. When I lost her, it withered me. I stopped worshiping; I stopped believing that the world can be good. I began believing that nothing good exists in this universe. The shrieks of my sister still live in my ears. I hear them often and never forget. I lost my humanity after I buried that fragile soul near the stream. The kid we were so worried about that we had to check on her all night was left there alone in the dark. In a grave.

They say, things turn worse before they get better. I guess it's one of those days when everything turned out to be heartbreaking. The day I lost her, that little girl with a bright smile, twinkling eyes, sparkle and glory emanating from her, was my last day on earth. I don't know why that sunshine was taken away from us or why a deity would allow it. Today, I visited an orphanage to bask in the beauty lingering in those little souls, and to find a piece of her somewhere in their familiar faces. She came to visit me in this two year old girl's smile. She waved at me from a six year old boy. She played with me among the group of joyous kids.

But then, I realised, she walked home without saying goodbye as her sun descended beyond the horizon. Maybe she knew I couldn't stand the sight of her leaving me. Maybe, she couldn't see me in a puddle of tears. Manya saw me right into my eyes. She knew how weak and vulnerable Shreyansh could grow. Poor soul. She was sorry about the inevitable.

I don't know who to blame for the tragedies in our lives. Acceptance doesn't come easily, but at least today, I had a shoulder to cry on. I had a hand to hold. I had someone who cared enough. In the midst of all these miseries, I managed.

I managed to smile.

Chapter 19

Since Riya had stated that people in college were talking about me, it didn't bother me anymore. Ever since I had conquered my fears, nothing could get to me. I was aware; it thrilled me, although I had no idea how long this carefree feeling would last.

When I entered the rusted gates of the college that day, I could feel all eyes on me. 'The girl dating the super-senior', I knew they must be talking. I walked to the front office lab, the door opened with a bang and everyone turned to look at me. I shrugged and moved to sit in the front row.

"Where were you yesterday? I got your proxy," Shruti asked, setting her funny specs over her nose.

"No kidding? How did you manage to skip through Yogesh sir?"

"It's easy to hide behind tall people," she grinned. "Where were you, though?"

"I was tired, stayed in the PG."

"I thought I saw you near Shrey sir's flat," Sagar said from behind.

"She was at his flat! Weren't you?" Maryam asked. I frowned and looked at her in disgust.

"I don't know. Maybe she was," Sagar replied.

"Shut up, guys," Shruti turned. "Sagar, if you don't have proper knowledge, don't talk rubbish about people. Maryam, being a girl, you should know how such accusations must feel."

They made faces and then laughed. How insensitive it was of them to laugh and talk about all those things, like it was normal to malign someone's reputation. I was certainly not pleased by this sudden attention. The practical went on and I left only when everyone was done. Maybe Shruti understood my silence, but she left me too.

I walked to the mess; it was full of a chaotic crowd, eating without a care in this world. Sagar and Maryam were sitting with Rohan's group, as I crossed them by and they laughed like madness unleashed. My eyes looked for Shrey as I made my way amidst the students and fetched some food.

"Your lover is absent today," Rohan shouted and everyone turned to look at me. His voice, his eyes, his presence disgusted me. I ignored him as I saw Riya sitting on the next table. I breathed a sigh of relief and moved towards her. To my surprise, she put her bag on the vacant seat, and without looking at me, she rolled her eyes. I was left stranded.

"Lonely lover," someone from their group spoke again. I had had enough of this. In disgust, I dumped my plate and left the mess.

I sat on the wall by the mess and held my head in my hands. I could sense everyone laughing at me, picturing me and Shrey in every inappropriate way possible. Through the window, I saw Mayank with a plate full of food strolling around for a vacant seat. He hadn't been in class when I wanted him there. Maybe he would have bashed Sagar's head. That would have been nasty, Mayank murmuring 'so cool' with his hands covered in blood). He saw me through the window too and came out.

"What's up with you?" he chirped. I shook my head.

"Look, I heard about it. Shruti told me everything. They-" he pointed back to the mess "-are a bunch of jerks, narcissistic losers."

I smiled, "Okay, so what are we going to do?"

"There." He slid the plate to me and hopped on the wall himself. "You don't skip food because of people who don't matter."

I smiled, my soul smiled, and the calm solidarity that embraced me smiled. It felt good to recognize I wasn't completely alone just yet. Mayank was there with his funny demeanour and 'so cool' talks. I could see his lips moving, but my mind was elsewhere. I missed Shrey. I had never stopped missing him since the previous day; his lonely eyes, his sombre smile like sad poetry humming in my ears during twilight.

I bunked my remaining classes. Mayank asked me to join him, but I turned him down. I needed some solitude to clean out the dirt in my mind. I crashed on the lawn, then the locker room, but it was lonely everywhere. It's crazy how you seek solitude, but once you find it, it gets lonely.

I was the first one to leave college that day, and the first one to reach the PG. All this while, I struggled to beat back my emotions from calling Shrey and telling him everything. Instead, in the back of my mind, the self obsessed Manya convinced me to deal with her own shit.

Everything started churning inside me then. It was getting harder to remain content. I wanted answers. Everyone was talking about Shrey and me. I asked myself this question again and again. What was it between us that had sparked my desires and other people's thoughts? When these questions became unbearable, I gave up and called him. He picked up after three rings.

"Hi, Manya." His voice was husky.

"Since when have you been in bed?"

"I don't know, since yesterday afternoon maybe."

"What about food and daily chores?"

"Manya, I am grown up enough not to shit and piss in bed," he laughed and I joined him. "And, I had an apple."

"Maybe you aren't grown enough to take care of your food. How could an apple feed your bulky muscles?" He laughed again, it was soothing.

"They swing with my mood," he said after a pause.

"No, don't bullshit the bullshitter. You're meeting me at eight, Sardar ji's dhaba."

"Aye aye, Captain. See you."

I took a jacket and a cap out of the cupboard. Riya was still out; I waited for her to come back so I might tell her where I was going. I wanted peace with her. I didn't have it in me to fight anymore. She didn't show up till 7:30. I'd had enough patience and left for the dhaba.

I was right about freezing outside. The cold wind rammed against my jacket and cap. My ears were cold. I wondered if I was the only one out here who could catch cold through their ears. Perhaps, I was an alien. Thankfully, the dhaba wasn't far. Shrey was sitting right where I had seen him once before. Maybe it was his favourite table.

"You're here early?"

"I am a man of my code, I never make a lady wait."

"But you drink in front of them?" I said, sitting down. The chair felt cold and wet from dew.

"This is not alcohol. Beer is just Bournvita for a man," he winked.

"Isn't bournvita supposed to be for kids?" I asked.

"You can't smell sarcasm, can you?" he smirked, I patted his hand and smiled.

He called Raju to order food. Raju smiled at him as Shrey shook his hand. Raju admired him and Shrey never failed to show his soft side to him. We gave our order and Raju left after chatting a bit.

"So, I guess you didn't just call me here for the food," he asked.

"Well, yes. I wanted to talk to you and I couldn't stop myself."

"You don't have to stop yourself to talk to me EVER."

I smiled. "Yes, but I am afraid you won't like the conversation."

"Don't you think I should decide that?"

I nodded, "Okay, maybe you weren't noticing, but people are talking about us."

He sighed, "I know Manya ,and I am sorry for whatever happened today, behind my back."

"How do you know that?"

He smiled, "I have my contacts."

"Mayank told you, didn't he?! His stomach can't digest anything. Creep," I leaned backward, crossing my hands over my chest.

He laughed, and it was real. "He was just concerned about you, Manya. And you shouldn't blame him for that. He doesn't think you can handle this." He looked into my eyes, "Can you?"

I huffed and the air formed a cloud and then vanished. "I can, if I am clear about things between us," I said, staring back.

He leaned forward, his gaze still intact. "Do you really want to talk about this, knowing how it ended the last time?"

"Yes I do, I have to. People are talking about us, gossiping and fantasizing about us, and I don't even know if it is significant or not. Is there even a shred of truth regarding something between us? What about that kiss? We didn't talk about it after that. I didn't tell anyone either, because I wanted it to be our secret. But now this secret is suffocating me."

His face fell in disappointment, and he broke the gaze. "Manya, what should I say? What should I tell you?" He took a long breath. "Why do you have to throw me under the bus when you know I want to survive?"

"Shrey, I know it's hard for you. But you don't know what's going on inside my head. Riya isn't talking to me because of this, my batchmates are making fun of me, and seniors are their usual selves, bullying, robbing and disturbing my peace. I want answers, otherwise my head will burst."

"I don't have answers for you. I don't even know what it is between us. But, I do know that we have an ethereal connection," he smiled. "If you're seeking a tag for it, I can't give you one. I don't know what to call it, calling it anything would be degrading the meaning of it, the purity and authenticity of it. We do have something. I won't deny that, and I'm brave enough to tell everyone. Are you?" I shook my head, I wanted him to continue.

"I know, Manya, it's complicated and messed up. Everything inside my head is messed up too, I don't know if I can accept the terms and tags others want to give us. I don't want to live on their terms, but I promise you to stay here, and we'll figure out what it is between us..." He held my hand.

My nerves jolted awake at his touch. My brain was unsatisfied with his answer, but my heart gave up to that smile. I smiled back. We finished our dinner and I fought my way out to pay for it.

I grabbed my jacket then and got up to leave when he held my hand and stopped me. "Are you going already?" he asked. I nodded. It was dark and I was supposed to be in my bed, or Sheila aunty would have kicked my ass.

"Can I walk with you?"

"I don't know, can you?" I shrugged.

"Come on, don't be mad at me." He wrapped his fingers around mine and I could feel warmth in his skin for the first time. Mist embraced the dark lonely road. Lights from the houses around us twinkled like stars. For a moment, I felt as though we were walking through the night sky. I felt at peace with him. He looked at me, I could feel his presence next to me. I wanted this walk to last for an eternity.

"Well, that's it then, thank you for dinner," he said, breaking away. I didn't realise when we reached the PG.

"Thanks to you, Shrey. I needed someone to talk to."

"Or do you mean, only me?" he winked, rubbing his hands. It was getting colder.

He stood there as I walked into my PG. His eyes seeked me out, craving to stop me, luring me to run away with him. He stood there, leaning into the fences, staring at me. I wanted him to run over to me, grab me by my waist and kiss the chaos out of me. Instead, he stayed there, kissing me goodnight with his eyes.

It was at that moment, at that very moment, I knew that those eyes would haunt my nights forever.

17th December

I breathe one moment and die the next. It's a challenge to control myself sometimes. I'll talk non-stop and laugh like nothing is wrong with me. This is a mirage. I pretend to live a normal life, like a normal human being. I transform and all I am left with are ruptured thoughts in my mind and my withering consciousness. I drown deeper with the passing of time. Deeper and deeper. I am scared. I'm terrified that one day, I won't make it to the living. I feel like I am gasping for air, screaming for help. I want to live. No one understands me, no one can help. People wonder why I am struggling when they're all living just fine. It makes me jealous and I feel sick with envy when I observe the way they take it all for granted. They have the capability to live a normal life. It disgusts me.

I wondered about this for a long while and now the time came. She questioned US. She questioned things I have been asking myself, every day, every night, in every breath I inhale. I think there are some connections you cannot define. How can you bind an ethereal something to a definition? These are soulful connections and they are beyond the realm of human comprehension.

We both share that mystical connection, I won't be able to give it a name. It's beautiful, and I think beautiful things are better when left as they are, instead of defined for the glory that is. But this society, this society never lets us breathe the way we want to. Why can't we simply live the way we want to live and build our world around our ideals? Why don't people let us live the way we want to?

Me? It doesn't bother me the way it used to. I have grown a thick skin to all the petty comments that judgmental people raise at me. But she...she is naive, she is meant to remain soft and not grow as cold as I am. She is beautiful the way she is, honest and gentle. I hope I allow her to remain like that. I wish this society lets her stay the way she is. I don't want her to be destroyed on account of falling for me. Gosh, she's falling for me! Why is she falling for me? I am not meant to be loved. I can't be loved. If I do, It will lead to destruction. Of myself. Of others around me. I run. I scream. I can't escape this dream. When I want to live and breathe Love and sow seeds. Of my desires and cravings. That I want to seek and give So, I lay here in peace. Letting the ashes of myself devour me. For Phoenix is tired And now won't be able to rise from this.

Chapter 20

If I could wish for 'forever', I would wish to live in that moment every time, when he stayed there looking at me. I would've run to him, but I had to leave, treasuring the moment in only memory. From the window, I saw him lighting another cigarette, walking, lost in the fog.

The light from my room illuminated the dark corridor. Riya was sitting on my bed. "Where were you?" she asked.

"It shouldn't concern you."

"It did, you haven't done this before."

"Yeah, there's always a first time."

"What do you want to say?"

"You ignored me at college for the FIRST time too."

"I did because I didn't want to dive into your WAR."

"My war? Okay then, let's maintain distance. Don't interfere in my life."

"Fine, do whatever the hell you want."

"Get off my bed."

"Screw you and your filthy bed, Manya," she said and climbed into her own bed.

"Oh, thank you." I shoved my middle finger at her and pulled the blanket over me. It's unbelievable how some people can cheer your mood up when you're screwed, and fuck your mood when you're happy.

I didn't blame her for being a bitch to me. What bothered me was that she talked as though nothing had happened. When she was amidst the crowd, she cared for her reputation. There it didn't matter to her whether I was living or dying. At the PG when she was alone, she sought my presence and wanted to know my whereabouts, not thinking about my feelings towards her; a selfish act which I never expected from her. We weren't in school anymore where you could ignore someone and then come back with a candy as truce.

It was finally the weekend after that fateful week of college and chaos. The bright sun rays escaped through the curtains and woke me up. Riya wasn't in her bed. I looked at the watch–it was eleven already, which meant no breakfast. Riya had ditched me for the weekend. I smiled, it was lonely and felt like home.

I slipped out of bed, got fresh and brushed. The water felt cold. I couldn't gather the courage to wash my face. While preparing coffee, I took some chips and cup cakes from Riya's cupboard and sat in the balcony. The sun had awakened from its slumber.

Everyone was outside their houses. Kids played on the road while the elders sat on their porches, soaking up the sunlight. It was warm and soothing. Almost everyone was out of their homes in Dehradun that day, enjoying the bright cosy weekend.

I sat there in the balcony, reading a book about the chaos of life and how to find solace. The author advised ways to find inner peace even in the toughest of times. She explained how we run all of our lives in search of peace, but we never search for it within ourselves. Peace lies inside us, but we insist on seeking it elsewhere. The book further talked about how to find the salvation one is chasing. Obviously, without going into the jungle and turning into a monk.

I looked down at the kids playing on the road and found peace there, on their faces and in their eyes. It made me believe that peace existed somewhere in a corner of our existence. Somehow, we lose it as we grow up.

My lonely weekend ended there on that balcony. I sat there the entire day thinking about everything and nothing. I decided to find inner peace. Though melancholic and lost, I sometimes found peace in Shrey's eyes. I don't know if it was peace, helplessness, or resolve.

Riya came back late, slipped on her pyjamas and went to the dining room without me. It didn't matter to me. Nothing mattered to me anymore. I'd sat alone in the dining room and ate before anyone. I didn't even wait for Soumya and went to sleep early for the next day at college. I had to wake up early to write some practical assignments for bakery, otherwise Mr. Rahul would have kicked my ass.

Unfortunately, I woke up just in time to get ready. I ran to college without taking a shower. That arrogant bitch had woken up early and left without me. The old rusted gate closed behind me and I stepped into my practical class only to realise that it was filled, except the first row. I was nervous now, desperate to escape the wrath of Mr. Rahul. Mayank waved at me from the second row as I occupied the first, just ahead of him. No student sat beside me.

"Alright, settle down," Mr. Rahul said, closing the door behind him. "Take out your practical assignments. Those who didn't complete it, stand away from your desk." I was doomed. I looked behind, everyone had it.

"Manya, where is yours?" he asked, coming to my table.

"I am sorry, sir, I couldn't complete it."

"Not again, Manya, What's wrong with you? You were so good in the first semester. What happened now?" I couldn't gather the courage to look up and answer.

"You're going to make this pudding alone today. This is your punishment and last chance." I nodded and thanked him.

"If someone is willing to help her, they can," he said to the class. I turned back and as expected, no one volunteered. Shruti hid herself in the crowd, her small stature helping again. I didn't expect her to come forward and suffer with me anyway, so I was okay.

«Sir, may I help her?" I turned back and shook my head. *No Mayank, you can't. You are already in a lot of trouble because of me,* I thought. But he just grinned like an idiot, a cool idiot. Mayank looked at Mr. Rahul with his puppy-dog eyes and he nodded.

"You didn't have to do that," I told him as he came to my table with his bag.

He patted my back and smiled, «We're in this together, Manya." I felt relieved that my recent tension with Riya hadn't acted as a negative catalyst between Mayank and me.

The pudding took a lot of our time and effort, but we pulled it off somehow. It was ready before the time was up. He talked as I completed my assignment, waiting for the seniors to come pick up the pudding. It was to be served at the staff lunch that day.

I didn't know, however, that the devil himself would come to pick it up. Rohan and Sarthak stood there smiling. Some attention hungry whores surrounded them. "So, who made the pudding today?" Rohan sung in his hoarse voice. I hid behind my table. "Manya," someone said and I sunk deeper.

"Juliet, oh Juliet. I call thee for pudding, give me your pudding," Rohan's voice echoed, trailed by the giggles of his followers.

"Sick people," I muttered.

"Here is the pudding, sir." Mayank took it out and gave it to them.

"Did he ask you for it?" Sarthak said. Mayank shook his head, smiling.

"So, go back and tell her to bring it to us."

"But sir, we made it together."

"Can't you understand one simple thing? Crazy," Sarthak glared at him.

"Do as you're told, kid," Rohan said and Mayank followed with a smile.

"Such jerks," I whispered when he came back.

"I know, take this cool pudding and shut their mouths," he said.

I took the pudding from him and walked towards Rohan. He pushed his finger into the pudding, took it out and licked it. "It's raw, bake it for five more minutes," he said.

"It will burn," Mayank mumbled from behind.

"Are you deaf? You crazy stupid jerk. Do as you are fucking told," Sarthak shrieked.

I took the pudding before things could get ugly, and slid it into the oven. We stood there praying. I knew they were wrong, but fear made me do it. After five minutes, Mayank took it out and from the look and smell of it, we both knew that the inevitable had happened.

"Guess, I was wrong," Rohan grinned. I wanted to punch his face, but somehow suppressed my emotions.

"What's this smell about?" Mr. Rahul came in just then. The worst timing! Stars were aligned to fuck me up that day.

"Manya burned the pudding, sir." Sarthak smiled at me.

"You did what? Neither did you complete your work, nor do you do your practicals properly. What will we serve at the restaurant now?" he said at the top of his voice. His brows were tensed and face flushed red. I had never seen him that angry. "Go, dump this and make another. No food for you today and no help either. You have an hour. Otherwise, I'm going to cut your assessment marks and attendance. Rohan, come back by 2 PM. The rest of you students may mark your attendance and leave." Rohan and Sarthak left grinning.

"I'm sorry," Mayank said meekly.

"It's not your fault."

"Still, do you want me to save you something to eat?"

"No, I have lost my appetite. Save a seat for the lectures, if you can."

"I will and good luck." He left with his bag. Mr. Rahul left after a while too. It took me forever to dump the burnt pudding. All my effort had been a waste. Somehow, I managed to make it again, but it wasn't like the one before, just okay enough to be served. The clock struck 2 by the time it got baked, and I waited for those jerks to come back.

"I didn't know that you were the one who burnt the pudding." A voice echoed in my ear and it sounded familiar, like a song in my head. I turned back, it was Shrey. He was standing by my table, smiling, hands in his pockets.

"Don't you dare laugh," I said. "What are you doing here?"

"I am here to pick up the order. I'm sorry you had to face this," he said.

"No, you're not, no one is. If you had come earlier, this wouldn't have happened."

"Oh right, how on earth would I have known that they would do this?"

"You must have, you both were best friends. Who else would him and his bloody intentions better?"

"Oh, come on, Manya. I was busy in other chores. You're being unreasonable."

"Yes, you are always busy and you always have reasons for everything, but not for things that matter." I pushed the pudding towards him. "Take it and go." He stood there looked at me for a while, then left with the pudding. I had poured all my frustration and anger out on him. All I got in return was a calm nod. God, this silence was eating me alive. I didn't know how to get through his walls, how to make him talk.

I took my bag. Lunch was over and everyone was in the lecture room. I sat on the stairs. I decided to go in late to class to avoid any mockery. I knew Rohan's toads would target me again. The stairs by the lecture room never failed to provide solitude and peace.

"Bunking class?" A voice echoed from down the stairs. I looked down, but couldn't recognize the person.

"No, there's still time," I replied, puzzled. She came up. Her face looked more familiar up close.

"Oh yes, you don't know me. I am in second year. I just came back from my industrial training. I am Deepika. You're Manya, right?" Shrey had told me about her, but how on earth did she know my name?

"I can understand your dilemma here, I know a lot about you. You're quite famous around here," she smirked.

"I can smell the sarcasm." I burned within.

"No, no pun intended. People talk about you like they talked about me." She sat beside me.

"Can you stop talking in riddles, please?"

"Pardon me, it's just that you're hot property in college right now. A connection with the hottest senior has its pros and cons."

"Who?" I asked.

"Shreyansh, of course. Don't tell me you weren't aware?"

"How were you connected to him and how are you so sure that we are connected?" I asked.

"The college is talking about you. Even the people in training want to know who Manya is. I was in the same place like you last year. The college was talking about me and him, but it faded away quickly enough. The fun doesn't last, anguish does."

"You were his what?"

"I don't know what we were or what we wanted to be, but we were close, too close for people's comfort. He didn't want any commitment, only the closeness and intimacy that came with it." I raised my brows, wondering where and what she was getting into. "Yes, we had this thing going on for a while, but it didn't last. I was afraid that I might lose myself and my conscience. I hope that same thing doesn't happen to you. Maybe you're just another rose in his garden, like I was."

10TH January

Approach me with innumerable questions in your eyes, then slit my throat and watch me bleed in pain and agony. Rip my heart out and mock me because it still beats fast. Pierce my flesh with a thousand needles and as I scream in agony, you enjoy the sound of my suffering because it sounds melodious to you. Leave me alone to wither and decorate your room with the petals of my soul, artefacts of the time we've shared. But love, you could never make me talk about myself, my wandering thoughts and my depths.

Every time I open up to someone, I regret it. My stupid little heart can't fathom the idea that people genuinely want to know me, instead of wanting to know me out of curiosity on a superficial level.

I don't want to pour out myself and turn hollow again. I've tried it before. I've tried it again and again. Every time, I've failed terribly, I lost a part of myself, I became hollow. It's exhausting to push people away when all they want is to know who I am, but I never know if the devil is masquerading as an angel or not.

Sometimes I secretly wish for someone to hold onto me, no matter how much I try to run away. Some days, I'm looking to escape, while other days I want to be captured, to be quelled and understood.

Anxiety talks to me, it captures me and never leaves my side. It's terrible to be me. It's terrible to be with me. Yet, she wants parts of me that I fight to keep hidden. I always hide it in plain sight in front of humans that feed on us like vampires and leave us to worry.

That's the thing about anxious people. They push you away because they think they aren't good enough. But somewhere inside them, there lays a heart full of fears which wants to conquer all of its demons and come out alive. The heart longs to feel good, to love and to live. If you're lucky, you'll find someone who takes the time to find that heart of yours, a lost treasure for the ages, suddenly found. Let them show you the beauty you've never believed in. Let them be your mirror, the window into the beauty of your soul.

Chapter 21

Deepika left after bombing my world. It's strange how someone can play with our mind and alter our thoughts. A stubborn symphony then takes hold inside us only to give way to insecurity, anxiety, confusion.

After she left, I decided to bunk my lecture. I couldn't fathom the idea of anyone else having Shreyansh. I sat in the lawn, lost in chaotic thought, when some guys jumped over the fence. The wall near the staff quarters was short and surrounded by bushes, which made it a perfect escape point. The guards didn't allow us to leave before five, that's why some outsiders escape through it.

I was wearing chef pants that day, so I took the risk of my life. The fog hid me as I crawled through the bushes. The guys looked back, clapping, cheering for me. I ran to the wall, pressed my feet on the hay of prickly grass and jumped over the wall. I screwed up the jump and collapsed upside down on the other side. By God's grace, there was a bed of grass there, otherwise I would've broken at least a couple of bones. They laughed at me as I dusted off my clothes, then cheered on for me. I flashed a faint smile.

"You're so cool, maybe the first girl to ever escape college like this," one of them said. I had never seen them before, so I figured they must be from Deepika's batch. All I know was they were sweet, minded their own business, and left me alone.

The words 'you're the first' got stuck in my mind, and I wondered if I was his first choice. While Deepika was there, would I be able to travel through the crowd to him? With all these thoughts, the walk to the PG felt long.

The door banged, thumped, and knocked. I thought I was dreaming about someone scolding me in a rage, but I soon realized that someone was at the door. I got up with a jolt and opened it.

"Where the hell were you?" Mrs. Shila asked fuming.

"Umm..sleeping aunty."

"Sleeping? Look at the watch," she snarled. It was 9:30 PM. I had been sleeping for five straight hours. It happened a lot lately. I usually fell asleep whenever I was tensed. "You missed your dinner again, this has happened ten times in a month now. Do you know how much food gets wasted? Can't you tell me beforehand?" I shook my head apologetically. "You come home late, you skip meals, you don't inform me. I think it's time to talk to your parents," she said, pulling out her phone from her baggy cardigan's jacket.

"No, no. Please don't call them," I pleaded. That was the last thing I wanted right now.

"This is your last warning. I am going to leave you for now, this better not happen again." She slammed the door in my face. Everyone was trying to stick it to my ass. My mind was messed up to the point of no return. I was too far gone to come back to my senses. Suddenly, somebody knocked at the door again.

"Who the fuck is it now? It's open," I yelled.

"What's up with you? Haan?" Riya opened the door. She stood there with a plate in her hand, still in her college uniform.

"Nothing. Why are you wandering in your college dress?"

"My psycho roommate decided to lock herself in her room. I knocked, but she didn't open, so I had to wander around in this pathetic uniform," she said, sitting beside me.

I smiled. Her sarcastic tone was missing this time. "I'm sorry. I overslept."

"I figured. Here, I got you some food." She passed the plate to me. "What's up with you?"

"Nothing, why?" I started stuffing my hungry stomach.

"Never lie to your mother. You weren't at breakfast, or lunch, and now you've skipped dinner too." She had genuine concern in her eyes, so I told her about everything, except Deepika.

"Wicked," she smirked. "But why did you let out all your frustration on poor Shrey?"

"Poor? You don't know what's been going around," I replied, still digging into the plate. "Everything is so messed up."

"Yeah. I can see. I heard about all the rumours."

"And you still ignored me, you cold hearted witch."

"I ignored you because you asked me to." She took the plate and slide it under her bed, where it collided with others and made a noise. "We have a full stack of these plates now. We should start selling them," she grinned.

I laughed. "Do you want to know now?"

She nodded. I told her everything Shrey and I had talked about during dinner. I connected it with the things Deepika had told me about them, the relationship they had had, the rumours about them and the reason why they had drifted apart.

"I knew Shrey was bad news," she blurted out as soon as I finished.

"What?"

"Yes, he's playing around. That chauvinistic pig thinks that girls are toys. He's toying with you, just like he did with Deepika."

"He's not like that. He didn't do anything to me. It was I who initiated the kiss. What made you think that?"

"What about the time in Dhanaulti? I know these guys. I've dealt with them. You're new to this."

"It was I that time too. I kissed him. And he's not like other guys you've met."

"Just because you initiated the kiss doesn't mean that he didn't want it, he reverted back the second time, right? I am telling you, don't get involved with him. Delhi guys are so cunning," she said. "He's ruining you beyond repair."

"So, does that mean Rehan is sick too?"

"Don't bring Rehan into this."

"Why? He's so goody-goody and Shrey is the devil? You're not helping here, Riya, you're making things worse. I asked you for advice, not to make things sound hopeless and accuse Shrey. Why does he always have to be the culprit?"

"Because he is the culprit. The truth is, no one really likes him." She took a pause. "Even I don't like him. He's creepy."

"Shut up, Riya, enough is enough."

"What the hell is wrong with you, Manya? You believe in him? Over me?" Her eyes shut in disgust.

"Yes, because you're wrong this time. He never said anything against you. It's you who have a grudge against him, and maybe I shouldn't have told you anything."

"Yeah right, don't. I won't listen anything from now. Go ruin yourself. Be his hoe or whatever you like. I don't care now," she said, standing from my bed.

"You know what, go away. I am done with you. I don't want to talk to you ever again."

"I'm not interested either," she said and turned out the lights. I held my head in my hands, unable to unleash the flood of tears behind my eyes.

Sometimes, even the people closest to you do not see eye to eye with you. It hurts, but what can you do about it? When you can't alter your own beliefs, how can you expect them to change theirs? All you can try is to forget your differences and move on.

Sometimes, it's not easy to move on. Sometimes, you find yourself stuck in an abyss. That's what the quarrel with Riya did to me. The nights to follow, I fell apart bit by bit, but found the strength to gather myself somehow the next morning.

Two weeks passed after we fought. A lot happened during that time. There was a week of intense tests with isolated studying. We were two humans in a room, studying separately. The silence bothered me. Only humans have the capability to act like total strangers in the same room, under the same roof. Mayank, Soumya and the other PG people constantly tried to sort things between us, but neither of us budged. Everyone was astonished at how the night and stars could stay apart, but we managed.

The other batch of 2nd years was filling in. They were better than the other half that went for training. There wasn't a sign of ragging, intro, or chaos this time. There wasn't a sign of any further connection between Deepika and Shrey. *Was I jealous?*

Shrey had come to me the day before the tests were supposed to begin. He stood there in front of me with a poker face. I was sitting in my class alone, while everyone else was still at the mess.

"How are you?" he asked.

"Do you really want to know?"

"Why would I come here and ask if I didn't want to know?"

"I'm surviving. Why do you care?"

"I do, I came here to ask if you want any help with your tests," he sighed. "Wait a minute, Manya, are you mad at me because of the other day?"

"Partially, and I don't want any help."

"What's the other part?" he asked, sitting on the table, leaning towards me.

I didn't let myself get distracted by those hazel eyes. "The other part is where you didn't tell the whole story about you and Deepika."

"And who told you about rest?" he asked.

"Before I tell you, I just have to say that I didn't expect that you of all people would lie to me." I threw my books in my bag, ready to leave. He grabbed my hand and I turned me to look at him.

"I didn't do anything, Manya. As always, you're misguided. Someone's been playing with your head."

"Yes, like you did. But you playing with my head hurts more, Shrey. Deepika told me everything about you...about you both."

"And you believed her over me?" He loosened his grip on my hand. "After all this time that we've known each other, you believed everything she said. I don't even know what she told you, what lies she fed to you."

"I believed her. I'm a woman, and I know a woman doesn't lie about her own character. She won't malign herself."

"Oh, Manya. Well, here's what I know. You're so innocent, you don't know to what extent people can go to get into your head to ruin you."

"I am not so innocent to let you or anyone else play with my mind anymore. I am done with you people. I don't want to talk to you again," I said, picking up my bag.

"Fine, keep dwelling in lies," he said and left before I could. People had now started to come in for the lectures, so I stayed.

"What are you looking at dumbass?! Get out of my way," I heard him shouting at someone.

"What's up his ass?" someone asked.

"Maybe another love quarrel." They laughed, passing by me. I sighed.

I could hear people whispering about me, weaving webs of fascinating lies to sell in the college gossip market.

For another two weeks, I dragged myself like a corpse from my PG to college. Everything around me felt empty, while I was in a.vacuum. Nothing made sense to me. There was a battle raging inside my head that I wasn't quite sure how to win. It was already lost, unknown to me.

I had no one to talk to, no one to share anything with. Mayank was there, but he couldn't truly help. He was emotionally immune, didn't seem to think much, and couldn't understand. He was too cool for the shits of life. I had to seek someone out. This tension was boiling up inside, ready to erupt. She was the only one I could go to, so my feet led me to her. I knocked on the door, but there was no answer. I turned around thinking that she had perhaps slept since it was late.

"What do you want this late?" Soumya came out, rubbing her eyes. "Come on in." She had the room all to herself now. Her roommate had shifted to the hostel, just for getting good grades. Licking boots always helped. I sat on the couch by the door.

"Hey, come here inside the blanket, it's cold," she said.

"I'm fine."

"Come on in, kid," she ordered, and I followed. "Now tell me, what do you want?"

"I just wanted someone to talk to, someone I could trust," I said. She nodded.

"I want you to tell me everything that existed between Shrey and Deepika. Is he really the guy he projects himself to be?" I took a pillow and crushed it between my legs.

"First of all, there wasn't anything between them. Don't let your imagination run wild. Second, you astonish me. Do you really want to know who Shrey is? After all that he has done for you?" she asked, leaning against the wall.

"There wasn't anything between them? Nothing intimate? Surely something must be, right?"

"Who told you that? How did you get to know about things that don't even exist?"

"Deepika did, she told me everything," I sighed.

"Damn it. These fucking hostlers, their evil minds never rest. Don't you get it? They are playing with your head. It's so easy to get inside your head, Manya. And honestly, I'm furious now. Why do you believe in anything anybody says so quickly?"

"I know that, but I couldn't help it. Did she lie to me?"

"Yes, she did. Probably another mind game of theirs."

"What game? What did she lie about? Stop riddling around, Soumya. Don't make it more complicated. I'm miserable here."

"Okay, so it started when Deepika came to college and took an instant liking to Shrey. We had just been promoted to 2nd year, new seniors, and all the attention we were getting was raging wildly in us. Shreyansh, being his charismatic self, often found himself at the centre of everyone's attention. He wasn't like he is now. He was lively, happy, and yes, in a relationship too." She took a pause. "Deepika started falling for him, but it was unrequited. Shreyansh was loyal to his girlfriend. Deepika was just a friend to him, but she wanted more. Her devotion for him travelled through the college and hostel, as she used to blabber about him to everyone she met. It was her who brought all those rumours upon herself. Shreyansh still supported her, ignoring everything, even the rumours that could destroy him. He even got scolded by Reshma ma'am and received innumerable warnings from her. Then he went to training, the breakup happened and everything changed. He wasn't the same after that in any way, shape or form. The guy couldn't save himself, how could he have saved others? Her? The lively guy turned away and into himself. He stopped talking to everyone, including Deepika, and you already know the rest. This is the only truth."

"Oh, damn. Oh, my God. I am so stupid. Why am I like this? Why do I ruin everything?" I held my head in my hands. She pulled me close to her and hugged me tight. I needed it.

"I don't blame you. People like us who care for others are vanishing from the world. The world ruins us, demolishes us, plays with us until we give up and feel nothing. Like they did to Shrey," she said, breaking the embrace.

"What do I do now? How can I possibly make things right? How do I apologize to Shrey?"

"I don't know, Manya. At this point, I can only tell you one thing: follow your heart and everything will be all right."

26th January

What will you and I have without love?

Yes, tragedy.

Yes, melancholy.

But at some point, it's soothing and enchanting. Hate as much as you can, curse it, yearn for it, burn in it or live in it. There wouldn't be anything without love. There wouldn't be me or you without it. Tragedies connect people and sometimes love blossoms in it. Two insecure people can take away each other's vulnerability. You know, that's why I feel for tragic people and the tragedies that connect them.

She somehow fell for me because of this vulnerability that lives inside me. It's like she had a thing for it.

All her life, she lived a fairytale, as she had told me. But I wasn't anywhere close to a fairytale. I was a delusional disparity against a cruel reality, a living nightmare. Maybe that's what pulled her towards me. She was exhausted of fairy tales and happy endings; she wanted thrill and found it in me.

I do believe now that love finds its way. It is finding its way to me, into me. It's filling the cracks in me, but for how long? For how long will it fill the cracks, when I am going to shed for eternity. It'll run its course, it'll be over soon. The fear consumes me. It occurs to me: what if one fine day, she forgets about me as though I never existed?

'What if's and 'but's steal my peace. She'll get tired and stop showering her devotion over me. If then she keeps on loving me, robbed of every possession, I'll embrace her, I'll know that her love won't just run its course.

I'll find peace.

I'll love her then.

And I know it'll be forever with ease.

Chapter 22

February was another frigid month. This was the time when all the hotel management colleges from around the country came to Dehradun to participate in a competition organised by the All India Group of Hotel Management. Our college, being the top ranked, organized it every year at this time.

People arrived in their fancy college uniforms and gathered in the canopied playground of our college. Mist enveloped everything in its path, escaping through the tent's joints. For the first time, every student of our college was seen sporting the same attire, a black coat with white shirt and trousers, adorned with ties. We looked royal. I inhaled pride.

While I scanned the crowd for Deepika, my heart apologetically searched for Shrey. To my dismay, our college had allotted some small errands for us to run, and mine required both concentration and precision. I had to escort the participants to their stations and make sure that they had all the necessary things they required.

I walked around like a woman in-charge, with files in my hand. Only I knew how difficult it had been to win this job from others, or how many errands I had to run for Ms. Reshma to get this privilege. After due motivation from Soumya, I had gained enough energy to make amends, starting within myself.

While I managed people and the files, my classmates managed guest accommodations, served drinks and snacks, while some of them were in the kitchen, assisting our seniors. While the second year was busy with supervising work in the kitchen, and the food & beverage service, the third year dealt with contest participation.

Since a majority of participants were seniors, it was hard to instruct them around, specially since I had a knack for bumping into rowdy bullies.

"Hey junior, what's your name?" one of the guys from a Delhi college asked. *What a lecher*, I thought.

"Manya."

"Full name?"

"Don't try, sir."

"Don't try what?"

"I am not available. I have work. Since you're settled, I should leave."

"What the..."

"Enough boys, she got you," the girls in their group laughed as I left.

All the participants were now settled, so I decided to check on my own college. All the colleges were represented by their college flag above their station. Ours was in a far corner, beside the jury's stage. Some of them looked at me and smiled, while others made faces and turned away. I was fortunate to catch the attention of the one I wanted.

"What are you doing here?" Deepika asked, making her way out.

"Whatever you're doing."

"Don't play games with me. I am participating."

"So, only you get to play games?"

"What are you talking about?" she asked.

"You lied to me about everything! How could you be so insensitive? How could you be such a heartless bitch?"

She laughed, "Maybe that's how you take revenge. I wanted it from Shrey, you dragged yourself into it like a puppy. Little puppy, go away, shoo…this isn't your fight."

"I don't care. You have made it my fight now and I won't let you spoil things for me anymore," I said. I was ready to leave when Tanya decided to come out from her hiding.

"You're a puppet and we'll keep playing with you and your miserable life! There's nothing you can do about it now and there never will be. You'd better go away before we make you piss in your pants." She laughed like a devil. "Come, Deepika, baby, we've a competition to win." They walked away, laughing at my miserable plight.

I stood there like a dumb puppet. I had to make a decision then and there, whether I would continue being stuck there, or if I would drive myself away from this. I decided to go with the latter. "Drive away, Manya," I told myself.

I looked into my file. These two were participating in the 'salad making' competition. A cruel smirk formed over my lips. They were about to get a taste of their own medicine.

I looked for Mayank; a partner in crime is a prerequisite. Though I would admit that she scared me, Tanya wasn't a girl with any morals. Whatever she did, she did without empathy. But the time of fear was now over. It was time to fight fire with fire. I found Mayank hopping around the participants with a platter of raw vegetables.

"Arey…*sabzi wale bhaiya*?" I shouted.

He stopped and turned around. "Yeah, you have all the right to call me that because you have a file in your hand. Still, not funny."

I laughed, "You're a cool *sabzi wala* though."

"Haha...still not funny. Unlike you, I have work to do, so piss off."

"Call me your saviour. I'm taking you away for a mission. Put the platter down."

He slid the platter under a table immediately. "Cool! This sounds so cool. Come on, tell me about it." I dragged him into a corner where all the things were kept. There were two second year guys doing the inventory, but no one else.

"So, we're going to ruin someone's party and I need your help."

"Looks like an undercover mission, cool! I'm up for it."

"Are they making mayonnaise for the salad, or are we giving it to them?" I asked.

"Yes, we're providing them with it. Why do you ask?"

"Just listen. Get the mayonnaise, salt, pepper, a spoon, and come with me. Oh, and stay silent."

He nodded and grabbed the things I'd asked him to. We moved to a more discreet location. I took the mayonnaise and mixed a handful of salt and pepper in it with caution. We couldn't afford to get caught.

"Good Lord, are you trying to kill someone?"

"Worse, I am going to piss someone off beyond death," I smirked.

"I don't understand."

"You don't have to. Do whatever I tell you. Now, go and give this bowl to Tanya. After that, I'll fill you in on the plan."

Like an obedient kid, he took the bowl and gave it to them. I stood away to avoid their attention. They took it without suspicion and blurted out something, laughing at Mayank.

"What did they say?" I asked when he came back.

"Oh, nothing. They said, 'You're a crack head, but sweet. Thank you, crazy.' and then they laughed," he said.

„Such arrogant and rude bitches."

"But they were cool, they called me sweet."

"Yes, you with your raging hormones only focused on that."

"Oh, I don't know what games you guys play," he said. "Now tell me about this evil plan of yours."

"That mayonnaise is the sole plan. They're participating in salad making and the plan is to ruin their salad."

"What the fuck? Why did you do that? Our college will lose."

"I don't care. They had it coming by bothering me and my friend.» I patted his shoulder.

"You're so evil but okay, cool!" he exclaimed. I shrugged, and turned to leave.

"Where you going?" he called after me.

"Leaving. Do your work, *sabji wale*. I'm going to wander around a bit." He cursed, kicked dust and left. He was always so nice, innocent and gullible that I pitied him for falling into other people's traps. Insensitive people played with him and his mind. Perhaps I had been one such person too.

I crossed paths with some seniors and asked them about Shrey. He wasn't with them. I walked by the reception and found him standing there with Maryam and a second year girl. They wore sarees while Shrey had on a black suit. I waved at him from the stairs, and he raised his brows.

"What are you doing here?" I asked. Maryam looked at me, I stared back. She turned away and whispered something to the other girl, to which they both laughed with their plastic faces.

"Are we on talking terms again?" he smirked.

I smiled. It was never too hard to win him over. Maybe he couldn't remain angry at people for long. "It's hard to stay mad at you, Shrey."

"I thank my charms daily before going to bed," he winked.

I laughed, and it echoed through the empty reception hall. "I repeat, what are you doing here with these plastic faced witches?" I asked.

"You're in a strange mood," he smiled, to which I shrugged. "Alas, I have no choice but to bear with them. Ms. Reshma asked me to use my charms to welcome the Chief Guests."

"Who's coming?"

"I don't know."

"Really? The Head of Hotel Management Groups of India is coming. I don't know the man's name though."

"Ramesh Malhotra?" he said.

"Yes, yes, him. I heard he's quite influential."

"Maybe that's why I'm here," he grinned.

I patted his hand. "And them?"

"They are fair, tall and dumb. That's why," he said. I laughed looking at them.

"I'll meet you near the library, I think they're here," he said. I saw Maryam and the other 2nd year girl rushing towards the gate with several of our professors. Shrey walked after them without a care in the world. I went back to the stairs by the library and waited for him for what felt like an eternity.

He came back with his coat in his hand and his tie loose around his neck. "You wanted to talk?" he asked, sitting beside me.

"How do you know?" I looked at him.

"I can read it on your face," he answered.

"So now you are psychic too?"

"I've been doing that for years now."

I imitated his tone to which he smiled and slapped my back.

"Ouch, okay. So, back to the point. I'm sorry," I said.

"I didn't hear you, what did you just say? Pardon me?" he grinned.

"I am seriously sorry," I whispered in his ear.

"Sorry, SIR?" I slapped his hand. "Apology accepted, dear junior. But why now?" he asked.

"Just learning to read people and their agenda myself," I said.

"Someone's growing up," he smiled.

"Had to, intend to, or else I won't be able to survive here."

"You know what?" He took a deep breath. "This innocence I see in your eyes is on the verge of extinction. I don't see it in people now. The carnivores of feelings and emotions seek you out. You're their prey, their fun, their entertainment and fodder for their gossip. If you intend to fight for your survival, you might fail now and then, but these failures and these scars will lead you somewhere."

"Yes, I learned that. Thank you for always understanding me. You're my safe home in this barren world." He wrapped his strong arms around my shoulders and embraced me. In that moment, we were complete, we were us. Like in a parallel universe, we were together and safe from the chaos around us.

The competition started after the Chief Guest's speech. Shrey, Soumya and I wandered around with nothing to do. Riya was, as usual, busy with her society friends as well as the 'other people.' Shrey and Soumya had told us already how biased these competitions were. Colleges had to maintain a set image so everyone could enjoy a fixed success.

Everything looked good from the outside: the vivid rangolis highlighting social issues like dowry and female infanticide were thought provoking and pleasing to the eye, the salads were experimental and amusing, then there was poster making and flower arrangement which were both a feast for the senses.

"Hey, they're about to examine the salad preparation. We should go see," I told everyone.

We stopped at a distance from the table where all the salads by different participants lay. I was thrilled. This was my moment. The inspection jury tasted each salad and talked about it with the participants. Tanya and Deepika stood there, full of pride over their own preparation. Their salad seemed far above the rest. It looked pleasing and unique compared to everyone else's.

The jury looked pleased and praised the appearance. Tanya smiled and grabbed Deepika's hand. One of the jury members then dug his fork into it, tasted it, and spit it out the next second. "What the hell...is this a joke?" he balked in disgust, gulping down the glass of water before him.

Everyone looked at them. "What's wrong, sir?» Deepika and Tanya asked together.

"Taste it," he shouted, a nerve popping out of his forehead.

Tanya tasted it and spit it out herself. Rohan grabbed a water bottle for her and rubbed her back. "Good job, kid, good acting," the old man said in anger. The other jury member gathered herself and asked, "What's the matter?"

"They put salt and chilli powder in their salad to make it different. Cheeky kids." The old man said irritatedly and smiled in a mocking way.

The jury and other participants laughed. Other people gathered around too as we laughed at them. Their faces flushed red in embarrassment. I had never thought that I would see them in such a dire state.

They were ridiculed by the crowd, disqualified, and even got scolded by Ms. Reshma. The show was over and I moved away smiling, basking in the success of my prank.

"We pulled it off, it was so cool." Mayank patted my back.

"Pulled off what? Did you guys do it?" Soumya asked in surprise, while Shrey raised his brows.

"Yes, it was her 'cool' plan," Mayank said. I smirked at them.

Though Soumya patted my back, I already felt like the world was under my feet.

"You're wicked!" Shrey exclaimed with a straight face.

1st February

My heart had been keeping surveillance over you and I saw you talking to them the way you never did to me. You spoke to everyone around you, but forgot about my servile existence.

My mind races back to us, to our moments, to our conversations, to those days when I found myself smiling. Perhaps I still smile in a parallel universe. You see, it faded away as soon as the cruel world dragged me to the present, into your bleak presence now and it hurts. Believe me, I tried putting in the best of my efforts to keep my soul from wandering back to you. I imagine you running back to me. Here, you would have walked to me, kissed me all over, cursed yourself for my damp face and dabbed my the eyelashes. You would have held me tight, and in that one moment, we would have understood that if it's love, it always remains, despite the sad eyes, swollen face, numbness, dry lips, mum words.

Although we would have known that we were not good enough for each other, it would have come with the realization that being apart would leave us in a much worse condition, which neither of us wanted to witness. Perhaps it was too cliché, and you didn't want to come running back to me. I didn't let you in even when you promised me all that I wanted to hear.

Maybe things are supposed to end with sadness and melancholic nights.

Chapter 23

Pain, when it sets in, seeps into our nerves and occupies a permanent place inside us like a parasite. It feeds on our longings. It grows colossal as time progresses, eventually swallowing us whole. Anguish can last forever and linger, but happiness rarely does.

I realized this soon enough, rather a week after the prank, when I was relishing the success of my sweet revenge. I was enjoying the aftermath of Tanya and Deepika's embarrassment when I was suddenly caught off guard and found myself ambushed by a sudden turn of events.

It was food and beverages practical that day. We had to work with the seniors so as to get ready for the final practicals. I tried to maintain my distance from Rohan and his gang who were hovering around the juniors, ordering them around and overloading them with work. Shreyansh and Soumya were busy helping the attendants prepare for the practicals.

"Why are we just wiping this cutlery? Will they ever teach us anything or not?" Shruti asked, settling her spectacles. I shrugged. "My specs are getting foggy from these vapours," she continued, making me laugh. We were assigned the duty of wiping the entire cutlery in the pantry, so we decided to stay there, away from the seniors.

"Having a good time, ladies?" Rohan whispered. Think of the devil…

"No, sir. What good time might we have in wiping these?" Shruti said.

"Aren't you always complaining? Go and bring more cutlery from the tables and the sideboards," Rohan ordered. Shruti rolled her eyes at me and left.

"I know what you did to Tanya and she won't spare you for this," Rohan said to me as he mixed the clean cutlery with the dirty ones and left.

Shruti came back in with a platter full of more cutlery, and it took us over an hour to wipe them clean. Everyone was sitting on the pavement beside the training restaurant when we came out. The sun was shining bright and kissed everyone in beams of amber and orange. People sat there, scattered in groups. Rohan, Tanya, Sarthak, Maryam, Sagar were on one side, while Shreyansh, Soumya, Mayank, Nisha and others were on the other.

I sat beside Shrey and he smiled at me. "Are you smiling because I was burdened with their outburst?" I asked him.

"No, I smiled because you kept your cool," he said.

"Bitch, you bitch. I know you pranked me at the competition." Tanya rushed towards me and my eyes met with hrs. Rohan ran after her and said, "Tanya, no! Not here!"

"No Rohan, I can't stand it anymore." She threw Rohan's hand aside.

"What are you talking about?" I asked.

"What am I talking about? Aren't you a cunning bitch." For a moment, I was scared. She looked as if she was going to punch me right in my face.

"Please mind your words ma'am, else I'll forget that you're a senior," I said.

"Like you minded your respect or remembered that Shreyansh is your senior when you started meeting and cuddling with him? If you aren't a bitch, what are you? A whore?"

"Enough, don't create a scene here." Rohan grabbed her hand and tried to pull her away.

"Yes, take your puppy away and chain her," Shrey said.

My eyes had already started shedding tears by then as I screamed at her, "You don't have any right to say this, you pathetic creature."

"I may not, but Sagar does. He saw you both embracing and kissing. When we were busy at the competition, you both were having your fun," she smirked. Sagar shifted on his feet, hiding behind others. I looked at him with rage in my eyes. I took a step toward him, but Shrey held my hand.

"Enough now. Before maligning someone else's image, peek inside your own conscience, Tanya. How would you like it if I started telling people about all the places you've kissed Rohan at, about how you made out in the girls' hostel, and so on. What would happen to you then?" Shrey said aloud and everyone started whispering and giggling. Tanya's jaw dropped and drop of sweat formed on her forehead.

"See, I told you to stay in control!" Rohan whispered, loud enough for us to hear.

"This isn't over, Manya. You started it, but we'll end this," Tanya said.

"Shoo..away, puppy. We'll see," Soumya said and hugged me. Tanya intimidated me. I didn't know how she had figured out that I was the one behind the salty salad. Mayank wouldn't have told her.

Mr. Anuj came after a while and we rushed inside the restaurant. "Okay everyone, gather up and close the door." We formed a circle around him as he began to speak. "Your practical examinations are drawing near. Third years' will be taught later. It's first years' turn today. Your seniors will teach you how to set up the restaurant, tables and cutlery, and also how to serve. Tanya and Shreyansh will divide the duties and will be the restaurant managers for today. I'll be in my office and will return at lunch. Please be responsible seniors and obedient juniors," he smiled and left with his file.

I shook my head as the attendant wasn't there again. We were left alone to the mercy of our seniors again, and I knew Tanya sniffed blood. A wicked smile formed on her lips. She glared at me, as if to burn me with her eyes–Medusa preparing to turn me into stone. I looked away in disgust. After assigning easy duties to her group, she burdened the others with a heavy workload and then came to me at the end. Shrey was silent all this while. "Now you, Manya," she spoke. "You'll clear the tables, wipe the cutlery and plates after lunch, and put them in the store room."

"But…"

She interrupted me, "No 'buts'. Do as you're told. I am in-charge."

I walked back to my place in anger. Shrey, having heard her, came into the middle of the circle. "Oh please, Tanya, you talk like you own everyone. Everyone's not your toy. This college belongs to all of us and you can't bully some juniors just because you've got a personal vendetta against them. She and the others won't do the things you've told them to do. It'll all be divided equally among everyone. Even you and me."

"Shrey, don't…"

"Am I clear?" Shrey said firmly and Tanya's lips got sealed. Everyone nodded at him. Tanya stormed off to the store room, her heels tapping loudly on the wooden floor. Rohan looked at Shrey and nodded. To my surprise, their lips curved up in identical smiles. Perhaps a soft truce was still alive and breathing between them.

Mayank came to meet me in the pantry after lunch. I was wiping plates and settling them. "Are you okay?" he asked, pulling out his duster, and started wiping the plates with me.

"Yes, I am. I feel less burdened today," I smiled.

He stood near me and grabbed my hand. "We're here with you," he said.

I smiled at him. "Dragging yourself into my mess again?"

"It's not your mess alone. It's ours. You're not alone in this," he whispered.

"I've given you enough trouble. Don't suffer for me anymore, please."

"Oh, Manya. You're so kind. I am so sorry. I feel bad now," he sighed.

"Why?" I asked.

"Tanya came to me the day before with Rohan. They threatened me and told me that they'd screw up my practicals if I didn't tell them who gave me the bowl of mayonnaise. They said that a crazy crack head like me couldn't come up with such a cruel prank. I had to tell them. I'm so sorry. It's so not cool." I felt bad for him, but was glad that he told me the truth without me having to ask him for it.

"It's not your fault," I said.

He smiled at me. "Thank you for understanding."

I nodded, "Always."

It takes courage to open up to people and tear down the walls you've built around yourself, even more to pour out everything you've been hiding behind a facade of lies. When they leave you, they take away all of your secrets with them.

Rohan and Shreyansh were living examples, best friends turned into foes. They still participated in a strange dance of enmity with one another. There were flickering moments of near reconciliation, although both were too egoistic to acknowledge it. Sometimes, I felt like they were pretending, playing the enemy game.

Soumya had told me that Rohan and his mates always wanted to have fun, pranking and playing around. When Shreyansh was lively and fun loving, he was the architect of these pranks while Rohan put them into action. Soumya always talked about how much he enjoyed those pranks.

Rohan would often ask her about him. Apparently, he really was concerned about how Shrey was coping with his family and health problems. She tried bringing them together, but her efforts always ended in vain. She then left it to time and believed that they would eventually reconcile. She said, "Someday, they'll get back together like two long lost pals who've been travelling on the same road, finally realizing that home was always within each other. I'll cry tears of joy when they do."

"But girls like Tanya and Deepika are thirsty for blood and unscrupulous," Soumya continued. "They like to play with people and when they get bored. Now since you've raged a war, be ready for the blows to come," she warned.

As she had predicted, they began chasing me right from that day of the practical. At first, I thought I was just overthinking it, but I saw them wherever I went. In practical classes, the mess, lecture rooms, corridors, girls' locker room, everywhere. I could feel eyes glued on me all the time. Something was brewing, I could sense it. If not Tanya, then Deepika; if not Deepika, then Maryam, watching every move of mine. They wouldn't leave me alone. Wherever I went, I would hear giggles around me, and whenever I would stand or talk to Shreyansh, pairs of eyes would constantly be fixed on us.

Still, I dismissed the idea of sharing the concern with others. Maybe I was being delusional, I felt. But then, Reshma ma'am started staring at me too. Whenever I saw her, I found her staring at me like I was a culprit. Tests were drawing closer, so I decided not to worry about it too much and focus on pulling up my grades, even though I found it difficult not to overthink. It further affected my studies.

For Riya, I was no more than a refugee in her life. She wouldn't look at me or talk to me. The tests drew nearer, still she didn't ask for any help with studying. I decided, on the other hand, not to disturb anyone with my problems. I wasn't that selfish.

20th February

You are a puppet and life is a game. People around you and God himself are mere spectators. You play this game, dress your character with vivid emotions and desires, talk to people around you and try to learn about them. You try to see if your cravings are complementary, or if they can satisfy them with utmost care. If they meet the criteria, you collapse under the burden of a type of debt that comes with a price.

No, you're not weak or lazy, you just wanted to feel normal and see if you fitted in. The actual truth is, normal is depressing. I'm not normal. It's hard for me to talk to normal people; they're boring and dislike me, as I hate them. I think I repel them because they think I'm complicated and different from them.

The herd doesn't know that I only talk about deep and meaningful things. It's never just chit-chat with me. Conversations like that take singular effort, and are difficult to pull off every day with everyone you meet. You can't easily find people ready to have deep, lengthy, meaningful conversations, especially if short conversations are working fine for them. So, I keep my distance from them and stay to myself as much as I can.

The truth is, each one of us has fears we run away from. One of my biggest fears is that I will stop appreciating my own existence, that I can live my present and future without once looking back. While the past teaches me how to be better, it haunts me too. Sometimes, I fear it will destroy this present improved self.

While fighting through this, I've won and learned to carve a future where I won't have to fight anything anymore. There won't be any place for my demons or my past there because only I know how difficult it is to last.

I have stopped here and there, time to time, to appreciate, to breathe, and to embrace the beauty in the humans around me. I've learned to cherish the people who've stayed and to be thankful for those who didn't, for they have made me truly appreciate those who did, and have taught me to not take them for granted. I still struggle to let go and not to peek back at the filled pages of my existence, yet I visit them far too often, only to see myself still breaking and withering; unchanged. I've learned to endure the pain and turn a blind eye to them when I start to break. It's hard to let go of the things that shaped me into this thing I've become. Maybe one fine winter morning, I'll gather enough courage and finally dig into the grave of my past, and seal it back in its frigid grace.

Only then will I be whole again.

Chapter 24

The lecture rooms were empty. Winter vanished gradually as the sun held its head high up in the sky. As the date of our sessional exams approached, people could be seen sitting in the corridors and stairs in groups. Our group sat on the floor of the corridor. "So, this is it. College life is over for you guys. Isn't it cool, you don't have to suffer anymore?" Mayank asked.

"My boy, the suffering starts here," Shrey replied.

"Why?" Mayank asked.

"Because dumbo, we'll get busy with life," Soumya said, hitting Mayank playfully. "The fun only lasted till here. After this, it's just job, earning, then marriage and kids, and whoosh…there goes your life in torture."

"I hope you make time for me too. I'm sure you would give time to Mayank," I said. She smiled and gripped my hand, "Of course, I will. But I am uncertain about Mayank."

Mayank threw a puppy face at her, and she pulled his chin.

Shrey arched his back against the wall. His face glowed in the sunlight. "Would you reach out to me?" I asked.

His eyes were closed. "What do you think?"

"I think you'll get busy with your life, and you won't have time for me or any one of us."

"No, Manya." He turned to me and continued, "I won't ever forget you. I'll never be too busy to think about you or talk to you." He wrapped his arms around my shoulders. I smiled.

"Manya…Manya…" Someone called for me, while Shrey loosened his grip and sat straight. I was so lost in my thoughts that I didn't see Ms. Reshma standing near the lecture room, staring at us. A circle of students had formed around her, giggling and whispering. I cursed myself for being so lost in my thoughts and stood straight.

"Yes ma'am..." I muttered.

"Come with me, I want to have a word with you," she ordered.

I shivered in panic and looked back at Shrey. He blinked and muttered, "Don't worry." How couldn't I worry? I gave them a reason to get under my skin.

"Well, come on, I don't have the whole day," Ms. Reshma yelled at me. I followed her into her office towards the basement. She sat on her chair and signalled me to sit across the table from her.

"What's wrong with you, Manya?" she asked.

"Nothing," I replied meekly.

"Well, I sense that everything is wrong. You haven't been yourself. I just checked your sheets, you barely passed. I checked with the other teachers, and it's same story. Is everything okay?"

I nodded, shifting uncomfortable in my chair.

"You started really well. The other professors considered you a bright prospect. But you and your grades slipped with time. Is something bothering you? Share with me, is it about a senior? Is someone's bullying you?" I shook my head. I could've told her about Tanya and everything, but only a month was remaining in their third year and I didn't want to ruin it for them. Despite all that they had done to me, I still felt that there was a shred of humanity in their beating hearts and I didn't want to malign it.

"Manya... Manya.. "

"Yes ma'am. Sorry."

"You don't seem okay to me. Is it something related to Shreyansh? I warned him and Rohan to stay away from juniors last year too. Are you involved with him?" She stared at me.

"No…no, ma'am. What are you saying? He's a good senior and a friend who is always willing to help. There's nothing else going on."

"I've heard something from some of the other girls. Maybe they were wrong." Her gaze was fixed on me. "You aren't lying to me, are you?"

«No ma'am, I wouldn't dare," I muttered.

"Alright, Manya. I trust you. You can always reach out to me. Just stay out of trouble. You're under my radar," she said.

"Thank you," I whispered.

"You may leave now."

I got up and closed the door behind me. I wanted to go home and crumple up into a ball on my bed. This was exhausting.

Shrey was waiting for me at the stairs. "What took you so long? Everything good?"

"Yes," I muttered.

"Doesn't look like it from your face. You look like you've seen a ghost."

"Yeah, a ghost. Maybe of my future self," I said, leaning on the railing.

"What did Reshma ma'am say?"

"She warned me about skipping classes, poor grades, my performance and asked if everything's okay." I paused for a moment, and thought of telling him that Reshma ma'am had asked me about us too, but decided against it.

"And, what did you tell her?"

"I told her everything's alright."

"You've learned the art of lying here," he smiled.

I shrugged, "And she told me I am in trouble."

"What kind?"

"I don't know. Stop asking too many things. My mind is already fucked up."

He slipped his hand inside his pocket and kicked the floor. "What do we do now?"

"I want to go home, but there's still time," I shrugged.

"You told me that you escaped the college by jumping over the wall once," he grinned. I smiled. The corridors were empty, so I looked around and ran out of the building. His laughter echoed behind as he ran after me. In no time, we were on the other side of the wall.

The dampness over the wall had made the edges slippery. I tumbled over and fell upon Shrey on the other side. Both of us landed on a stack of hey. We giggled and got up, flecks of grass sticking to our hair and clothes, while our shoes were stained with mud. We were a sight, artistic and dirty.

"Where should we go now?" I asked as we approached the road. The sun was still out.

"How about tea? I bet you have never had tea like this in your life."

"Where?"

"Follow me, junior," he signalled.

We crossed the road in front of the college gate like criminals, tip-toeing and looking around. It was turning out to be a fun day–confusion, complaints, trouble, adventure and an escape–like a classic Hitchcock movie, and we were living it.

The tea joint was next to our college, near the open wild fields. The barn shade above us was woven, while the chairs and tables in the front were laid under the dense shade of trees in the field. My nostrils filled up with the fragrance of mustard.

"*Kya haal hein, kaka?*(How are you, old man?)" Shrey asked the owner there.

"*Thik hein, beta.* (I am good, son.)" he replied, smiling. His cheeks wrinkled and eyes creased with years of wisdom.

"*Do chai* (Two cups of tea)," Shrey said.

"*Abhi lo* (Coming right away)."

We crashed on the chairs, arching our backs to stretch out the ache of our fall. The setting sun cast an abstract painting of shadows through the branches. It was fascinating. Shrey looked at me as if he wanted to say something, but he just smiled instead. I sipped my tea in silence and allowed the aroma to fill my soul.

"Hey, kiddo…enough of your over-thinking, okay?" He pulled his chair closer to mine.

"Her warning and expressions made it clear that she meant business." I took a sip, then gulped down the entire cup. It wasn't enough, so he ordered more in large glasses.

"Ms. Reshma has always been that way. She cares for people, that's why she does it. She's a softie in a coconut shell."

"I am still scared," I said.

He wrapped his arms around my backrest. "It's humane to be scared. Everything will be alright."

The soft evening wind hit my face as it began wandering and exploring the horizon. He grabbed my hand suddenly and jerked it down under the table. "Ouch," I muttered.

"Manya, hide!"

"But, why?"

"Just hide."

"But where?"

"Damn, Manya. No use now. We're doomed," he said. "Did he see us?" he asked the old man.

"*Dekh liya beta, tumhre liye hei aaya tha laage* (He saw you. It seems like he had come for you only)," Kaka said.

"Scoundrel informer. Damn it!" Shrey shrieked, kicking the chair.

"What's wrong? Who saw us?"

"Someone ratted us out, maybe saw us escaping. One of the guards, Mr. Thakur's bootlicker, came to spy on us. Mr. Thakur must have sent him," he said.

"What? What the fuck? What should we do now?"

"Let me think, calm down please. Everything will be okay," he tried to console me.

"Do you want me to believe that? No, Shrey. A big NO. I am in trouble, I was stupid to come out today with you."

He stayed silent. I didn't want him to be quite, as I was getting impatient. I wanted to hear something, anything, but only the rustling of leaves and the howling breeze danced with the chaos inside me. Silence descended upon us and slowly devoured me.

Maybe Shrey knew that it was bad. Mr. Thakur always wanted to tighten the screws over him. Shrey had always been on his hit list, and the hatred was mutual. I was the sacrificial lamb being led to the slaughter, a casualty of Thakur's revenge.

I looked at him. His head was hung low and his feet were digging through the dirt. I'd had enough, and got up in frustration to leave. "Where are you going?" he asked.

"Home. Where else?"

"Stay for some more time, please."

"Why? Are you waiting for Mr. Thakur to come here now?"

"I'm sorry. Just stay."

"We're screwed, Shrey. Ms. Reshma asked me about us today. She wanted to know if you were involved with me. Your fling with Deepika has tarnished your image. She looked at me like she knew that we're involved."

"What? Why didn't you tell me before? Why did you lie?"

"What, why? I'm sorry, Shrey. I've never been in this place before. Yes, I imagined that if I ever got stuck, you would always save me. There was a time when I wanted to be stuck, just to see you save me from everything, but now I don't like it. I don't like the idea of being stuck, when I know you won't save me. For the first time, I feel alone in your presence. Can you save me? Save me from myself?" I yelled at him. "I know, you won't. I look back and see my old self safe from all this trouble. I guess I was afraid all this while. That's why I never entered a relationship, or let my feelings for someone consume me to the point of no return. In you, I saw all of these reasons to lose myself because I knew that you'd find me. But now, I've lost all hope of being found. And now, when I'm drowning, I am drowning with the regret of relying on you and us as a whole."

I turned to leave, but he gripped me by my shoulders. That moment, that very moment, I lost it. There was helplessness in his eyes and pain magnified in them like I'd never seen before. The saviour needed saving. The knight who had shielded me from the wrath of the world until now stood there in a withered armour, helpless and wounded. Who was I to save him when I couldn't even save myself? I released myself from his grip and walked away. I knew I shouldn't have left that day, that moment, but I had mastered the art of quitting.

5th March

Have you ever felt defeated and guilty of ruining someone? I am guilty of creating an apocalypse instead of creating life. When Vaani left, she was my executioner; she ruined me, leading to my apocalypse. At that time, I promised myself that I wouldn't ever ruin anyone, rather I'd try to save everyone I met. But now, I think I've turned into the same monster I was running away from. I ruined Manya and in turn, ruined myself.

Does love only lead to destruction?

If yes, I find myself in the ruins again.

You don't know how hard it is for me to reject the love.

Believe me, I try. I get up daily, look in the mirror and tell myself that I want love, and then shower it on everyone I meet. For reasons, I can't. I just can't. I don't have it in me anymore. I don't crave it anymore. There was a time when I did and I was let down. I'm over it now, but I just can't return to being that same person anymore. I can't love and give love the way they show in movies and books. My idea of love is different. Maybe, even alien.

Sometimes, I feel as if I am the loneliest person in the world. If I ever get blown away in my chaos, no one will bother to find me because I don't exist for them. I am an invisible entity, diminishing from this world. The only thing that soothes my withering soul is my dark room, my bed and the window in front of it. The sun comes up and goes down; the moon wakes up and goes back to its slumber. All the while, I remain there aghast and worn out, ready to turn into dirt.

Oh Manya, I call for you now. I implore you to go, leave me and go away. Please, take the leading position, take a step forward. Leave me and go.

Let me know I never mattered to you, and that you are not even bothered about how much I love you. Express your anguish by telling me that I made your life worse than hell, and chant prayers wishing me dead.

Step on all my dreams and crush them abruptly, direct weapons of your hate towards me. Add a spark to the fire burning inside me, then come out of nowhere to extinguish it intentionally.

Justify all my fears and make them into a movie to play inside me. Encourage me till I vomit all those desires and then let me fall, don't try to even rescue me.

Bark, that I never deserved you and that I'm just a hollow piece of crap you have encountered in your life. Make me thank you for it, so that I make myself hate you for this.

Please, do not save me. Because if you'll lend your hand, I won't be able to help but hold it tight forever. It might hurt you, a little more than you might be able to bear.

But just for one last time, let me tell you this.

"I've never loved anyone more, my darling, than when I saw you walking away from me that evening."

Chapter 25

It's important to have some parts of yourself hidden inside you that should only belong to you; parts no one should ever know. You will always have things that are just yours then, and no one will be able to take that away, be it emotions, feelings, people, desires or cravings. Every time you share these things, you're left more vulnerable than before. Once your mystery has been exposed, there's nothing left inside you to lure someone. If you bare yourself whole, there are bound to be repercussions–your capacity for self-love might dwindle, a skewed path through a daunting maze, a never ending search, banishment from the self.

The world is a strange place and humans are strange in different ways. They'll attempt to dig through you until they've found some treasure. Once they've got it, they will discard you, leaving you an empty shell. You're left in the lurch then as you don't interest them anymore.

I struggled to drag my defeated and worn out self back to the PG. I felt my impending doom drawing near. Despite my inclination to blame Shrey, I knew it was my fault, my reckless behaviour, which had got me into this mess. But wasn't he supposed to hold me together when I was breaking apart, instead of breaking with me?

Riya was already there when I reached my room. I checked my watch, she was early. "Where have you been?" she asked.

"Leave me alone."

"Where the fuck were you?" she shouted.

I held my hand high. "Don't shout at me. Whoever is asking you questions, tell them we're not talking..."

"Shut up, bitch. Just shut up. Soumya, Mayank, Shruti, some others and I were called by Mr. Thakur. He was fuming, asked about you, Shreyansh and more. We were ridiculed as well. You're a fucked up story now, Manya." She sounded rueful.

I crashed on my bed. "I am sorry, Riya..."

"No, you're not, you self-centred bitch. You don't care about anyone. You only care when you're in trouble. But now, no one's going to save you. No one can. Not even your saviour, Shreyansh."

She banged the door and walked out. I lay on my bed, swallowing all the hatred and venom thrown at me. I was getting used to it. My mind and my body were growing numb to it. I closed my eyes and saw those helpless hazel eyes. I cursed myself and they vanished, only to appear again in my dreams this time, framed inside a nightmare.

The next morning began with a wave of tragedy, and I felt the storm closing in on me. The Food Production practical was about to start when someone from staff came calling for me. Mr. Thakur wanted me in his office. It was enough to get everyone's attention, even Mr. Yogesh's. It is not a pretty sight when the disciplinarian in-charge summons you. "What did you do?" Shruti whispered. I shrugged and moved away. I didn't want to answer anybody.

Mr. Thakur's office was near the Principal's, beside the reception. It was the first time I was there. Shrey was already sitting opposite Mr. Thakur, and an intense staring game was going on between them. My eyes explored his office. He seemed like a man with an artistic taste. Paintings covered the walls, and small sculptures were dispersed throughout. A large window on the left of his chair gave a clear view of the college gate. His table featured a small picture of him smiling along with two other people, notably our Principal and the

Head of some management group. The sculpture near the table attracted my attention the most. It was of a couple separated by some space, walking in opposite directions. How ironic!

"Have a seat, Manya," he ordered. I sat there and looked at Shrey. He didn't blink or look at me. His gaze was fixed on Mr. Thakur. "Where were you both after mess yesterday?" he asked. We both looked at each other and stayed silent.

"After Ms. Reshma asked you to go speak to her, where did you go, Manya?"

"I…I…went to class," I stuttered.

"I hate liars, Manya. I checked the attendance register and you weren't there." Mr. Thakur stared into my eyes. I felt like he was looking right into my soul. Arching his back against the chair, he spoke again, "What about you, Mr. Shreyansh? I know you won't lie."

"I escaped from the college through the wall. I wasn't feeling good," Shrey replied in a cold tone.

"I assume you felt well enough to enjoy tea?" Mr. Thakur smirked. "Were you alone?" Shrey nodded. I looked at Shrey but he was still playing the staring game.

"Are you sure, Mr. Shreyansh?"

"I don't nod to things I am unsure of," Shrey replied.

"Alright. What about the rumours I heard about you and Mr. Shreyansh?" He turned to me.

"What rumours?" I asked meekly.

"You two walk hand in hand in college, sneak out whenever you feel like it, act as though it's not a college, but a garden for love birds. I've unfortunately heard about more intimate things you might have participated in."

"What are you trying to insinuate, sir?" I asked.

"You know what I mean, Manya. Don't lie to me again or continue trying to play cat and mouse games with me. We have a strict policy that addresses inappropriate behaviour. You both were found to have broken that policy, not to mention, the guards caught you off the premises during college hours, and without permission too. I regret to inform you that we may need to inform your parents and ask them to come meet us. We have a lot of things to discuss," Mr. Thakur threw a bomb, and it promised to explode.

"But...but...sir..." I stuttered in panic. For all the wrong that I had done, I never intended for my parents to get caught up in my storm. I didn't want them to hear that their innocent little girl wasn't the same anymore, that she wasn't who they thought she was. All my life, whatever I had done, I did to make them happy. I wanted to see their heads held high, proud of me, not bowed low in shame as a consequence of my naïve actions. Shrey looked at me, but I wanted him to look away. I was about to lose it all as my eyes itched to shed all the pain.

"Excuse me, sir. You said you heard about it. What kind of a person would stoop so low as to tell you such things anyway?" Shrey asked.

"I am not obligated to answer your questions, Mr. Shreyansh," Mr. Thakur said.

"You say that you have a strict policy? I beg to differ," Shrey said.

"What?" Mr. Thakur raised his brows.

"You've been neglecting your policy. You watch people hold hands, hug, kiss, and whatever else...no, no, not whatever else–making out too," Shrey sighed.

"Let me stop you there. Are you trying to tell me that I am not doing my job properly and that this college is under a serious threat for inappropriate behaviour? Who are you attempting to accuse?"

"That's exactly what I wanted to hear, sir. You turn a blind eye to this because these culprits are your informers. They bring others to you, that's why you leave them alone. You say you 'heard' about us from them, but what they told you might not even be true. I have HEARD that people lie just to escape or cover their own wrong doings," Shrey said and leaned back. I gasped for breath. *Why was he doing this?*

"How dare you say that to me? You mind your tongue with me. You know what? I've had enough, no one can save you now." Mr. Thakur slammed his fist on the table. "And you, Ms. Manya, you may leave now. I think it's time for Mr. Shreyansh to learn his lesson once and for all." I stood up and looked at Shrey, but he wasn't looking at me. Before walking out of the office, I looked back to catch his eyes. He never turned around, but only sat there like a statue. I had never seen Shrey like that. It was different. He was different.

Outside Mr. Thakur's office, a herd had formed waiting for some spicy news. It wasn't everyday that a girl got caught escaping from college with a super senior on a romantic excursion. It was the first time for them and they were excited to see someone's world come crashing down.

No one came near me–I repelled them. Not one person asked me if I were okay. Not even my people. Prejudice is a funny concept. I could hear both of them arguing in the office still, but it wasn't clear. Each passing moment caused more and more panic in me.

Shrey came out of the office after a while and slammed the door behind him. Without looking at me, he walked away. I ran behind him, calling out, "Shrey, Shrey, stop please."

He stopped and turned. His face was blank and his eyes were red, as if blood would spill out of them any moment.

"Am I safe? Are they going to restrict me? Is he going to call my parents?" I blabbered.

His expression changed, his brows furrowed, and his intense gaze fixed on me. I was scared. "Manya, think about other people for once. Stop being so selfish, so self centred that you lose the people around you who care," he said. "The world doesn't revolve around you." He turned to leave. I stood there helpless and scared. "You're safe for now, go and celebrate." He looked back and smiled, moving out the door. Something slithered in me through that smile. I had never seen such a painful sight in my entire life.

Everyone looked at me as I stood there confused, scared and defeated. There was pleasure in some eyes, pity in others, sympathy in some and amusement in the rest.

In mine, there was only devastation.

7th March

"*I felt like crying but nothing came out. It was just a sort of sad sickness, sick sad, when you can't feel any worse. I think you know it. I think everybody knows it now and then, but I think I have known it pretty often, too often.*" -Charles Bukowski

I wake up to an anchor on my chest and the thumping of drums inside my head. I can't breathe, this big knot in my throat chokes me. It feels as though there is a huge stone of my desires taking away my breath. It is attached to my spine, trying to pull me down into a dark place. Something or someone is trying to swallow me whole. I am worn out and fragile. I don't possess the strength to fight anymore. So, I lie here, stuck to the core. There are people around me, staring right into my eyes. They come to meet me in my dark room.

«Get up!" they command me, all the faces fumingly facing me.

I whisper, "I can't."

They say, "Get up and get dressed. Move out from this dark room and come into the light."

I tell them, "It's hard, I can't do it, I can't ignore it anymore, I want to seek help. I don't want to feel trapped."

They say, "No. Stop being weak. Fix your own problems and let others breathe."

But, I can't do it.

This isn't me. Help me, please. I feel trapped inside my body. My depression has possessed me and taken over this body. I'm inside, hiding in a deep dark corner, scared and fragile. Please listen, I need you, I need you all. Why don't they listen? Why can't they understand?

They say they want to help me, but all they do is punish me each time. I tell them all, I don't want to be here anymore. Yet, they say, "Get over it," like it is some kind of a show.

I scream, I cry, and now I can't fight.

I am weak and lonely, but no one understands that this loneliness only belongs to me. It was nothing that anyone else created. It's all by my own wrongdoings. Now that I've grown used to it, and made a home in it, I can't escape it anymore. I feel my end will be this.

In this.

I welcomed Vaani and Manya in, but they couldn't cope with the idea of staying with me in it. So, I'll stay here till the end of my time. Sometimes, it gets hard to stop myself from wandering, and then I feel like running away from everyone and everything. The running never works out, because whenever I try, I collapse, I tremble and try again, only to collapse again and again. I end up face down in the dirt with a hope of breathing again.

And tonight, just like last night and all the nights before, I will close my eyes and stop thinking about my chaos. Instead, I will focus on how happy I was before. I cease to grapple with the memory of that day when she wrapped her arms around me on that frigid winter night; those kisses, her warmth, her half-asleep face pecking me all over my face. I mustn't replay these memories anymore. The past was never mine to hold, but those were my quietest and happiest moments all along.

"Meeting her was a mere reason to live. I was made and meant to suffer, and to burn in this chaos all along."

Chapter 26

It had been a week since I last saw him. His eyes haunted my nights all this while. I ran away from them, only to be engulfed by them further. My home wasn't safe anymore, the fire in those eyes had left me homeless. Only soot and ash remained.

As the week rolled on, the news spread like wildfire to every corner of the college. Everyone now knew that Shreyansh had gotten suspended, and wouldn't be permitted to give the final exams. The gossip continued to twist and turn around me in a whirlwind of whispers echoing through the hallways. People named me the mastermind behind the entire incident. 'Despite being the main culprit, MANYA escaped unscathed.' This deteriorated my psyche even more.

I no longer held my head high. The esteem and pride that I once felt in spite of everything, dissipated. Tanya, Deepika and their crew lost interest in me. I was too deflated to thrill them anymore. Their interest diverted to destroying others.

They weren't the only ones. The people who had been with me through everything, in struggle and fun, distanced themselves from me. The trouble that reeked from me repelled them. During practicals, I would stand alone in a corner, lost. No one talked to me–Shruti, Maryam, Sagar, Nisha, not even Mayank–everyone despised me. Riya and Mayank would often talk and eat together at the mess, while I ate somewhere in a corner. Even at lectures, I would sit alone, banished and shunned. I felt empty. After all, I'd fought to live my life my way. I wanted to be a good friend.

It was Sunday evening after a weekend spent in overthinking and anguish. This was all new to me as I'd never been sleep deprived before. These days, whenever I closed my eyes, all I could see was *red,* his red eyes staring right into the depths of my soul. I woke up most nights gasping for breath. That day changed everything. He scared me for the first time, he repelled me.

My phone rang. I knew my father was calling. It rang twice, but I ignored it. After a while, Riya's phone rang too.

"Hello?" she answered in her sweet mushy voice. "Yes, uncle. Namaste. Yes, she's here. Wait, I'll give it to her." She held her hand over the mic and glared at me. "Next time, pick up your phone. I am not your babysitter."

I took the phone from her and answered, "Yes, dad."

"Where are you? I've been calling your phone, but no response. Are you okay? Is everything okay?"

"Yes," I mumbled.

"I got a mail from your college this morning. It stated that you're slipping in your grades, performance in practicals, strange behaviour, rebellion, lethargic actions and so on. This was the first warning and by the language of it, I assume it to be the last."

"It's nothing, they're sending it to everyone's parents."

Riya looked at me.

"It doesn't look like it to me. You weren't like that before, what happened now?" I turned numb. "Did you choose to go to a college so far away just to behave like this? I wasn't expecting such irresponsible actions from you. You fought with us to go there and you defied our choices only to malign our name?"

"I…I…am sorry, dad," I stuttered. He was fuming, though such anger usually took decades to erupt in him.

"No, you're not. You should have told me about it, but you chose to remain silent. I never knew my Manya could be such a good liar. We will deal with this my way now. One more mail against you and I'll bring you back to Bangalore. We are done for now."

"But dad…dad…" I was panting. He disconnected. The phone slipped from my hand.

"Hey, are you okay?" Riya asked. I couldn't speak, I felt choked. I wanted to puke out the emotions, the anguish, everything, but to no avail. I felt dizzy and collapsed on the bed.

I was drained, but no one understood and no one attempted to. My mind was filled with chaos and regret, and my body was giving up on me. It felt too difficult to carry on, and everything felt overwhelming–this world and the people in it. Each breath brought pangs of utter pain, yet no one understood. They all saw a naïve selfish girl enjoying the spring of adulthood, as opposed to a fallen soul suffering the frigid autumn.

The lump in my throat got tougher to gulp down. It felt like I was in the middle of an ocean, drowning. The more I struggled to swim, the more I sunk down into an abyss. Darkness surrounded me, as if it were the end of me.

"Manya, Manya, Manya."

I heard someone calling for me, but I was too tired to respond. Someone shook my body, I could feel it, but my body wasn't in my control. I felt like a corpse sprawled on the bed.

"Soumya, Soumya, come here fast." The words echoed in my ears. My eyes were burning, I closed them and a flood of tears escaped in waves. I was ready, my body was ready, it was time to succumb to chaos.

What felt like a decade long slumber ended with a sprinkling of water on my face. Through my blurry vision, I found myself surrounded by Soumya and Riya. Their hair brushed over my face while their eyes were fixed on me. I tried to move, but couldn't. "Shhh...don't move," Riya whispered. I smiled at her. "Am I alive?" the words escaped from my mouth somehow.

They laughed with flooded eyes. Despite my wrongdoings and naivety, they were still there. "You scared the shit out of us. You passed out." They spoke together, while I just smiled. This had never happened to me before, and I hoped for it to never happen again.

We sat together that night, talking for hours like nothing had ever went wrong between us. We were the old lost pals, rejoicing in the company we had missed.

"How's everything with Rehan?" I asked Riya.

"Good, great. Just waiting for the vacations."

"My vacations are over, this college life was no less than a vacation. I have to join the hotel as soon as exams finish," Soumya sighed.

"Who else has a job besides you?" I asked.

"Mostly everyone," she said. "I know you want to know about Shrey. No, he doesn't have it yet."

"Why not?" Riya and I asked and looked at one another.

"I don't know what he wants. He could easily grab a handful of jobs, but he skipped all the interviews. That guy is in trouble, always fighting and sabotaging himself. "

"You didn't mention this before," I said.

"I never expected you to get so involved with him, and I certainly didn't expect things to end like this. You kept drowning into him as if he was quicksand. Did you like it?"

I shrugged.

"See, I told you," Riya said. I glared at her and she smiled, pulling my cheeks.

"I won't disagree with Riya. When someone tells you about their instincts, try to listen, understand and heed their warning," Soumya said.

"Not when your heart rules your mind and every instinct fails," I said.

"I know, it's not your fault, but for now, focus on yourself and the sessional exams. Try to divert your mind from all the chaos and trouble." Soumya patted my back.

But it wasn't okay. How could it be okay? How could I be okay? I found myself thinking about him all the time. It felt like he was there in my mind, in me. I couldn't shut him out. I'd been in this exact situation so many times before, and I wasn't surprised when it happened repeatedly. I'd been here so long, and it was the same story every time. I closed my eyes and there he was. I had wanted him for long, but I was getting tired. I didn't know how to let go and I didn't want to either, but I knew I'd have to eventually. I knew I'd never be happy or at peace without him, but I was also aware that the longer I saved myself for him, the more I lost myself. The notice board was crowded that day, the date of churning was out. It was the last week of March, before the sessionals started in April. March brings change; a metamorphosis of the world. Spring blooms out of the barren soil, as well as the human soul. Flowers bloom, even over scars. Sunshine cleanses both our habitat and our conscience. I was under the process, ready to bloom out of the muck and mire that encapsulated my seed.

I'd survived scorching heat, flood waters, and a monsoon full of anguish and struggle. Autumn saw my leaves wither, winter froze my heart, but spring with its blooming buds cradled my ashes and I emerged a phoenix.

I found Mayank clicking pictures of the date-sheet on the notice board. I hadn't spoken to him in more than a couple of weeks. He wouldn't pick up my calls or reply to my texts. I waved at him, but he ignored me again, and walked away.

"Mayank!" I yelled, running after him.

"What do you want?"

"I want you to stop and at least tell me what's wrong."

"I don't want to talk to you."

I held his hand, but he escaped my grip. "Tell me, how are you and how Sh-" He stopped me.

"Do you really want to know about him?" he asked. "No, you don't. Keep your self-centredness to yourself and away from him."

"Why are you saying this? I didn't do anything to him. I am not selfish, I care about him."

Mayank held his hand up. "Stop with your bullshit."

"Tell me then? What's the truth? Where did I go wrong?"

"I don't know about anyone else, but I expected you to be careful with Shrey after everything he did for you." He stared at me. "He self-destructed, and he did it all for you!"

"What? How?" I asked. His serious demeanour scared me.

"He took the fall for you, saved you and took all the blame on himself. His father was called, but he refused to come after they told him about everything. Shrey was scolded by his father and I don't know what else. He told me this a few nights back while we were high and wasted."

"Where is he? He's not picking my calls or replying to my texts. I want to talk to him," I said.

"I don't know. Maybe by being with you, I have turned selfish too. I study in my room and don't go out or get involved in any trouble ," he said.

"Can you please do something? I want to talk to him. Please, Mayank, do something." My eyes were already swimming. Maybe Mayank understood my helplessness, and he held my hand and nodded.

The smell of spring began to stink. The fragrant blooming buds filled my nostrils with their sickening sweetness. Those buds that were meant to bloom again and fill my world with fragrance were now plucked, crushed and stepped over. Their fragrance disgusted me. The garden of my life was barren and infertile without him. I could lie to others and pretend he didn't matter to me, but how could I lie to myself? All of this took a toll on my mind and I craved for an escape. My escape, my home, my getaway–Shreyansh, in whom I wanted to lose myself, was lost himself.

I waited for what seemed like forever. Two days seem long enough when you're filtering through a myriad of thoughts in your mind. Mayank texted me in the evening after two days.

'He just went out to Sardar ji's dhaba. Go talk to him.'

'Thank you, Mayank.'

'But make sure you don't piss him off more. He's already suffering a lot.'

I wished I could quote John Green to him then, "There's a thing about pain, it demands to be felt."

But for how long? How long before this pain vanished and we stopped feeling at all?

I dressed up, ready to leave, when Riya blocked my way. "Where are you going?" she asked.

"I need to see Shrey and talk to him," I said.

"WTF? Why?"

"Because he saved me from everything and threw himself into a downward spiral."

Riya sat on the bed, looking down. "It's late, I must come with you."

"No, this is between me and him now. This needs to end today. I can't survive this storm of anguish anymore," I told her and slammed the door behind me.

20th March

I know I've made your life difficult, Manya. I know how difficult it was to love and embrace me. I know how in doing so, I destroyed you in pieces. I know how deeply I altered your life and changed it into a disaster of epic proportions. I want to tell you how you altered my life into something deep and passionately good. You changed me, making me more human and lively than ever before. I learned the meaning of both love and tranquillity from you. You transformed me into something I always longed to be, but couldn't ever become. I always desired to feel worthy and valued. By painting my barren world with colourful hues, you made me into Vincent Van Gogh's 'Starry Night'.

I began loving the idea of getting out of bed and began to appreciate my life a little bit more. I'd learned to live with a dead soul, but you provided me hope of living again and feeling everything a little bit more than before. I am grateful that you didn't ask me to try to fit into the frame of a happy person anymore. I was living in peace–a peace I got for free–and like every other free thing, it came with a cliché tag–I HAVE TO PAY FOR IT. I have to pay the requisite price for it, a price that promised to take everything away. Even you...

But so did you. You paid the price for investing in me, and I'm sorry you had to do this. It pains me to think that I led you to nothing but destruction. I became a living nightmare to the girl my dreams were made of. For a moment, I thought us to be perfect, but like every other perfect thing, we must be put to rest.

22nd March

So today, Today, I let her know, that I wished the best for her and I'll always pray for her betterment. You know I wanted her to have goodness, don't you? And you know, I escorted myself to a path opposite of her. I traversed away Very far from her. I forfeited myself when I wanted her to accept and love me. I should have told her to love me harder, to crave for me deeper. But I didn't, for I wanted my darling to remain free in her sky; not to be trapped in my abyss of miseries and withering desires. And so, I condemned myself, and shackled to the core of this abyss, slowly decaying, craving her, yet moving away.

Chapter 27

The night was dark and deserted, but my conscience was darker and gloomy. There weren't too many people around when I reached the dhaba. His bike was lying on the ground. I wondered why, since he had never been this careless with his bike before–he adored it like his baby. I saw him sitting at his usual place with his face turned away from me. I approached him and tapped him on his shoulder. He turned around and I quickly sat down opposite him.

"Who's that…Manya....you? For heaven's sake, why can't you leave me alone?" He got up, but I held his hand and pushed him back down. He was tipsy. Two empty beer bottles were strewn around his chair, and a cigarette butt or two sat on the table, covered in ash.

"Please stay and listen. My position isn't any better than yours," I pleaded.

He laughed, "But, you aren't drinking on debt like me." He took a pause. "Disowned and left to suffer."

"I am on the path to being disowned myself. My father called and warned me to behave, or else I'll have to go home. He even yelled at me for the first time in my life," I said, trying to comfort him.

"Well, that's not even close to what I'm going through, but it's a start." He shook my hand, "Okay then, good luck to you. Bye." He got up.

"I am not done yet, please sit."

He reluctantly slid back into his chair. His face looked sallow and sunken, and he had dark circles under his eyes. Those gorgeous deep eyes were dull and lost today. His hair were ruffled and fell over his forehead. He looked like a distant shadow of himself. "Why did you do that, Shrey? Why did you save me?" I asked.

"I did nothing, they let you off easy."

"Mayank told me everything. Why did you sacrifice yourself for me? Why did you destroy yourself?" My eyes were already stinging with threatening tears.

He looked at me. "Curse him, he can't digest any secrets. He's not the type of man a real man can talk to." He laughed.

I laughed too, but stopped when I felt the ache. I had been trying for so long to hold up, but in that moment every wall came crashing down. Laughter turned into crying and tears fell from my eyes like a flood. Shrey grabbed my hand. "Hey, hey, hey, it's okay. Ssshh…everything's fine," he whispered. He slid his chair closer to mine and started caressing my back. I coughed twice, and he handed me his beer can. I gulped it down. It tasted awful, but it was a relief. He ordered two more cans and I decided to get drunk with him.

"This silence, your silence is eating me, scaring me. Say something, anything..." I sobbed.

"You want to know why I did what I did?" He looked at me, and I nodded.

"Remember the day you left me at the tea joint? I could see that you were terrified, you were scared of me. I repelled you. You thought for a while that I was ruining you, dragging you into peril with me."

"I didn't, Shrey-"

He stopped me. "It's okay, Manya. In front of Mr. Thakur the next day, it did feel like I had ruined you, spoiled you, led you down a path of destruction. I couldn't have lived with that. My demons had consumed the girl I wanted to save and preserve and protect. How could I have allowed that to happen? That's why I went ahead and scarified myself for slaughter. I felt like a knight then, but now, I don't know what to do with this thing inside me."

"And what is that?" I asked.

"It feels like I have this rage, this hatred inside, and it's eating me alive. It's getting bigger and bigger, ready to come out of me. My lungs, ribs, heart, everything is filling up. I don't know for how long will I be able to hold it at bay, or survive like this. It does come out every now and then, destroying everything and everyone in its wake. I poured everything out to my father and it's building up again."

"Hatred? But for whom?" I asked.

"For myself, for what I am and what I do to the people around me. I am such a disappointment, a disgrace to my family and a pain for my dad. I've been a big disappointment, I still am, and I just made it worse. He doesn't want to see me or hear anything from me. It's bad this time, very bad. We can never be like the father-son we once were."

"It can be stitched back together. Everything will be okay, he'll understand," I said, but he shook his head. "What about your mom, then?"

"Like always, she won't say anything. My father didn't let me talk to her, but I know that even if she did, she wouldn't say anything. She would stay silent like always and watch me burn. Even when my father used to beat me, abuse me when I was still in school, she would just stay silent."

"Everything will be okay, Shrey." I rubbed his back as he drowned his beer and lit another cigarette.

"Nothing will be okay, Manya. I've been lying to myself for a long time now, but things are only getting worse. I don't know for how long I can fight with myself now. I feel like there's a person inside me, telling me that I'll never be happy again."

"Why do you think so?" I held his hand. "What's going on inside you? What are you thinking?"

"My head is on fire. There are scars all over my body that no one can see. They haven't healed even a bit over the past years, and now they're bleeding again. I am covered in the blood of my anguish." He took a long puff. "These gory sores make it hard to take things one day at a time. Sometimes, I feel like rowing a lifeboat to no shore. My boat is filled with anger, sadness and loneliness. They're going to drown me and the boat with it. I yearn for relief, but to no avail. Sometimes, I just lay in bed, covered in sweat, my heart and head aching, just staring at the ceiling. Sometimes, I cry with dry eyes. I don't leave the house because the anxiety doesn't let me." He coughed, gulped the beer down and lit another cigarette.

"Shreyansh…don't…" I tried to take his cigarette away.

"No, Manya, let me. I know I won't be happy again, I can't be loved again. I am someone that happiness will always elude. I wouldn't know what to do with it," he sighed.

"Why do you think that? What am I here for? What am I doing sitting here after everything? You're not ready to accept love when I am ready to give it to you. Why are you so scared when I am not…" I looked into his eyes. "If you are stating your vulnerability to me, please trust that I won't exploit it."

"How can I believe that when the very people who brought me into this world discarded me, couldn't love me. Why should I trust you? How can anyone love me–someone so broken and miserable? It's not love, it's nothing. How can you be so sure?" He took a long drag of the cigarette.

"I know this is love. I am sure about it. I know it because you are everything I have ever wanted. I think about you just to be happy. You and your thoughts make the shittiest of my days okay. I look at you and wonder how it would feel to wake up every morning next to you. I see a person that never ceases to love others, often forgetting about himself. You say you only have tragedy in you, well I love tragic people because they have been through many aspects of life, and yet survived. I find love and emotions buried deep in you that need to be freed."

He looked away. I could see his eyes growing moist. "Manya, this is just a mirage. You love the idea of me, and someday this idea would be replaced too. This is infatuation you're dwelling in. One day, you'll wake up from this and realise that I was just a dream. What you feel is not real. I am not real."

"It's easy to say this, right? At least don't insult someone's feelings. You are ridiculing my emotions and discarding me like trash. How long will you toss me around like this? How long before I rid myself of everything and kill myself? Why can't you care enough? What have I done to deserve this, Shrey?" I kicked the empty beer bottles. "I can't be a part of this or continue to be your friend, knowing that it will always be unrequited because I will always love you and you will always see me as that one helpless person who you could never love in return."

"That's it? Tired already? You were planning to take births for me, right? And now, you're frustrated within an hour? See, that's what I was telling you. People leave me, and it never surprises me. It amazes me when they decide to stay. I've grown thick skin for goodbyes now, it doesn't hurt me anymore. How could it hurt the hollow me? Out of all goodbyes, yours will hurt the most, though. But I'll bear it. That's what I do when people leave me to suffer." He lit a third stick.

I snatched it from between his lips and threw it away. He lit another, I threw it away again. He lit yet another and moved away from me. "Uhhh…I hate you, Shreyansh Thakur."

"Everyone does, tell me something new." He blew out a cloud of smoke.

"You are a coward, Shrey, just looking for an escape from your problems. You don't have the courage to face them head-on. All your life, you've just run away from your problems. You find a scapegoat to blame for your problems, and for now, it's me. I take all the blame on me, does that make you any less miserable? Everyone has their own set of problems, Shreyansh, but that doesn't mean you cry and mourn forever like a little kid." He got up, looked at me and smiled. It was then that I knew I had fucked up. What the fuck had I done? I pulled on his jacket. "I am sorry, Shreyansh. I am so sorry…"

There was melancholy in his eyes, yet he smiled at me. I wished for it to rain that night and to have his arms around me. "I've hurt you, I know, Shreyansh…"

"So, you know?"

"Can we please forget about this? I blurted it out in frustration. Please forgive me."

"How easy it is to say sorry, right? *Sorry Shreyansh*, snap your fingers and it's gone, right? The hurt, the words that wounded me, everything gone, just like that. Maybe you people forget that I am a human too with feelings that get hurt, who cries when no one is looking. I wished that you would see the mess in me as an art that is worthy of treasure, but no. I am just a miserable, hopeless, and melancholic guy. I wish all the happiness in the world for you though, even mine." He smiled and turned.

I grabbed his jacket tighter and my tears fell on it.

I felt that sting in my heart, the pain before your heart completely falls apart. I looked at him with a blank expression, I couldn't hide from him now that I was so close to breaking. His gaze peered right through me as he said, "Goodbye, Manya," and walked away. I turned around, not letting any emotions show until I had walked away from the dhaba, pieces of my heart trailing behind me in a veil of sorrow.

His words echoed in my mind, intensifying the darkness that hovered in the evening chill. I couldn't say anything, I'd gone catatonic as I moved to my PG. I could see his melancholy eyes in the distance as I walked away from him. There was an eerie silence between us with a haunting feeling of finality. My feet struggled to move forward, making it difficult to drag my lethargic body. I could've collapsed any moment. From the distance, I heard the engine of his bike roar to life. It was menacing. I craved for him to drive to me and embrace me. I stopped there and waited for him, but only silence remained.

My shattered heart had had enough, and it finally let go. I decided to walk away from his life. I couldn't save him if he didn't want to be saved. I knew I would curse myself forever for letting him go, for not having enough patience, for not trying hard enough. But I was tired.

I told myself that this was the last I'd ever hear from him. I was just steps away from the dhaba, when a loud and piercing crash echoed behind me. It felt like someone had hammered something right next to my ear. A loud wail followed and I felt a chill run down my spine. The hair on my neck bristled and I stood there frozen for a few minutes. I didn't have it in me to turn around, to see what had happened. I wanted to run away, but my mind went blank. It didn't want to believe the worst.

Everything was silent for a moment. I could hear people running and shouting behind me. In a split second, everything I'd lived until then flashed before my eyes, then. A warm stream crept from my eyes and my breath became deeper and heavier. I finally turned around. In the distance, I could see people gathered around a truck and his bike which had crashed into it. I didn't want to believe it. I told myself to run away, but my body didn't budge. My heart yearned to stay. My heart empowered my mind and I ran towards the crowd.

A cold breeze slapped across my face as I pushed through the crowd. My body shivered in fear, weakness and helplessness consuming me. I couldn't move, but just stayed there for a moment, dwelling in the void. If I hadn't moved, he might've always remained a memory. I didn't want him to be just a memory of a forgotten past. I pushed the people aside, soon to realize that I was standing in a pool of blood. In that gory river of blood lied in peace a person, but not the one I always dreamt of.

My legs gave away and I collapsed in the blood. My trembling hands supported me as I gasped for breath. My lungs refused to take in the air diluted with his blood. Still trembling, I dragged myself onto my knees. That beautiful face, the sculpted jawline, those exquisite lips and a pristine complexion that would turn dirty if touched, were all red, stained, bruised and cut from every possible angle. I held his head up and put it in my lap.

No, that couldn't be my Shreyansh. It was a mere body, motionless and lifeless. It wasn't him. I heard people shouting around me, but I calmed myself down, convincing myself that it couldn't be him. This blood soaked and bruised body could not be him. I couldn't let it be him. My blurred vision made it difficult for me to see anything. There was red all around, an ocean of blood and a lifeless rose lying peacefully in my arms.

My heart and lungs suddenly came to life, and a gush of air escaped my mouth. I muttered something, but no words formed. I tried again. Nothing. Mute. With all my will, I screamed and words came out. "Help..." It gave way to wailing. Someone pulled him away from my embrace. "*Sab thik hojana hei, fikar naa kari* (Everything will be alright, don't worry)," I heard.

As I lifted myself up, blood dripped from my clothes like drops of rubies. I was soaked in his mortality. "*Gaaddii laayi itthhee* (Bring the car here)." I looked at them, taking his lifeless carcass and stuffing it in a car. I followed them. "Careful." I would whisper again and again. I sat with him, his head back in my lap. "Drive fast, please," I muttered.

The evening was getting darker, swallowing us whole. With everything evanescing, the light I sought was also fading, travelling away from the world of mortals, shattering the vile of life. Somewhere deep inside, I wished him to be free of this pain, to be released from everything; I wanted his suffering to end. He'd already suffered through hell and it was his time for freedom, time to relinquish all the misery, to sleep in permanent peace.

I rubbed his forehead and smiled at him.

But it was blood, just blood, nothing but red and a carcass on my lap.

3rd April

Dear Manya,

"Through the long years I sought peace. I *found* ecstasy, I *found* anguish, I *found* madness, I *found* loneliness. I *found* the solitary pain that gnaws the heart, but peace I did not *find*. Now, withered & near my end, since I am losing all my will and strength, I have known you, And, knowing you, I have found both ecstasy & peace, I know rest. After so many lonely years, I know what life & love may be, now, if I sleep, I shall sleep fulfilled."

-Bertrand Russell

No matter how much I write, how many poems I dedicate to you, I bleed to fit you inside me. I cannot explain the depth of the simple truth that I, Shreyansh Thakur, love you and wish for your best.

Always & forever.

Chapter 28

The silence of the hospital tormented my soul. The corridor leading to the operation theatre looked like a graveyard. The smell of death lingered in the air, stagnant and stale. I could smell it, feel it.

I was dead myself. A dead soul and a dead heart in a withering body that was about to give up soon. There was blood on me of the life that was slipping away, the life he was fighting for inside the room, inches away from me.

Shreyansh hated hospitals, he had told me, for it reeked of helplessness. That feeling had stayed with him for a long time after the death of his niece. "I felt trapped, scared, haunted; the wailing and the melancholy that followed her death haunted my nights and days. It hovered around me, inside me. I was paranoid for a long time. Maybe, I still am. After that, whenever I pass by a hospital or go inside one, everything flashes in front of my eyes like a scene from a tragic movie. That's why I can't stand hospitals." There he was now himself, swimming between life and death, back at one such hospital.

The earth under me moved as my phone started vibrating. "Where the fuck are you, Manya?" It was Riya. "Ask her if she's with Shrey. He'll bring her to the PG," Soumya's voice echoed from behind.

"He…he can't…"

"What are you saying? Where are you two?" Riya asked.

"I am at the hospital, this big one near the tower. He... he...was hit. There was blood...a lot of it...Riya..." I couldn't breathe. She said something, but it was all vague. The blood, those bruises, the scars flashed in front of my eyes. The phone slipped from my hand and everything went black.

"Manya, Manya?" I felt someone shaking my body.

"Manya? It's us."

"Stop him. He's leaving," I muttered.

"She's in shock. Get water, Mayank." Some sprinkles rained over my face. I gasped and was back to the cruel reality.

"Get up and sit here on the bench, otherwise you'll catch a cold. Mayank, water?!" Soumya held me up.

They were silent for a while. I wanted them to ask me how it happened, how he had ended up here, how things had resulted in this, but they didn't. Maybe all this seemed natural to them, like an accident, but it wasn't. It had been orchestrated by me and my wild desires. I was the culprit. I was the reason for it.

"He'll be okay," Soumya filled the silence.

"Yes, he will be," Riya and Mayank followed.

"You both are following your mother," I smiled. Soumya gently slapped my head and they laughed.

"Wait, who signed the papers and brought him here?" Riya asked.

"I don't know. I can't remember," I said. "Someone in a turban.»

"Must be Kuku Paaji. I saw him coming out of the hospital," Mayank said.

A rushing sound of feet from the far end of the corridor approached us. The door at the end slammed open and Rohan entered.

"What the fuck is he doing here?!" I got up in rage. My weak legs found energy in hatred.

"Calm down, I called him to get the number of Shrey's parents," Mayank said, holding me by my shoulder.

"Where is he?" Rohan asked. Mayank pointed to the operation room.

"I called his parents, they must be on their way."

"You didn't have to come," I muttered.

"Manya…no…" Soumya started.

"It's okay, Soumya," Rohan stopped her.

"What happened to your clothes?" Riya asked. His clothes were ragged in parts, covered in mud and barn. His face was dirty and his hair a mess.

"I had to jump over the wall. I didn't want the warden to know about this. It was dark and the guards were on their rounds, so I slipped over the wall in haste and fell face down," he shrugged.

I wanted to walk away from them, to seek solace in some fresh air. I wanted to run away as far as I could. There were sounds behind me, they were talking, giggling. I ran away, the door slammed behind me and I stepped out of the hospital. My lungs got filled with fresh midnight air; it was unusually cold. I closed my eyes and breathed in some more, sitting down on the pavement beside the front door of the hospital. Darkness evaded the light, and suddenly, I wasn't alone.

"Here, you might need it." Rohan passed a cigarette to me. I took it, one drag, two drags, three…four. He slipped two more cigarettes between his lips, lit both, then gave one more to me.

"You are both alike," I said.

"Excuse me?"

"You and Shrey are alike."

"Yes, we are. We were. I don't know." He blew out a cloud of smoke.

"Rohan, I've done something terrible. I know you won't judge me because of this mutual hatred we have."

"I don't hate you. I never did. And, yes, you can share it with me."

"I am responsible for this, for his condition. He was on the edge and I pushed him off."

"It's okay, Manya. He will be alright. He'll climb back."

"Nothing will be the same again. He needed someone to save him, but I just pushed him into the abyss. I am the culprit. I could've done better with a little patience."

"No, you are not. There isn't anything you could've done. How could you have saved someone who doesn't want to be saved? Yet you tried, right? Remember that you tried. He was always this stubborn and selfless, not sharing his anguish with anyone and burning within."

"No, Rohan. How can you push someone away who is in need? Something had to be done and I didn't try hard enough. I made it worse. I made it difficult for him. I might have killed him, Rohan." Tears escaped from my eyes.

"Ssshhh…it'll be okay." He hugged me.

We went inside after a while. Shrey was still behind those closed doors. I lost count of the hours passing. Minutes felt like decades. It wasn't hours for me, it was a life after life, waiting and lingering in pain. Morning arrived and the hospital came to life.

Some people came barging in through the door at the far end of the corridor. Rohan got up in haste and rushed towards them. He greeted them and touched their feet. "Shrey's parents, his sister and her husband," Soumya whispered to me. I looked at the young woman and my breath got stuck in my throat. She had the same facial features, her eyes were as deep as his, with pupils dancing in rhythm. I could see the reflection of my soul in her eyes. The man holding her by the shoulder was tall, strongly built and fair. They were talking to Rohan, while occasionally looking at me. Was he telling them that I had killed him, that I pushed him to a point of no return?

His parents moved closer to the operation room and sat on the bench beside it. They crossed us without noticing either Soumya or Mayank. His mother looked lost and scared. His father looked down, defeated and numb. Everyone surrounded them, while I sat alone.

His sister came and sat beside me. "You look exactly like he told me," she said.

"You look like him," I told her. She smiled at me, and I had to reciprocate. Silence prevailed for a moment. I looked at his father, he was silent, staring the wall ahead without blinking. Maybe he was thinking that the person he despised his whole life would soon leave the world. I hated every bit of him.

"Did you bring him here?" she asked.

"Yes di…"

"Meet, my name is Meet."

"I'm Manya..."

"I know your name. Shrey has told me a lot about you," she said. My lips trembled.

"He will live," she assured me, grabbing my hand.

"Huh?"

"My brother will live." Her tired eyes welled up with tears. "He has survived everything else, he will survive this too. He's a survivor, he will fight his way out of hell fire for his sister. He will fight death for me. He won't leave me hanging here. He…he…will live." Her voice cracked; it was painful and heartbreaking.

"Yes, yes. He will live." I held her and she hid herself in my arms, sobbing under her breath. "It's okay, Meet di, he will be fine." I rubbed her back. I wished I could convince her that nothing would take her brother away, not even death, and that he'd swim back from afterlife to the shores of the living, back to us. If he did, I wouldn't push him away this time.

The door opened and a middle aged doctor came out like a ray of hope. I thought for a moment that my prayers had been answered. Meet broke our embrace and rushed towards him. Everyone surrounded him, except me and one other person.

I sat there because I knew it was my doing. He sat there because he knew it was his. Both culprits sat there looking at each other. I could see the helplessness in his eyes and maybe he could see it in my mine, but there was something more there. It was the *guilt* of having let Shrey down. His father seemed cold and distant.

His mother and Meet clinched the doctor's arm. I couldn't hear anything, but just watched their lips moving. The doctor shook his head and they stopped. Meet let out a sound I had never heard before, a wail that pierced right through my heart and reverberated off the walls. His mother collapsed down to the floor from the arms of Meet's husband.

My vision blurred and I felt drowsy. My breath was stuck in my throat. I stood up, wanting to escape. *Run,* someone shouted in my ear, *run away*. I ran out. I couldn't hear anything, it was just silence, plain horrid silence. People were talking but no words fell in my ears. My eyes were dry too, perhaps having run out of tears.

"Hey, are you okay?" A hand grabbed my shoulder. I broke free, yet everyone looked at me. All eyes were on me. *Murderer, killer, you killed him,* they seemed to shout at me. I couldn't hold it in anymore. I ran out and threw up on the pavement. I heaved again, there was more…

Everything was out, the beer and the food…every bit of him.

I gasped, but felt light. I calmed myself down, refusing to believe that he was dead.

He could never be dead.

People like Shreyansh could never die.

They lived.

They lived forever.

They left a part of themselves in everyone, in his sister, his mother, Rohan, Riya, Soumya, Mayank, and me.

He will…breathe. He will always live in me, in my soul, heart, and conscience.

I closed my eyes and took a deep breath; there he was, smiling, his hazel eyes twinkling. I opened my eyes and a rain of tears showered down my cheeks.

Everything that I had been holding in came out.

Every bit of him.

Everything that remained of him…

4th April

Last night, I dreamt that I was driving around the city, the way I always do when anguish becomes too heavy and thoughts become stones pinning me down. Then I ride my phoenix, and from the ashes of melancholy, I rise again. I was wandering around in twilight, feeling the breeze and hearing the wind calling for me, memories hitting my face with all the misery I hide.

Somehow, everything carries me to you and I ended up in front of your house. The light from your room illuminated the dark aisle which led me to you. I saw your silhouette by the window and tried to call for you, but then I stopped myself and watched you comb your hair while looking at the moon. With uneven breath and reluctant steps, I walked to the door and pushed it ajar. I saw you then, sitting by your bed, reading a book I had lent you. Everything bubbled up from my conscience as I saw you emptying yourself from the very eyes that once showered life and care over me.

I saw your tired self crawl into bed, resting your head on the cushion, as if on my lap. I moved my fingers over your head and traced the world under my hand. You looked at me and smiled, and told me to stay there until the end of time–when there would be no pain, no worry, no hatred, no one to part us, even if everything ended. I looked at you for the final time and kissed your forehead, whispering a last goodbye.

I dreamt that I came back last night...

Chapter 29

Sometimes, I woke up at night, gasping for breath and panting with my throat dry. The constant heaviness and ache in my chest remained unwavering. Then it struck me that I wasn't even asleep.

The thought of him gone was hard to digest. I couldn't stop myself from believing that I could've saved him, and now with him gone, this void would never fill up. I felt as though I'd be incomplete forever. I'd had sleepless nights before, nights spent in overthinking, but this was different. There was something terrible about these nights, something terrifying.

Sometimes, I could feel a presence by my headboard, as if he were sitting there caressing my head and looking at me with those hazel eyes. Yes, I saw those hazel eyes everywhere in the darkness–by the couch, in my cupboard, by the door. I truly believed that he was hiding somewhere, looking out for me, about to reveal himself at any second.

Sometimes, I would feel his arms around me and I'd smile. "Shrey, you're here. Hug me to sleep," I'd say, and hug my pillow and cry. I wish I could alter time and walk back to erase him from my life altogether, erase the very day our eyes had first met. I accept that before him, I had never felt the true thrill of love, emotions, or feelings, nor did I feel this pain of loneliness, or helplessness, but why adorn my life with those memories? I still felt his alcohol stained lips and smokey breath in mine.

The places we visited together haunted me and I decided to never return to them. That staircase in college always reminded me of him and those corridors reeked of his presence. I feared that if I went there, I'd find him leaning against the wall in one corner, smiling with his bright hazel eyes.

He wouldn't ever know the huge void that lived in my chest, or the longing I felt as if I was only a half of a nonexistent whole. How could he have left me hanging there with only silence and suffering? After promising to always be by my side, he had run away and become the composer of this suffering and longing. Why hadn't I been enough for him? Why couldn't he trust me enough with all the pain, anguish and trauma he had?

Someone ask him to come back, please.

I will never turn my back on him.

Everything will be okay. Everything will be fine.

I am sorry, Shreyansh..

I am sorry...

But there was no forgiveness for me. I was doing a terrible job at forgetting him. I often dreamt about him, his eyes and face appeared so easily behind my eye-lids. It was especially difficult the week after I lost him.

I lay there like a corpse, my gaze stuck at the ceiling. The sun travelled across the sky, peeking in through the gaps in the shades on my window. The moon followed and dressed me in its silk and cream, surrounded by a shroud of darkness. I, a bride of murk, lay there mourning for my groom who was mere dirt now, never to be mine. Perhaps we had a chance to be together in the after-life.

"Manya, you need to gather yourself up. Shrey would've hated to see you like this," Riya said.

"Riya, you could've come up with something new, you know that. I expected better from you, at least. And, yeah, Shrey would've disliked it, but he's not here to give a fuck, so please don't pull him into this. He has no right to stay in our lives anymore."

"Manya..."

"No, Riya. I'm okay." I wiped my eyes. "There's no mourning over a selfish person who went away without thinking about me, his sister and the others." I gasped and started sobbing. Riya hugged me tight. I could feel her tears dropping on my head, like a shower of sympathy. I promised her that I'd pick myself up and not mourn for him, but it was hollow, just like myself.

It pained me to have to pretend. Shrey was always pretending and faking being okay, so I embraced it with open arms. By doing this, I felt closer to him than ever, by *living for others*. It was like our private secret.

The entire student community at college was in grief, mourning the loss of someone they had crushed and thrown away. The atmosphere at college was sombre, and silence prevailed like at a graveyard. They looked at me like I was a widow, and Shrey a martyr. Their sympathy sickened me. It repelled me to the point where I felt like running away from everything. I didn't want to be a part of their pseudo group mourning. They were all actors playing a part in a melodramatic movie. When the movie ends, the mourning would too.

The college went on like nothing had happened, but just a hitch and that was it. The examinations started as planned with the practicals. I could still see remnants of sorrow that his departure had left behind. Nothing gets past eyes that both see and hide. I saw pain in Reshma ma'am's eyes, helplessness and guilt in Mr. Thakur's. They pampered me because I had lost something. Questions weren't hard in the viva, and the attendants would check on me from time to time. *Why all this sympathy, this care, for a cold-hearted killer?*

The murk around me didn't settle, however, the guilt didn't vanish and the shiver of fear remained. The good that came from Shrey's demise was a reconciliation between the hostellers and the outsiders; the college stood united.

I grabbed my plate at the mess, and people nodded at me. The most chaotic place in the college was now muted. My favourite table by the window was vacant, and I acquired it. This was the very place where I had started my first day–the tears, the bullying, that stare, and those eyes. *Damn those eyes, would they ever leave me alone?* I froze, lost in the memories of the past.

"Hey, Manya." Someone slapped my back and it melted me.

"Reminiscing the past?" It was Riya.

I nodded. She sat down next to me with her plate.

Then came Mayank. "That's a cool place. May I sit here?" I shifted to make space for him.

Soumya came after. "Shift, kiddo."

"Can we sit here?" Sagar and Shruti were next. I looked at them puzzled. What was up with all of them? We had never sat together before.

"Practicals are over, how's your exam preparation?" Soumya asked.

"Good…good…good…" everyone replied.

"Cool," Mayank added and everyone laughed. It was good to indulge in a bit of happiness after a while. After all, it had been a bad week, month, and year for me.

"What about you, Manya?" Soumya asked. "You can always come to me for studies." I nodded.

"Yeah, she's under my surveillance now," Riya chimed in.

"It's you who needs more help," Mayank grinned and Riya slapped his head.

"Or we can study together at the library," Shruti suggested and Sagar nodded. Rumour was that they were dating. Perhaps that was what had brought a change in the bully that Sagar was.

"Guys, I appreciate your concern, but I really am alright. All this attention is getting kind of irritating in fact," I grinned. "I'll catch you later." I stood up and carried my plate away to dump it. There she stood, waiting for me. The muscles in my hand twitched and I felt like throwing the plate with the leftover food at her face. Just then, I saw Rohan and stopped.

He smiled and waved at me. "How are you holding up, strong girl?"

"Good. How about you?"

"I've been better," he smiled. There was a valley under his eyes.

"Hello, Manya. I wanted to talk, but couldn't gather the courage. Shr…"

"Just shut that dirty mouth of yours. I swear, if you take his name, I will grab you by your hair and shove your face in the dumpster. I don't fear getting expelled anymore." I dumped the plate and turned away.

I knew that I had to stand up for myself now and be strong to face everything, since Shrey wasn't around to save me anymore. "Manya, Manya," someone called after me. The voice echoed in my ears, I knew who she was.

"Donot,Irepeat,donotsayanything,"Isaidwithoutturning. She held my hand, "Please, Manya, I beg you. Please talk to me." I'd never seen or heard Deepika like that before. She was a walking mess. She had no makeup on, her eyes were red with deep dark-circles around them. Her perfect red lips were patchy. "I can't hold this inside me anymore. It's killing me already, little by little."

I nodded. We sat on the stairs outside the mess. She couldn't speak and seemed to be in deep turmoil. I understood that she was embarrassed about the things she'd done. "So, Deepika..?"

"I can't sleep, Manya. I tried, but cannot."

"Why?"

"Every time I close my eyes, his image dances in front of me. I keep seeing his perfect sweet smile. His eyes shine in the darkness when I turn off the lights." Her voice was trembling. "I know people will call me insane if I tell them this. Despite everything I did to him, he always met me with a smile. I am sorry, Manya." Tears dropped from her eyes.

Why was she apologising to me? And why now? He was gone, away to a better place and far from this cruel world. All these sorries were only for themselves.

"Manya..." she sobbed, "This guilt in me, this pain, these sleepless nights — will they ever subside? Those eyes, that smile…they still haunt me. Will they ever go away?" There it was, the question I had been asking myself, contemplating it over and over again, but not reaching any answer.

"I don't know, Deepika. I don't know," I sighed and patted her back.

That evening, my father called me. After rejecting his calls for weeks, I felt like talking to him. I wanted to listen to the voice that used to calm my nerves when I was a kid.

"Hello, dad."

"Are you okay? You sound low." He didn't ask me about the unanswered calls.

"Yeah. I'm okay. I've been stressed lately. Practicals just ended and I'm going to write the exams soon."

"I know you will do well. Don't take stress. Daddy is here, *beta*."

"I'm sorry, dad."

"Don't be, *beta*. I can understand the loss, your loss. You can always talk to me about anything that's bothering you."

"Who told you?"

"When you didn't take our calls for a week, your mother called Riya. She told us everything. I am sorry. I shouldn't have yelled at you."

I thought, *Yeah, you shouldn't have, dad. The anger you brought out in me that day, the fear, the loss of understanding changed something major in me and that something ruined everything.*

"Are you there, Manya?"

"Yes, yes. I am okay, you don't have to say sorry. It was my fault."

"No, it wasn't. Oh, my poor Manu. Should I come to Doon to pick you up?" he asked.

"No, dad, I'll be fine."

Everything that I've been through this year has made me tough, dad. I wish I could tell you how much your Manu changed and transformed from being your naïve daughter to a cold and numb woman.

My mother sobbed and cried as I told her about Shrey. I used to sing his praises to her before. Maybe I still had her sensitive side in me, hidden somewhere, buried for good.

Chapter 30

In the pursuit of accomplishment, people often turn selfish, and I don't usually blame them. If you can't make your own self happy, how can you possibly spread happiness?

I tried to take a break from my mourning and guilt, and tried to make myself busy. Every once in a while, I slipped into agony. I clawed my way out of this state by developing and repeating a mantra: *Once he was my home, now I live in his void. Once I survived by him, now I am surviving because of him.*

I wanted the session to be over as soon as possible. The frequent pampering and calls from my parents made me weak and home-sick. The lecturers went easy on everyone, a mourning gifted to the poor students. Everyone wanted to finish with the exams and leave this dreadful year behind.

It was the last day of exams. I sat in the examination hall and looked outside. Birds chirped, leaves rustled, and branches danced to and fro. There was such peace outside, but none inside. We are such ephemeral creatures; living every moment that's fleeting without a promise of tomorrow.

The speaker in the classroom blared, "Attention students...I wish you guys good luck for the fold of this session and year." It was Principal Verma. "I wish luck to the 3rd year students for their future, and to the 1st and 2nd year students to work harder next year." We exchanged glances in the classroom. "We have had a tough year. We lost a bright young student who had brilliant prospects in future. Let's all stand up and close our eyes for him, and hope that he rests in peace. Let us pray for his soul."

I wanted to believe that he was honest with his words and genuinely wanted to express his remorse, but my mind told me that it was just a plain lie fabricated for the sake of formality. What more could I expect from people who didn't acknowledge mental illness as something serious? They were afraid for their reputation, what if people got to know that it was a 'drunk & drive accident'.

I got up from my seat and all heads turned towards me. Mr. Yogesh looked at me puzzled. I walked over to him, slammed my answer sheet at his desk and walked away. "Manya, where you going?" he shrieked after me.

I turned and glared at him. "Sir, I can't be a part of this mockery. He deserved better, not this formality. All of us should've given him something better." I turned to look at everyone sitting there, their heads now bent low. I knew that they wouldn't ever understand the depth of my misery, but I felt good and walked away. I held my head high while people from other classes stared at me.

My feet carried me upstairs and I found the place where it had all started. My hands moved over the railings to feeling for his impression, as if they were still there. I felt his fragrance still lingering in the air.

After counting the steps, I sat at the exact step where he had that day. The lecture room in front of me was empty. I could see a scared Manya standing there, bullied and ridiculed. I saw Shrey look at her from here. The exact moment flashed in front of my eyes and I smiled. Would I have escaped that day without looking at him? No, I couldn't wish that anymore. I would have taken on more embarrassing ordeals just to see him looking at me again, like that very first time.

I don't know if it was my insensitivity, but I felt happy for him. This world didn't deserve him, he was a nomad in this mad chaotic world. At last, he had got his peace, his redemption at the end of his journey. The chaos he had left behind was my burden to bear, painful as it was.

"Found you at last." I turned to find Rohan coming up the stairs.

«Huh?»

"I saw you leaving after the announcement. I couldn't be a part of that bullshit either, so I left too." He sat beside me.

"This is the place I saw him for the first time. I was standing there." I pointed to the door. "And he was sitting here."

"First day?"

I nodded.

"Right. After I bullied and insulted you?" He turned his head away.

"Yeah. It's okay. I forgave you already," I said.

"But why? After all I had done to you, how could you?"

"One of the good things I learned from him," I smiled.

He smiled back. "Maybe you should try to forgive Tanya too."

I shook my head. "Maybe I can forgive him for leaving me here, but I can't forgive her or forget that she was the catalyst in his bane."

"How?" He raised his brows. "I know she acts like a bitch sometimes, but she's not that insensitive."

I laughed and he looked at me puzzled. "Not insensitive? She is robbed of every shred of sensitivity, not to mention humanity."

"How? Why are you saying that?" He asked.

"You wouldn't like the truth; hell, you wouldn't be able to digest it. So don't ask."

"Try me."

"Fine. This is going to blow you away. It's ugly and you're probably not going to like what you hear. Do you still want to listen?"

He nodded.

When Shrey died, I decided to bury everything with him, but some things shouldn't be buried as they only fester like untreated wounds. I knew it was going to destroy Rohan's relationship with Tanya, but I needed him to know. They both deserved their share of pain.

I told him how Tanya had lied and ended their friendship, I told him about her bullying me with Deepika, and how she tricked me into being ridiculed by Ms. Reshma who once adored me. I also told him about how she was the reason for Shreyansh's expulsion and my outburst at him.

His expression changed from shock to sorrow, to disgust, then anger. And at last, every emotion came flooding out.

"Hey, Rohan. I have been looking for you everywhere. Hi, Manya…» Tanya had chosen the worst moment to arrive.

Rohan got up in haste and stumbled down the stairs. Tanya tried to hold him, but he pushed her away. He swung his arms and bang! a tight hard slap fell on Tanya's cheek. The sound echoed through empty stairwell, followed by complete silence. Tears rushed down Rohan's cheeks. "How could you do that to me? To him? To us?" he sobbed.

"What have I done?" Tanya asked meekly and looked at us, puzzled.

"How could you separate two brothers? How could you destroy someone's life? How could you shut every gate of survival for him?" He broke down and crashed to his knees. "And how could I love an insensitive sadist bitch like you?"

Tanya bent down and grabbed him by his shoulders. "Don't you touch me, I don't know you, you're not the girl I loved," he sobbed and slapped her hands away.

Maybe the moment demanded it, or the human side of her finally overpowered the devil's side. Tanya started crying too. I was surprised at her tears. The woman who took pleasure in tormenting others was crying. "I did it for my love, the love I have for you. Shrey hated me, despised me from the start. I just wanted to separate him from you, so that he wouldn't separate us."

"He would never have separated us, and he never hated you. It was he who asked me to approach you in the first place and told me how nice you were, how honest and bold, that we would make a good couple. Why would he have a reason to hate you?"

"I am so sorry, Rohan. I love you. I just love you so much that I ruined everything." She wrapped her arms around him and held him. He hid himself in her arms and howled. It stung my ears, painful and intimidating. They both cried, and nobody spoke for a few minutes. It was Rohan who broke the embrace.

"I'll never forget this, Tanya. We will both live with this guilt forever. I don't even know what to do with you, or to you. My love for you is stopping me. I don't know what to do," he sobbed.

All my life, I had craved for love, affection and care, but when I received it, I let it slip by. I couldn't let that happen again as I watched a relationship dissolve in front of my eyes. How could I? And why? Because she was too naïve to think beyond her love? Or too selfish in thinking about their future and wanting to secure it? Everything I couldn't do, she did. She saved her relationship, stuck to him, did wrong, but all for love.

"Forgive her, Rohan," I sighed.

"What?" Rohan looked at me.

"Yes, please forgive her. She loves you and everything she did was for the sake of both of you. Forgive her or I won't forgive you."

"Oh Manya..." Tanya sobbed.

"But, how could I? She ruined everything, our friendship, your feelings, your emotions, your life *and him,*" Rohan said.

"If I can forgive both of you, why can't you do the same? To forgive is divine. Forgive her and you'll feel better."

"You talk like Shrey now," Rohan rubbed his eyes and smiled. "See, despite everything you did, she forgives you."

"I am sorry, Manya. I can't express how embarrassed and guilty I feel. You are such a good person–better than I could ever be. I'll surely try to improve." Tanya held my hand and sat in front of me.

"Shrey would've loved that."

"Do you think he will forgive us? Ever?" Tanya looked at Rohan and asked.

"He already did. The moment he took his last breath, he must have forgiven us all. The real question is, can we forgive ourselves?" I asked.

"I won't, I'll forever live with this guilt," Tanya said and Rohan nodded.

"We all will. We all will," I sighed.

It's funny how we dwell in regret and remorse after we lose someone. It makes us a lot more humane and sensitive. We begin to feel things we couldn't before. Then, slowly, we begin living again and everything changes. We transform into something else, someone else, someone better. What if we had been this humane before? What if they were still here with us, with our better selves? What if Shreyansh was still here?

«Finally we found her, the rebel, the legend, the myth. What are you doing up he…what the fuck?" Mayank looked at me, then at Rohan and Tanya, with his mouth wide open. "What are they doing here with you? Are they bothering you?"

Riya and Soumya were with him and Deepika was hiding behind them. She had been avoided Tanya and her group since the unfortunate event. "We're just reminiscing, feeling remorse, apologizing, and burning in guilt," Tanya said.

«Me too," I sighed.

«Me too," Rohan said and I smiled.

"Well, this looks cool. I want to join in." Mayank sat next to me.

"Sit, Soumya, we won't bite." Tanya smiled at her. Riya and Soumya looked at me puzzled. We all sat down together. Silence settled upon us and all the embarrassment, anger and guilt hovered over us.

We weren't enemies, friends, classmates, or batchmates anymore. We were people with regret in our eyes, sorrow in our hearts, guilt in our consciences and a great wide void within us.

"We should say something for him, for Shreyansh," Mayank said.

"Like?" I asked.

«Like what we feel, just let it out maybe?" Rohan added.

"Who wants to start?"

Everyone looked at each other. I knew I wouldn't be able to, so how could they?

"Caring, smiling, selfless, a saviour and healer, and the most beautiful human being I ever came across," Deepika said meekly. I smiled at her and she reciprocated.

"A friend, a brother, my family, a shield, a protector," Soumya said.

"Best friend, brother, partner in crime," Rohan added.

"Helping, best senior, handsome, my crush," Riya said shyly. I raised my brows at her and everyone smiled.

"Forgiving, strong, selfless," Tanya said.

"Cool..."

"Yeah, Mayank, stop there. It's enough for you. We understand," I said and everyone laughed.

In that careless laughter, we were all together; no bullying, no betrayal, no lies, no fighting, no back bitching between us. In that moment, we were just happy. He must have been looking at us, perhaps standing by the door of that lecture room, smiling with those hazel eyes. I knew he was looking at us and soaking in our words of salvation and redemption. It was all he had ever wanted. He had wanted to see the humanity in us. He had wanted us to have peace, both within and without. He had wanted us to have love for each other so that we could carry that love and happiness beyond this place and into the world outside. His investment in us had not been in vain, and I knew that he would have been happy.

He was dead, but he was also alive at the same time. He lived in us, among us. People like Shreyansh left a little bit of themselves in everyone they met.

As long as I breathe, Shrey will live in me, with me. I will cherish him in every breath I take. His work is done, his part is complete. I'm almost certain that he achieved *moksha,* rejoicing with his niece in heaven. It was time to set him free from all the shackles and bindings.

I shut my eyes tight. *I know I'll find you here, dancing eternally in my conscience. I didn't think I could do this, I don't want to do this, but I have to. I have to, Shreyansh.*

"Shreyansh Thakur, I set you free, for you were meant to fly and I can't cage you anymore."

Epilogue

Dear Manya,

I know you must think that I forgot all about you. I read all your texts, re-read them umpteen times. I saw all your calls and even wanted to pick up, but just couldn't. I'm sorry about that. But now, I cannot stand the burden of pain, to not reply or talk to you. I don't have that courage now. Not anymore. He's no longer here to fill me with strength.

I know you'll ask me if I am okay, and I'll ask you the same. I know we will both lie and say that we're fine, but deep inside we both know that nothing will ever be fine again.

I came there to collect his things and see you last weekend, but something inside me told me to go back without meeting you because I know what you'd have seen. You'd have seen him in me, I know. These eyes. I noticed you that day, looking dumbstruck into my eyes—one of the many things I shared with my brother. These eyes hide everything and yet speak everything. In front of you, they would have spoken everything I wanted to hide. I know because even my father wasn't able to save himself from these eyes.

He was sleeping in the dark when I went to his room after we cremated his body. I sat there, moving my hand over his forehead. He opened his eyes slightly and smiled at me. "Aagye, Shrey beta. I knew it. You won't be able to remain angry at your father for long. Punish me for everything, son, but don't leave your old man hanging here with this guilt, this ache." He closed his eyes and tears slid from them.

"It's me, dad, Meet. I'm not going to leave you, okay?" I held back my tears and for the first time in my life, I saw my father breaking, sobbing, and howling uncontrollably.

My mother, being my mother, just sat there facing his room like a morbid statue. You know what's even more shattering and scary? She smiled at moments. Who knows what she looks at? Her little son crawling to her? Him playing in his room with the toys he used to break the very day they were given to him? A young teen crying because he didn't want to go to school? A young man packing his bags to go to college?

Tears and pain follow. I know what truth consumes her now — her son covered in blood, bruised and deeply wounded, lying motionless in bed — a mere corpse, a lifeless body that she had brought into this world and raised into a beautiful soul, a gentleman. All of that, just to see him dead?

How could I do this to you? Tell me. How could I see you in pain and give you more pain? For everything you did, it was to make my brother happy, to make him feel loved. But you know, Manya, it was hard for him, near impossible for him to love with all the broken and shattered parts of his soul. Yet, my brother tried. He almost did it, he almost conquered his demons to feel love, to love you. I know how hard it was for him, and how difficult it became in the end.

I remember calling him before that fateful day. He was scared, lonely, and haunted. He told me about running away from everything, from everyone, to somewhere alone, somewhere peaceful. He wasn't talking about departing from this world; that's not what he wanted. My brother had always been a fighter, a survivor.

But where was he planning to go? Was he running away from us to someplace else? Was he searching for a place where he could be his normal self? Did he seek refuge while fighting his demons, conquering them and then planning to return to us reborn?

Unfortunately, none of that will happen now and we'll both suffer the brunt of these questions and guilt. Why couldn't we save him?

I know we could have, but we didn't. We allowed his life to slip away from our grasp like sand. Perhaps destiny played its part and we were only puppets following the trail of our predestined doom.

Manya, with tears in my eyes and longing in my soul, I am giving you this diary I found in his room. You deserve to know everything he wrote about you and whatever he went through. I wanted to tell you that you didn't kill him. You didn't kill our Shreyansh. We all did and we have to live with it.

You must've asked him before, "Will you stay?"

And I know he must have nodded to it, but wouldn't have answered it.

I am telling you this, He will stay. He will stay inside all of us. Hold yourself together, Manya, you're my strength now. Don't let this world break you again.

With love,

Meet.

About The Author

Vedant Saxena hails from Ghaziabad, and is a hotel management graduate from IHM Kurukshetra. He was a trainee at Le Méridien, New Delhi, before finding his niche in writing. He also founded an online magazine and blogging platform for aspiring writers called the 'Intellectual Owl'. He is a nyctophile who spends his nights writing, reading and thinking. He is also a self proclaimed grief-counsellor and motivator cum healer who loves to help people. He's counselled dozens of people out of suicidal thoughts, as well as people going through depression, anxiety and heartbreak. Apart from this, he loves to cook, read, travel and is a fitness freak.

You can reach out to him through:

Facebook – Vedant Saxena

Instagram–@Vedant_thereal

Twitter–@Vedant_thereal.

Mail – ved.saxena05@gmail.com

Annie Pruthi is an old soul nestled in the body of a 17-year-young teenage girl. She breathes air from the capital, New Delhi, India. An alumni of St. Anthony's School, she is now pursuing her Bachelor's from Gargi College, Delhi University. Being a true believer of values, her source of happiness is her family and her faith in goodness of a human. Apart from her love for writing prose and reading poetry carrying a deep sense of meaning, she also likes to dance and listen to Punjabi music. Her instinct drives her to read untold stories of those who wait to narrate it. She is a passionate dreamer at night and a ferocious chaser during the day.

Drop a 'Hello' and give voice to your voiceless stories to her at:

Instagram — @poetryandpoetess (Annie Pruthi)

Facebook — Annie Pruthi

Email — pruthiananya585@gmail.com